IN THE NAVEL OF THE MOON

IN THE NAVEL OF THE MOON

Paul St. Pierre

Douglas & McIntyre
Vancouver/Toronto

Douglas & McIntyre
1615 Venables Street
Vancouver, British Columbia V5L 2H1

Canadian Cataloguing in Publication Data

St. Pierre, Paul, 1923—
    In the navel of the moon

    ISBN 1-55054-054-8

    I. Title
PS8537.A5415 1992   C813'.54   C92-091460-8
PR9199.3.82415 1992

Cover photograph by Paul St. Pierre

Printed and bound in Canada by D.W. Friesen & Sons Ltd.
Printed on acid-free paper ∞

All the character and experiences depicted in this book are
fictional.

The author is grateful to Dibujos Musicales Ambríz of
Guadalajara, Mexico, for permission to reprint portions of the
songs "Mexico Lindo" by Chucho Monge, "Corrido del
Norte" by Pepe Guizar, "Cielito Lindo" by Quirino Mendoza
y Cortez and "Mañanitas Tapatias" from the collection *200
Joyas de la Cancion Mexicana.*

DEDICATED TO THE MEMORY OF
BENITO JUAREZ GARCÍA,
PRESIDENT OF MEXICO, 1858–1871

INTRODUCTION

A novel is like a joke: it is its own justification if good, and a waste of everybody's time if not. I say this because the idea persists that novels should come freighted with social significance, relevance and other codswallop. That is a notion best left with the pseudointellectuals who developed it in the first place. A novel's purpose is to tell a story. Nothing else matters.

Whether or not this book contains a good story, or stories, the readers will judge. At least I can say that it is free of environmentalism and all other forms of political correctness.

A few more things should be said here.

This is not the story of Mexico. I don't know what that story is. Neither do any of the Mexicans I know. Mexico is a huge country filled with people who scarcely know each other. It is an old country, and often mysterious. This book is set in one small village of one small state, and I have tried to make what happens in the story true to that little place and those people.

I have made a considerable effort to avoid stereotyping Mexicans, but doubtless here and there have failed. I'm sorry. I know of no typical Mexicans. In any Mexican community of more than a thousand people you can find every popular stereotype about Mexicans stood on its head by one person or another: man, woman or child. If there is one essential characteristic of the people south of the Rio Grande, it is that they sense, even if they cannot define, what Mexico is. They are sure they know who they are.

Language is another consideration. This book was written for English-speaking people, of whom I am one. Therefore, it is written entirely in the English language.

We all know that some things are better expressed in one language than in another. However, there is no act, scene or thought that cannot be translated, even if it suffers a bit in the process. Therefore, unless they are words of Spanish origin that can now be found in the Concise Oxford Dictionary, no Spanish words are used in this book, not even such commonly understood ones as señor and señorita. When I hear people tossing foreign words into English because "Oh dear, dear, English is so inadequate," I always suspect affectation. To a unilingual English-speaker, inadequate English beats incomprehensible Cantonese, Spanish, Chinook, Polish or academic jargon.

In the same spirit of trusting readers' common sense, I have retained the correct form of writing such figures as five thousand pesos or eight thousand pesos, that is, $5,000 and $8,000. The Mexicans have been using what we call the dollar symbol for many generations and feel they have as much right to it as Americans and Canadians. I have no licence to take it away from them.

If there are any readers who are led to believe that organ grinders' monkeys get tipped $10,000 American in Mexico City I would be grateful if they would get in touch with me with all possible speed; I have a few world-famous bridges in excellent condition to sell to them.

Most Canadians and Americans should not be startled to encounter $2,000 ice cream cones and $150,000 restaurant meals. If they will just be patient they will eventually pay such prices at home in their own mishandled currencies.

My thanks are due to the many people who read the manuscript and offered advice, particularly my wife, Melanie, who grew up bilingual in Texas and has a fluency in Spanish that goes far to make up for my slender vocabulary. And I would like to thank my publisher, Rob Sanders, without whose constant help and encouragement the thing would have been completed in half the time.

I am grateful for advice from Antonio Haas, columnist and author of the book *Mexico*, and to Maria Urquidi of the Mexican External Affairs Department.

I have also had the benefit of readings by Royal Canadian Mounted Police Inspector Lawson Eyman, retired, and RCMP Staff Sergeant Leon "Smokey" Stovern. Of course none of those I mention are responsible for any opinions expressed here on police work or on the state of the great republic of Mexico. As with any book, the final responsibility for everything it contains is the author's.

I am grateful for help from the writings of Alan Riding (*Distant Neighbors*), Antonio Haas (*Mexico*), Eugenio Toussant Aragon (*Who and What Was Pancho Villa?*) and Elaine Shannon (*Desperados*). Also extremely helpful to me were APA Publications' *Insight Guides—Mexico* (from which I extracted the translation of the old Aztec poem used to introduce the final chapter of the book); Dibujos Musicales Ambríz of Guadalajara, publishers of *Songs of Mexico*, and the Consulate General of Mexico in Vancouver, British Columbia.

In this, as in all fictional works, there is always a difficulty when using fictional characters in real situations. In 1988, there was a commissioner of the Royal Canadian Mounted Police, and only one. Yet he is not the commissioner who appears in these pages. My commissioner is a fictional creation, as are the NCO at the Canadian Embassy in Mexico City and Captain Alvarez of the Mexican force. So, too, are The Drunk, White Indian, Wolf Man, The Dark Horseman and all the rest. They are blendings of the characters of real people and, I hope, true to life. But their lives are fictional. I might as well also record that neither the city of Santander nor the pueblo of San Sebastian de Hidalgo appear on the map of Nayarit.

Here, I also express my profoundest thanks for the friendliness of the inhabitants of this small corner of the Mexican Republic, people who do not speak English and will never read this book. They have taught me many things about the world and, perhaps, about myself.

I would also like to say that writing *In the Navel of the Moon* was great fun, but some of my contemporaries have been dropping off rather suddenly of late, without time for the last rites, and I have become nervous about lying. Truth is, like my other books, it was a hard slog.

Casa Chucho
Teacapán, Sinaloa
Mexico
18 March 1992

CHAPTER 1

I REMEMBER ANGEL

Persons attempting to find a motive in this narrative will be prosecuted; persons attempting to find a moral in it will be banished; persons attempting to find a plot in it will be shot.
—Mark Twain, *The Adventures of Huckleberry Finn*

SAN SEBASTIAN DE HIDALGO, NAYARIT, MEXICO—Last night I was awakened by The Woman Who Wails, and never before have I heard such sadness in a human voice. She cried from a well of sorrow deep as the dark of eternal night.

I left my bed and went out of the rooftop bedroom into the moonlight, thinking perhaps I would see below some poor girl with the classic trouble of girls or a neighbour woman drowning in some other fathomless grief. There is sorrow enough for everyone in the village of San Sebastian de Hidalgo. But from the roof I could see only our dusty street, palm trees and the little houses of the neighbourhood, all in darkness.

The cries came from the foot of the garden, where the moon made patterns through the banana tree on the grey concrete-brick wall.

This was no mortal woman crying. It was the one the Mexicans call The Wailer.

Sooner or later, everyone in Mexico encounters The Woman Who Cries. Some say she is a mother who gave away her children in a time of famine and who now, brokenhearted, forever mourns them. Some say she is The Malinche, mistress of Cortés, endlessly lamenting her betrayal of her own Indian people to the Spaniards. It is known that The Wailer dates back to at least the time of the Spanish Conquest of Mexico. Some say she is older, older than the Aztecs, old as despair.

Her cries can never be forgotten, for they are not sorrow but utter heartbreak.

What I did next I cannot explain. I say only that I did it. I walked from the penthouse door to the edge of the roof and said, in my most sonorous Spanish, "Woman, go, with God." Immediately there was silence. Then the night sounds of the village washed back into the void: the crowing of the neighbour's fighting cocks, the barking of dogs and the absurd honking of a donkey.

I say only what happened. The truth of the matter I do not know. It was, no doubt, some night bird or an animal that happens to make sounds that put human souls in agony. It was not The Malinche, or any other ghost. I have no time or patience for superstition and, in any case, the people in San Sebastian already have more than they need; there is no reason to encourage more.

The Wailer is one more mystery in this vast, beautiful, exasperating land called Mexico, a word that is supposed to mean "bellybutton of the moon." I suppose it is a name as sensible and understandable as any other name might be.

I went downstairs to the kitchen and turned on the sixty-watt light bulb, which doesn't flicker much at that time of night when the village sleeps. I made coffee, laced it with Bacardi white rum and decided that there was a story to be told about San Sebastian, whether or not I could understand its meaning.

But how does one begin? What exactly is the story of these past few months? Which of the Seven Deadly Sins lifted this justifiably obscure Mexican village so high that even the international press could glimpse it?

It is no surprise that the lives of simple, ordinary people are as complex and passionate as those of the rich. Most of us older than eighteen know that. But here, where a thick layer of genteel courtesy overlies all social contact, the hungers and sins that lie beneath that surface seem blacker and more bitter when they emerge. Tears are saltier, and the laughter sometimes seems to verge on hysteria. There is nothing new under the sun, but here in San Sebastian life is more intense and often more surprising.

And all of it is set to song. Even now, half an hour after The Woman Who Cries has left, a shark fisherman who passes the door on the way to his boat on the beach is singing, to himself and the moon.

Voice of my guitar
Awaken me in the morning
I wish to rejoice
In my lovely land, Mexico.

He sings some ballad, usually one of love betrayed and hearts broken, every time he goes barefoot down this street to the dangerous little dugout that will carry him over the horizon so that he may, perhaps, come back twenty-four hours later with ten dollars worth of shark. He catches few shark. He sings well.

Farther up the narrow street, where another household is preparing for a new day, a stereo is playing. It will play all day. Sometimes the people in that house will sing along with a melody they admire. At all times the music is part of the household, like the walls with their chipped paint, the thatched roof and the pig tied to the palm tree in the yard.

In Mexico, everything is done to music. This isn't a country, it's an opera.

So on this morning I have decided to collect all my notes and memories of San Sebastian de Hidalgo, a village whose name is as long as its main street. Perhaps in the writing of it a truth now hidden from me will be found. At least I saw most of it happen, and what I did not see, I well know. So the events are clear and the characters, like Rivera and Orozco murals, are vivid. But what memory of these few months is most clear? Which characters are strongest?

I sat remembering, thinking, waiting for revelation until the sun jumped out of the eastern horizon, as if it had slept through the alarm, and started its headlong race across the tropical sky.

Of them all—Dark Horseman, The White Indian, Pretty Little One, the Falstaffian character we knew as Wilbur and all the rest—none comes more quickly to mind that the least consequential of them all, the boy called Angel. Angel—small, dark, proud and poor; his nickname was Fragment.

Why Angel?

Perhaps because he was the only child among us, and therefore a conundrum. We think we know children. We prefer to believe that they merely tread in the tracks our generation has made for them. But this is wrong. It is only our own generation we can hope to understand. Children have seen a different world and will spend their lives in a world different from the one you and I know, possibly slightly different but perhaps profoundly so.

In the grand opera played out here in bedraggled San Sebastian, I think I have understood all the older players. Of the boy's story I know only the beginning and will not live long enough to know the end. I wish I could.

CHAPTER 2

WITHOUT SIN, WITHOUT GLORY

Poetry was the maiden I loved, but politics was the harridan I married.
—Sir John A. Macdonald, first Canadian prime minister

In my notes of December 1988, I find this observation about Fragment. It was the day I was enlisted in the Syndic's cleanup-and-paintup campaign.

"In every town there's a kid who is different, usually to his intense sorrow. The Fragment is different in that he appears to have ceased to be a child by age eleven."

Several mornings I had noticed him, standing by the bus stop in the village square, a calm boy obviously reserved and indifferent to the horseplay of other youngsters on the street. He didn't seem passive; rather, there was a sort of intensity in him. His spring had been wound up, but the catch was on. And he had what I had come to believe was an essentially Mexican quality of limitless patience. In their history these people have sometimes been too patient for too long, and their rage when it expresses itself is atrociously cruel. One of every fifteen Mexicans was killed by other Mexicans in the great revolution.

Fragment was at his corner the morning I joined the Syndic in the bright, bold first day of his program. It was also the last day. Things sometimes go that way here.

I would have asked him about the boy, but San Sebastian's chief executive had spotted the banker and was urging me to come and meet this senior member of the small and exclusive body we know as middle-class people.

Although middle class, the banker was young and, as I later learned, earned little more than a labourer's wage. He was, however, a banker:

he wore a shirt with a necktie and a jacket and, truth to tell, was one or more notches higher on the social ladder than the Syndic himself, a fact they both tacitly accepted.

Like the Syndic, he praised my Spanish which, he said, was like the Spanish of the Mother Country. This is not necessarily a compliment. Linguists say that Mexican Spanish is richer and more expressive than European Spanish. But the young man probably meant it as a compliment. You seldom heard San Sebastian people even mention the name of Cortés or any of his motley band of soldiers, adventurers and psychopaths. In a land that loves statues, not one has been raised to Cortés. Yet old Spain is still sometimes called Mother.

"I have a problem with an American customer," said the banker. "He sent me two hundred American dollars for deposit, but by mistake it went into another American's account, and it is most complicated for me to move it. Now he keeps sending me telegram after telegram, asking where his money is."

"Have you wired him back?" I said. I knew the banker had no English, and the American client probably had no Spanish, but there are such things as translators.

"No, I haven't. But I think I might talk to him on the telephone sometime."

"The telephone. I see," I said.

"He lives in Oregon. Do you know any Oregon telephone numbers?"

No wonder all those billions of borrowed foreign dollars had disappeared in Mexico. They are probably still in the banking system, resting in the wrong accounts. No, I answered, I knew no Oregon phone numbers.

The Syndic began to speak with some passion about his campaign to get some of the rubbish off the streets around the square, to paint the iron benches and the ironwork of the bandstand, and perhaps to find some way to revive the sickly laurel trees that surrounded the central plaza, standing unevenly like recruits in their first army parade.

He had only a vague notion of what a paintup-and-cleanup campaign was, but he knew that American villages had such events and, as he so often said, what was good for Americans must be good for Mexicans.

The boy banker gave him courtesy but not much else. It would be unthinkable for Banamex, mightiest of all the nation's banks, to contribute its own money to this or any other cause. He put a folded bill in the Syndic's hand, and after we parted with the most earnest expressions of mutual good will, the Syndic unfolded it and discovered it to be a five-thousand-peso note, worth about two American dollars.

The woman who sells chickens in the corner store also gave, and so did the pharmacist, although that merchant first took the opportunity to lecture the Syndic on the need for better street-lighting, more policing and brighter fireworks at fiestas.

We preserved the separation of church and state while passing the little lime-green church where a plaster-of-Paris Christ watched us through the open doors. Some of my Mexican acquaintances crossed themselves when passing the door of the church, but the Syndic didn't. It is not proper, he said, for a government man such as himself to officially recognize the church.

"My friend," I said, "remember what Napoleon said. Religion is the only thing that keeps the poor from killing the rich."

He thought about this. "How practical!" he said. "How intelligent! This Napoleon, he is the president of Canada?"

No, I said, another country, and anyway he was long dead.

"He must have been a man of strong political instincts," said the Syndic.

His own surely were, although he was more a functionary than a politician. San Sebastian was far too small and poor to have municipal elections. It was one of several little pueblos that were wards of the city of Santander, fifty kilometres distant. Santander's elected president appointed syndics in the pueblos.

Syndics were half city manager, half chief of police. Two things they all had were the right to pack a pistol, which is no small perk, and a membership in the Party of the Institutional Revolution, the mighty PRI, which has governed Mexico for sixty uninterrupted years, longer than any other governing party on this planet.

The Syndic had a small building supply business, which he ran from his house, selling cement bricks, mortar and the steel reinforcing bars called rebar. Rebar stiffens every structure in the land, including, I sometimes suspect, the wives. Certainly the Syndic's wife had stiffener in her. She pretty well ran the business, probably better than he could, even if he were able to tear his attention away from politics long enough to give it some thought.

His cleanup-and-paintup campaign was a common practice of politicians anywhere: find a cause to support and if there is none, create one. It is a process I spent much of a working lifetime observing.

He was sincere, desperately so, and this has value in politics because voters forget that a completely sincere man can be totally wrong. But sincerity alone is seldom enough. Another quality is needed, which he seemed to lack. He had no presence. His face was pudgy and his clothes looked as though he regularly slept in them.

He had the further handicap of succeeding the late Don Jésus, who had been the oldest man in the village, as well as its syndic for many years.

Shortly before Don Jésus died in office, the Santander municipal government passed along to San Sebastian an unexpected windfall of subsidy money. Don Jésus knew exactly what to do with it. He wasted none on civic cleanup, sports fields for the kids or anything else useful. He invested the entire sum in improving the graveyard, and San Sebastian could now claim that its dead were better housed than its living, an achievement that made the villagers justly proud of themselves and Don Jésus.

My friend the new syndic, Cuauhtemoc López Barrientos, was overshadowed by the dead, and he didn't do very well with the living, being afflicted with an exaggerated respect for anybody American, wealthy or educated. Above all, he walked in terror of the PRI.

The Party of the Institutional Revolution, whatever those words mean, had no means of imposing terror, no party police, no torture chambers, none of the apparatus that has sustained single-party rule in some other nations. The PRI was an election machine that produced majorities, without much heed to what the voters put on their ballots, and then left the elected to get on with their dictatorial ways until another election performance was required. To Cuauhtemoc, however, it was the voice of the president himself that spoke to him through any official of the PRI.

We passed from the square onto the side streets, where people were burning their garbage on the street. None was too successful.

The houses of the poor we passed by. I mentioned that there were many poor, and a hundred or so pesos from each could be a fair amount of money, but he said no, a hundred times nothing was still nothing.

The widow Jiménez met us at the door of her prosperous two-storey home, insisting loudly that she was a good Catholic woman and that this house, bougainvillea and all, was a Catholic house.

When he finally got a chance to speak, the Syndic apologized for disturbing her and we left.

"She thinks we are Jehovah's Witnesses or else Mormon missionaries. I am afraid I do not have a presence that is memorable, like that of old Don Jésus," the Syndic sighed. "Don Jésus was, as they say, a man of affairs. When he spoke, no dogs barked. He had a presence that all men could recognize instantly."

"It sounds like what the Romans said of their good senators, that they had *gravitas*."

"I do not know about Romans. They live far from here. But Don Jésus had something that I do not." He shrugged. "It is God's will and of no importance." Obviously, it was of more importance to him than anything else.

I had agreed to accompany the Syndic this morning so that I could interpret for him when he approached gringos for donations. I'd been in San Sebastian long enough to have met most foreigners. Some were interesting. Others, who were there only because Mexico is the last place in this world where they could afford to have a servant problem, were not.

My nearest American neighbour, Wilbur, had no servant problems, or any other kind. Wilbur was problem-free, certified.

He was as old as I was but looked twenty years younger and acted like a school kid. When we rattled his gate he shouted, "Come in," without getting up from his deck chair. He was tanned a dark mahogany, which made his blue Paul Newman eyes all the more startling.

He was knitting, the most recent of his hobbies. On his lap lay a Smith & Wesson .38 revolver. A string, tied around one toe, led to an ingenious alarm system in a nearby hibiscus bush. Gardening was Wilbur's second most recent hobby.

He waved us forward, cheerily, with the pistol. The Syndic flinched, not at the sight of the pistol but because Wilbur was almost naked, wearing nothing except boxer shorts, a wide-brimmed hat and sandals.

"What are you up to now, Wilbur?" I said.

"Two things. I am knitting a scarf. If we invade Russia, I shall have a scarf to keep at least one brave American lad warm. That ensures me a place in history that will be denied the German general staff, which sent the German armies into Russia with no winter underwear.

But I suppose it's no great achievement to be smarter than an army general. The other thing I am doing is protecting my fields, as did my sturdy ancestors at Lexington."

"You had no sturdy ancestors at Lexington. Your ancestors were riding wild horses and carrying rapine and slaughter through the Pripet Marshes at that time."

"Like the authors of the Bible, I claim the right to utter allegorical statements."

He explained that an iguana had been munching his hibiscus, hence the revolver. When his toe twitched, even though he might be asleep in the deck chair, as so often he was, he would be able to awaken in time to shoot the creature.

Wilbur worked hard for his laughs, but who could blame him? He had flown Liberator bombers over Europe in the big war and had learned, through the process of unremitting terror, how lucky he was to be alive with nothing worse than a bleeding ulcer when the war ended.

He never lost his sense of amazed appreciation of every hour he had spent alive since he stopped going on bombing raids. After the war he took a couple of years to make a big, fat pile of money, a trick that comes easily to some Americans, and when he had enough he quit all pursuits except silly ones such as hunting iguanas or knitting wool scarves for people who would never wear them.

We all exchanged greetings in Spanish, of which Wilbur had good command, having married a small, lovely Mayan from Mérida with a face lifted from one of the carvings on the pyramids. Now, in her middle years, Guadalupe had taken on somewhat the shape of a pyramid, but none of the grace and charm had left her.

They had the perfect bilingual marriage. He never spoke a word of Spanish to her, nor did she ever address a word of English to him. It was amusing, at social gatherings, to watch them switch to their native tongues to address one another although each of them had been speaking fluently with other guests in the other language. We sometimes tried to trip them up, for the fun of it, but their marriage was too old, solid and stable for anything to change their ways.

"Where is Lupe?" I said.

"She went to see a sawbones in Arizona. Some tummy trouble. She'll be all right."

An odd way to say it. Why shouldn't she be all right? Not a care showed on his unlined face, and the baby-blue eyes shone warmly on the two of us.

A cleanup campaign. Why, of course. An excellent idea. He reached into his trousers, which he had flung on the tile floor of the patio, dragged out all the money in the pocket and handed it to the Syndic.

Later, on the street, we found that Wilbur's contribution was much the same as other people's. Did he perhaps keep the same amount of money always in one trouser pocket to make the grand gesture always possible? It seemed an unworthy thought, and I did not voice it to the Syndic.

He had asked me to join his excursion not only because he himself had no English but also because he was diffident about approaching gringos, all of whom, being crazy as well as wealthy, posed problems for him. Wilbur had no permit for the pistol, and if his patio wall was not so high almost certainly he would also be subject to arrest under the public decency laws for sitting there in his underwear. Why my company made the overlooking of such offences easier for the Syndic I cannot say, but it seemed to.

It suited me, in any case, to make the rounds of his village with him. I had been in San Sebastian only long enough be able to forget what day of the week it was. Much of my time, too much, perhaps, had been spent walking the empty beach beside the empty ocean and watching pelicans patrol the waves.

My brother-in-law, who was instrumental in my coming here, might have wished I were doing far more than that, but I had put peace of mind and ease before duty. I wished I'd learned the trick years ago.

So far I had exerted myself to nothing more than sending a picture postcard to him in Ottawa, writing on the back, "Weather here, wish you were beautiful." That, and making a few inconsequential notes to myself on the word processor at the house on Veracruz Street.

The next person we encountered was also a gringo: Little Margaret, formerly of Boston, formerly a nun, at this moment clad in the Mexican version of the Salvation Army uniform. She was a devout and practising Catholic. Despite having abandoned her vows she was, people said, more Catholic than the Pope. When gringo acquaintances pointed this out to her while she was approaching the men in the beer parlour for contributions to the Sally Ann, she would say, "Yes, yes, but they don't know it. Don't say anything."

11

If it was not the Sally Ann it would be a "Save the Whales" campaign or "Preserve the Speckled Snail Darter." Little Margaret could no more resist the impulse to do good than dogs can forbear to chase cats. When we encountered her she was in the act of killing a dog.

It had been struck by one of the few cars to use these streets, and one leg had been broken. It might have healed: the recuperative powers of those desperate curs was sometimes astonishing. But it would almost certainly have healed crooked, and the animal would have had a short life in the fierce competition of street life among other, stronger dogs.

"There, there," said Little Margaret, giving the dog a lethal injection with the syringe she customarily carried with her, "it will soon be all over. No more pain."

The dog quivered and was still. The carcass would lie there until it began to smell, and perhaps longer. A block away the night before, I had the miserable task of killing a half-dozen new-born pups with an iron bar. They had been taken from the bitch, wherever she was, and dumped in the street to die of thirst and hunger. The bloody little bodies were still there this morning, among the bread wrappers and plastic shopping bags.

"We are both on the same errand this morning," said the Syndic.

"The same?"

"Charitable collections," he said, but refrained from suggesting she rob the tambourine. We parted with vast expressions of mutual esteem and good will. When she was out of earshot, he sighed.

"Difficulty, Mr. Macko," he said.

Nobody in San Sebastian could handle Mac as a name, so when they addressed me formally it was as Mr. Macko.

"Little Margaret is a difficulty?" I said.

"The great President Juárez, when he made our laws, did not have ladies like Little Margaret clearly fixed in his mind."

"You mean the dog business?"

"Dog? Dog? Oh, the dog. That is of no importance. It is probably one of the Guzmán family dogs. The Guzmáns have plenty of dogs. No, she makes it difficult when she wears a religious uniform on the streets. The priest does not. He obeys the law. How do I explain to him that Little Margaret ignores our laws?"

"Within a week or two Little Margaret will no longer be in the Salvation Army dress. She is a sincere woman, Syndic, but all her sincerities are inconstant."

He was mildly reassured, and we went on to visit the Ochoa residence.

"Mr. Ochoa is so wealthy he can afford to do his own gardening," said the Syndic. Mr. Ochoa, a plump and pleasant man working an electric hedge-trimmer, smiled and was clearly flattered. He had made a comfortable sum running a manufacturing plant under the duty-free agreement at the Frontier Zone and he now lived part of the time in Cuernavaca and part in this handsome little house of snow-white cement, scarlet tiles and flowers.

I told him his garden was exquisite, and he said the same about my Spanish. We both lied a little. The people of San Sebastian loved flowers, and even the poorest cultivated some in their dusty yards, but the tropics cannot produce the profusion of colours and scents known to gardeners in the North Temperate Zone. Except for the bougainvillea, which they apparently imported from Brazil, Mexican blooms are showy but scanty and rather awkward in form and shape. Anybody in San Sebastian who saw a typical householder's garden in Victoria, British Columbia, would think he had died and gone to heaven, which is known to have the grandest of all flower displays.

Mr. Ochoa said, "I was pruning roses the other day when an American lady stopped her car and shouted through the gate at me, very loudly. Some American ladies speak very loudly. 'How much does the woman of this house pay you for that work?' she asked. I shouted back just as loudly, 'She pays me nothing. I take her to bed.' She became very red-faced and drove away. I should be ashamed; what would my mother say of me?"

He gave the Syndic high praise and a small donation.

On San Sebastian's best street, named Street of the Child Heroes, we visited the rather imposing estate of Henry Terwilliger III, of the Detroit automobile Terwilligers. He insisted we drink and only reluctantly allowed the Syndic, who would probably have been knocked on his ass by hard liquor, to settle for beer.

Although he had been resident here for part of each of the past thirty years, Henry had learned only about twenty words of Spanish, so I translated. Like any competent translator, I did not translate everything. The Syndic had no need to hear Henry's statement that the trouble with this country was that there was too goddamn much laughter and song. So their meeting went well, and the Syndic departed with a slightly larger donation than he had received elsewhere.

Other gringos being absent, off shopping or sleeping, we returned to the centre of the village and found the young doctor, recently graduated, who was serving his two-year rural service here. It is a first-class idea that medical students should repay part of the cost of their education by doctoring for two years in remote parts of Mexico when they graduate. As with so many good ideas, it doesn't always work.

Like compulsory military service, it is considered something to be endured with the least possible thought or effort, and villages are frequently subjected to physicians such as this one, who happened to be a wretched little yuppie.

It's not true what people say; I don't dislike all yuppies. However, I dislike all the ones I've ever met.

He took it upon himself to lecture the Syndic on the need for a functioning water system in the village, as if there were anybody living or dead who didn't know that.

"Instead of buying paint for benches in the square, why don't you take this money into Tepic, put it on the governor's table and say, 'Here. We have done our part. Here is our share. Now you bring us water from the mountains for our village.' "

The Syndic said it was an excellent thought. After all, the man was a doctor. He must know. We left with nothing.

"A cheap shot," I said. "Does that kid really believe that this state's governor doesn't know the difference in cost between a municipal water system and a can of paint?"

The Syndic shrugged. "He is a chilango. That's what we call Mexico City people. Chilangos."

"Is it a word of disrespect?" (It's always best to check when you're handling another language.)

"Yes, but the chilangos don't know it."

"You are a one," I said.

Since the gringo colonists were in short supply, I suggested we might go to see The Pretty Little One, a woman of formidable reputation who operated what came closest to being a tourist facility in San Sebastian. But the Syndic was reconsidering his program, something I suspected often happened.

"It is possible that it is not wise to go to the rich and ask the price of a can of paint," he said. "Rich people's minds do not operate like others. They always have a much more clear memory of having given money than they have of how much they gave." Better, perhaps, he said, to reserve the pockets of the rich for deeper dips. The poor had nothing, so it was pointless to approach them, and there were so few of the other kinds of people . . .

I suggested a beer at the canteen, a dark and noisome place where the interesting people were, but he insisted I visit his home. It stood near the square, a boat-fibreglassing operation in the house to the right, one of the thousand and one corner groceries in the house to the left, and his brickyard across the street. It was undistinguished from all the other houses, except that it displayed more flowers and fewer chickens, and there was no pig in the backyard.

In the main room, open to the street in the usual way from dawn to midnight, was much that you glimpsed through all other open doors on all other such streets. An overstuffed sofa, an overly coloured picture of Jesus with thorns in his heart, and a huge calendar depicting a Mexican pinup girl—she waved a rifle above her head and wore a bandoleer of bullets across large breasts that almost, but not quite, popped out of her dress. She was crying, "Land and Liberty!", the rallying cry of the Revolution, which had ended fifty or sixty years before she was born and long before her model of rifle was manufactured or Mexican women wore her gringo-style hairdo.

Had the Mexican Revolution, one of the greatest social convulsions in human history, somehow plucked a basic human heartstring with "Land and Liberty"?

Prosperity had not been part of it all. There wasn't much sign of it in the Syndic's house. There was a stereo, a TV, wedding photographs and ash trays made of seashells assembled in the shape of tom turkeys. Beyond was a kitchen from which came the smells you can never identify or forget: chilies, refried beans, roasted meat, smoke; the heart glows, the liver recoils.

From the street came other familiar smells—fibreglass resin from next door, donkey turds, and from somewhere not too far away the unmistakable scent of something dead and too long unburied.

His wife, Joanna, was a thin, pale woman whose name indicated descent from the wave of German immigrants into Sinaloa in the nineteenth century, the ones who brought Pilsner beer and the oom-pah-pah band music that, along with Spanish words, is now considered typically Mexican-Sinaloan. She urged me to take a seat, some coffee and my ease while she took Cuauhtemoc to the garden, obviously for chastisement.

"Politics" was the first word I heard her utter. I was reminded of when my brother Bert was elected an MP and went to Ottawa and his wife cried for two solid months. The Syndic's wife was too tough for tears but she had a tongue that had sharpened with use. I caught enough to learn that some customer had waited the entire morning for the bricks promised two weeks before and that he planned to take his business to Santander, where stores were reliable.

She was one of those women who cannot bear to say anything only one time, so she repeated it all and then repeated it again. I could hear him say, mildly, "You are a great asset, woman, for a man in political life. While you are with me, I shall never lose sight of my shortcomings."

So listening, I missed the entry of the Syndic's mother to the living room. She was in black, like most women over forty in San Sebastian, and walked with a cane. She had broad, bare feet in which the dust of ages had become permanently ingrained. She had passed old age and entered that rare state in which all aging ceases. She was one of those people whom God has simply forgotten to collect. They live simply, routinely, day after day, the count of the months and the years long abandoned.

This was the woman who had named her son, her only child as I later learned, after the last emperor of the Aztecs. You always wonder about such mothers.

I rose and introduced myself. She had brilliant black eyes, the last thing on her that could shine, for her teeth were gone. When she spoke, however, her voice was clear and her language perfect. She spoke all her names, which informed me that her Christian names were Rosa Carmen, that she was born into the Barrientos family and had married into the López family, and that she had been widowed and had not remarried. A full Mexican name is a family history. She then proceeded to the further formality, which is usually used perfunctorily in shortened form. Mrs. Barrientos, widow of López, did not use short forms of address. She said it all clearly, with meaning in every word: "It is an honour and a privilege to make your acquaintance, and I beg of you that you will consider my house to be your own house."

I bowed again. "You are most gracious to a stranger," I said.

"The stranger at our door may be God," she said.

I nodded agreement, which was about the best I could do in response, but her head was now turned towards proceedings in the backyard.

"My son the politician," she said, and grinned.

She invited me to sit, which I did. She remained leaning on the cane and summoning up memories.

"He could have gone to the priesthood or into politics; they're both pretty much the same thing, you know. Sometimes, when I hear my daughter-in-law, I think he made the wrong choice. He should have been a crow. But then I would have no grandchildren, or none that I could recognize."

"But he has been a politician only a very short time."

"He has always been as he is now. One who deserves more than he gets in this life." She pointed to the yard. "Listen to that. Is it any wonder that husbands take second fronts? I would, if I were a man."

"And, madam, since you are a woman and not a man, would you then take a lover?"

She giggled. "Who knows?" she said. "Who really knows? So much is changed now. The old women say change is bad. So does our crow. I am not so sure. The Bajaras girl up the street, she goes to technical school. Do you know what she plans to be? A bulldozer operator."

"Why not?" I said.

She rapped the cane on the floor. "Exactly. Why not? And that is why if I were a young wife again now I might take a lover instead of remaining with López. It might have been fun." She giggled again.

"You and your husband were not sympathetic?"

"He was all right but he wanted it to be forever Sunday. Not my type."

In three minutes we had passed from the stage of ritualized, almost petrified formalities to intimate conversation. It is one of the reasons that I will never spend much of the rest of my life away from this country.

She didn't tarry for the coffee. Joanna, the lecture over, also excused herself to attend to affairs in the brickyard. The Syndic and I finished a cup each. It was an effort because the stuff was instant and the water lukewarm.

He insisted on walking me home, as if I were a youngster who had

17

baby-sat at his home. The man was nothing if not considerate.

The boy was still waiting at the bus stop.

"His name is Angel," said the Syndic. "He is one of our poor."

"We have passed the homes of many poor people today."

"The truly poor," said the Syndic.

"Why does he stand there?"

"He has met every morning bus for four days. His school books are being sent from Santander, but the right bureaucrat is never active at the right moment in Santander, and nothing happens. The books are there, somewhere, in the great government stewpot, and he is entitled to them, by constitutional right."

"But nothing happens?" I said.

"But nothing happens. Nothing happens because he is poor. Because he is Indian. Because there is no place for that boy in the big, rich, modern state of Mexico."

There was a hardness in Cuauhtemoc's face that I hadn't seen before. He walked ahead to the boy, pulling the day's donations from his pocket in a crumpled wad, a gesture reminiscent of Wilbur's reach into his pants pocket. I stood away, but not so far that I couldn't eavesdrop.

"I must apologize to you, Angel. The plan for your books is changed. You are to take this money, buy a bus ticket and go, yourself, to Santander and buy new books. You have a list? Yes? Good. Buy all new books."

He put the money in the boy's hand and Angel, although he must have glimpsed the colour of $5,000 notes, did not count or even glance at it but poked it into his pants pocket.

"There is more there than you will need for books and bus fare, but that is money for your mother, you understand. It is money I owe to her."

The boy inclined his small, neat head a centimetre and murmured one word. "Thanks." He turned and walked toward the western side of the village, where the truly poor people lived in houses that were not houses.

"He didn't give you much thanks," I said.

"He was correct. You may not have noticed, but if you give a man in this village a light for his cigarette, he will thank you so profusely it's almost embarrassing. Give him a watch with diamonds on it and he may scarcely utter a word of thanks. He may take it home and throw it into a corner and leave it there for a few days before he wears it for the first time."

"That is strange."

"It is our way. It preserves dignity. Large presents can destroy dignity. I understand the boy. Pride is involved. Maybe, here, we have too much pride. I do not know."

I did not ask what he would say to the paintup-and-cleanup donors when no painting or cleaning took place. Probably they hadn't expected much to happen anyway.

At my house, Consuela, a big and handsome girl of twenty-five, daughter of The Pretty Little One, was doing the morning housework and singing. The bungalow's owners had never installed a stereo set.

"Sing on," I said. "Doves are just what I want to hear about today."

"What I can't understand is that these people don't own a stereo," she said.

"Maybe they can't afford one."

Consuela snorted. She was a big enough woman to snort strongly. "Any people who have enough money for glass in their windows have enough money for a stereo," she said.

I left her to her work and went to the word processor, where I unlocked my secret file by code word.

After typing awhile I said, "Consuela, what do the people in the village think of the Syndic?"

"He's a good enough man, I suppose. For a politician."

"But . . . ?"

"He is a decent man. That's it."

"But . . . ?"

"Well, you know. We have a saying about such a man. Without sin, without glory."

I wrote, "Without sin, without glory" beside the Syndic's name. Not that it accomplished anything except to make my notes a little longer that day. I had learned nothing.

Except for the two old women and the boy, every person I met that morning was already on my absurdly long list of suspects. They were among the many people in San Sebastian who might be guilty of supplying the English-speaking people of this continent with the goods for which they happily give all their money, namely, marijuana, cocaine and the semi-refined heroin known as Mexican Brown.

It was all too damn ridiculous for any more words and I shut down the word processor. I could hear Consuela singing.

"That's a familiar song," I said to her.

She laughed, another thing that Consuela did very well. "You should know that. It's almost our national song."

Some sententious ass, probably on a government cultural grant, once said he didn't care who wrote a country's laws as long as he could write its songs. I wondered if the little nit would have been able to write a song better known, more enduring, more loved than the anthem about a little cockroach who can't walk because he doesn't have a marijuana joint to smoke and whose boast is that he once saw Pancho Villa in his underwear.

CHAPTER 3

"I DON'T WANT TO GO TO WAR"

It is not a matter of a few holes in the dike which can be plugged with additional manpower. The dike is gone. . . . We will hear people say "Well, the problem is Mexico, the problem is Bolivia, the problem is Afghanistan, it is Colombia." The problem is in the hearts and minds of the American people who desire this flight from reality, this escape.
—Col. Ralph Milstead, director of public safety for the state of Arizona, testifying before the U.S. congressional committee on narcotics in 1986

My recruitment into a war whose cause I did not love came by chance, or whim; or, more exactly, by the unpredictable effects of sudden loneliness.

When my wife died, I was privately puzzled by how many people referred to ours as a perfect marriage. Even a couple of our kids seemed to have that idea.

She and I hadn't thought our marriage particularly good. We had talked of divorcing once, but didn't for the sake of the kids. We talked about it again years later when the kids had kids of their own, and that time we didn't split the blankets because of the grandchildren or because we were both white Anglo-Saxon Protestants from a small town in Ontario and of an older generation to whom divorce came hard.

It is in the first, passionate years that a couple is closest. Then resentments begin wedging them apart. The apologies never made pile up, and hearts grow colder.

My wife and I jogged along together somehow, but there existed between us neither war nor peace.

After the funeral, after the family members had gone back to their own homes and their own lives, I was left, in all honesty, with only a moderate sense of loss. What I did not expect was the appalling emptiness of the house. I was like a man alone on a raft and out of sight of the land.

It didn't help any to visit the curling club, which was also our town's social centre, because it was suddenly apparent to me that my friends didn't have much to offer in the way of conversation except to say that it was a remarkable spell of weather we were having.

One evening I went to the Shanghai Palace for some Szechwan cooking, and my old friend Ken Chow came over and put one hand on my shoulder.

"Poor Mac," he said, "Nobody even to fight with any more."

That did it. I started crying into the stir-fry. He brought me a big Scotch and sat beside me, not saying a word, just sitting, as a friend should. But the tears wouldn't stop, and he brought me my coat and offered to walk me home, but I said no thanks, pressed his hand and left him. He had tucked a mickey of Scotch into the coat pocket, I noticed.

I knew I had to break some old patterns and try to make some new ones. And it wasn't going to be good enough to dink around writing a Twenty-five Years Ago Today column for the paper I used to own. I needed something very new, very different. Either that or I was going to get old and silly and die earlier than was strictly necessary.

The same idea occurred to my older sister, I guess. All our lives she has had an unreasonable concern for my welfare. So, one thing leading to another, I ended up at the Royal Canadian Mounted Police headquarters in Ottawa, where my brother-in-law rates a two-window office and a pretty secretary. Higher ranks get secretaries who are smarter but long in the tooth.

"Spying is a gentleman's game, particularly if you're an unpaid spy," he said.

"I am no gentleman and don't want to be one. For God's sake, Harry, I'm an old, worn-out weekly newspaper editor."

"The best kind. Newspapermen spend all their lives spying on people. It's not second nature to you people, it's first nature."

"What's more to the point," I said, "I don't want to fight your war. It's a bad war and you are losing it. I say what I said when I still owned the paper: drugs should be as freely available in 1990 as they were in 1910. Your famous war on the drug trade is a pile of bullshit. Dangerous, harmful bullshit."

"A pailful of horseshit is the way we prefer to say it. We know we're trying to bale the river dry with a wicker basket. But we have to follow where the United States leads, and the Americans learned absolutely nothing from their experience with the prohibition of alchohol. They've built an even bigger industry to try to prohibit drugs, and they've created bigger criminals than Al Capone. All I can say is, and it might surprise you, once you get in the game and play by the rules, it's exhilarating."

I sang a song we both sang when we were younger, braver and more optimistic about the world.

> I don't want to join the army
> I don't want to go to war
> I'd rather hang around
> Picadilly underground
> And live on the earnings of a high born lady

He remembered it well and sang,

> Don't want a bay'net up my ass hole
> Don't want my bollocks shot away

But then he broke off and said "Mac, you'd enjoy it."

"I can't imagine why."

"You'll see, once you start. You'll be good. And you have that extraordinary gift for the Spanish language. Why, I don't know, but you do. Everybody says so."

"Because I spent ten years in the Spanish Club learning it. It's such a beautiful language. It's the closest, you know, to the original Latin, except maybe the Romance tongue in Switzerland. And we English-speakers are still using Latin two thousand years after it was supposed to have died."

"Spare me," he said, "I am having a hard enough time saying 'Pleased to meet you' in French, which is the politically correct language in this town. Tell me what you know about Mexico."

23

"Clara and I spent a week in Acapulco once and a day's stopover in Mexico City."

"Great! Your mind is clean and uncluttered by any facts. You're like the resident expert on the U.S.A.—he went to Disneyland with the kids once."

"Well, we were in Acapulco, I tell you."

"You could spend a week in Acapulco and never meet a Mexican. However, when you do meet them, you will like them. They will like you, too."

"How can possibly make a statement like that with no information whatever?"

In a gesture I was to encounter later in San Sebastian, he tapped a forefinger against the side of his forehead to signal that he was a man with second sight. I like my brother-in-law. He has style.

He also had an appealing offer. A friend, well, a friend of somebody, had a small, pleasant house in the small village of San Sebastian in the state of Nayarit. There was a maid service, which I could afford, and a cook I could also afford to hire if I lost my frying pan; also a wide, empty beach where you could watch the waves roll in from New Zealand and know that nothing was between you and that land.

"One very big shipment of heroin is going to move out of San Sebastian in the next half-year, and what we can't understand is, why San Sebastian? There are several thousand kilometres of equally empty beaches north and south.

"They're apparently going to run it from the beach to a freighter offshore, and she's going to unload it in Quatsino Sound on the west coast of Vancouver Island, which is why the Force is more concerned in this case than the Americans are. You might encounter Yanks, but probably not."

"How can you know all that?"

"It would not be healthy or helpful for you to know the answer to that question, Mac."

"Okay then, a different question. If you know so much, why not grab the damn stuff and be done with it all?"

He sighed. "Because then it's just another big drug haul. We will have some packets of Mexican Brown which the refiner got $50,000 for, and we will announce that street-sale value is $15 million dollars

24

or $10 million or $20 million or some other figure we snatch out of the air. It's all 'See what good boys are we.'

"Every other narcotics supplier between Colombia and Tuktoyaktuk will be so happy to learn that there's a vacancy in the supply line through Canada that he will buy a new Rolls-Royce on his predicted profits. In the confusion, one or two pedlars and an innocent citizen or two will get shot in parking lots in Vancouver and New York."

"Okay. Keep talking."

"Since San Sebastian's a new shipping point, at least as far as we know, the Mexicans figure the number one man will be hanging around to watch his investment. Or, what is also possible, he's been living in that town for years as a sober, upright citizen and has now got careless enough to be willing to have stuff parked under his bed. We think he'll be watching what his own people are doing and of course guarding it all against his competitors. It's a shipment too big to be left to the little errand boys we usually pick up."

"And you've all got the hots for Number One."

"To be honest, which we policeman sometimes aren't, if the Mexicans, the Americans and the Force had a choice between grabbing him or stopping the shipment, we'd take him and let the shipment go, and we'd give free pink Cadillacs to all the guys who carried it into the boats."

"Brother, have you ever heard about obsessions?"

He gave an apologetic smile. "Drugs are not a rational business."

"Make them rational for me. Try."

He put two hands on his letter opener and seemed to consider trying to break it. In the end he just held it.

"Almost all the people we pick up and throw into Hotel Crowbar are the same sort," he said. "Little people. Grubby. Usually none too bright. They're the world's losers, and I suppose if there was no drug trade they'd end up in jail anyway for stealing cars or pinching lawnmowers. Number One stays free and sassy. Have you any idea how much genuine satisfaction a policeman gets on those rare occasions when one of those well-manicured assholes go to prison, where, with any luck, some of his former employees will get together to gang-rape him?"

"The top people have, in other words, got up your nose."

"They live in good houses, drink good wines and send their kids to private schools. But I suppose policemen should tolerate that. There are a lot of other people up top who do not want, nor work, nor go to jail. Where the cheese binds, Mac, they laugh at us."

"It is, then, your pride that's hurting."

He had done it, bent the letter opener. He started to rebend it, thought better of the project and put it aside.

"Tell me something more, then," I said. "Tell me why you people keep trying."

"It's called discipline, Mac."

"And you and I know that isn't always sufficient."

"True. We put one or two spoiled policemen in jail every year. It's a wonder there aren't more. They're all playing Christ on the mountaintop. Every Constable Snottynose who handles a drug exhibit has wealth beyond his dreams right in his hands. All he has to do is make a few simple moves. As for the poor Mexicans, Christ, how do any of those poor bastards resist?"

"Are all the recording devices on in this office?"

"To hell with you and the horse you came in on."

My brother-in-law is the best kind of policeman. He is just like every other man. Vain. He is like a moose hunter. He wants the horns more than the meat.

"Don't go looking for a trophy to put on your wall," he said, using his second sight again. "You are not a policeman. You are a retired newspaperman who takes notes because maybe he's going to write a book. And maybe you will. A great love story, maybe, Mac. Get some sun. Get some rest. Catch some fish. Write us nice, chatty letters sometimes. Keep one eye and one ear open for us and we don't care what you do with the other ones."

"I haven't said I'll do it."

"But you will, for the sport of it."

"I take it you have a candidate for Number One in mind?"

"Truth is, Mac, no. Nobody except everybody. But the indications are that it's not one of the Mexican drug lords. Them we know. It looks as though this is a new operator, and maybe a foreigner. I'll give you a list of a dozen people, but that's all it is, a list of names. And be sure that if they are making millions in the new prohibition era, they won't be flashing it around for us to see."

He said there might be other spies or real policemen for Mexico or the U.S. in the region and if so, I, like a deceived husband, would be the last to know. He gave me a little talk about what he called "need to know," and it was clear my need was not great. Still, it was a good lecture, terse, profane and sensible. I do like Harry.

By this time it was clear I was to be a gossip writer and nothing more, and it was hard to tell if the main reason I was going was the Force's drug war or my sister's anxiety to send me to someplace that was sunny. Well, it was indoor work and no heavy lifting. He passed me his list of non-suspects. "You'll notice quite a few are gringos. There is a little gringo colony in San Sebastian."

"Did you know," I said, "that the word gringo originated when the American Army under Winfield Scott invaded Mexico and the soldiers were singing 'Green grow the rushes O'?"

"You're not all that expert on language," he said. "Gringo is an old word for foreigner that was being used in Spain before General Scott was a gleam in his daddy's eye."

I was beginning to learn something new, which has always pleased me, once I recovered from schooling, that is. Maybe newspapering is what made me that way.

"One happy thing. The Central Intelligence Agency has got no pet drug lords it's protecting in San Sebastian. We get a sly word on this from the American drug enforcement people. If the guy we think is a hoodlum and a grade A prick turns out to be a hero of the anti-Communist campaign, they tell us that our investigation just isn't going to go anywhere. They haven't said those words this time and everybody is grateful. The CIA is the American version of the KGB, but it's worse; the Soviet government still has some control of the KGB."

"If you fellows said publicly the kind of things you say privately, we might have a little better world, Harry."

"I'm talking this way to let you know how much I trust you."

So I joined him in a war in which neither of us much believed, like many good soldiers in many wars in many countries. Except that in my case the Queen wasn't going to give me a shilling for enlisting.

CHAPTER 4

TWO MEN NAMED DOROTHY
AND ONE CREAM PUFF

What is this Hague Conference?. . . It seems to me a funny thing to make rules about war. It is not a game. What is the difference between civilized war and other kinds of war? If you and I are having a fight in a canteen we are not going to pull out a little book out of our pockets to read rules.

It says here that you must not use lead bullets. I don't see why not. They do the work.

—Gen. Francisco Villa, quoted in *Insurgent Mexico* by John Reed

San Sebastian de Hidalgo lacked many things, such as a waterworks, a shopping mall and a statue of a revolutionary hero in the main square, but it never lacked surprises. Therefore, it was not strange to find a 1951 MG TD, gleaming in red and chrome, stuffed into a gravel pile in the plaza.

The owner sat behind the wheel, surrounded by all the friends he had just met. He talked to them in good Spanish with an accent to it that was uncannily familiar but eluded me. He was a well-set-up man in his thirties and had a mahogany face with carbuncles on it and a mop of pale yellow hair that would, as he got older, become wispy and fade so gradually into snow-white that nobody would ever be able to say exactly when it ceased being yellow. This is a characteristic of many Scandinavians, but it wasn't the singsong of Norwegians that I heard poking through his Spanish.

He saw the licence plate on my old Chevy, which I had trundled down to the square that day, and switched to English. "Tell me, friend, I just couldn't help asking. Where in the hell is Ontario?"

Then I placed the accent, that crooning twang. It registered on me at the same moment that I saw that he, too, had Ontario plates. I said, "It's a part of Canada that is run by the Mohawks and the Swampy Cree. The capital city is the Mississauga reserve."

He liked that, and laughed. "You're pretty close," he said. "I guess you can take the boy off the reserve, but you can't take the reserve out of his mouth."

He got out of the car and we shook hands. He shook like an Indian, too. Limply, anxious to get his hand back from you. I wondered how he'd manage in San Sebastian, where a handshake starts with palm-to-palm contact; you next grab thumbs, then wrists, then back up through the sequence. There is also the embrace, the double embrace: kisses to the air and kisses on the cheeks.

He did seem to have established some sympathetic connection with the crowd in the square, and I noticed that the boy Angel was now standing guard over the sports car, not daring to touch the gleaming metal himself but daring to warn other kids away.

"I tried a short cut across the front of the church, but she settled into a nest of gravel here that doesn't seem to have any bottom."

"It doesn't. Our town's syndic had the gravel delivered for use on the streets, but now he can't get any machines for spreading it, so it just sits here. It's been there a month, as a matter of fact. One of the new bus drivers even got stuck in it."

"Makes me feel right at home," he said. "The lumber for new houses on our reserve sat in the snow for three years while they straightened out the paperwork." He had a nice style, this blond Indian with the khaki-coloured eyes. He was going to get along well in San Sebastian, although how well I didn't then see.

Some men had shown up to replace the boys around the TD. Clarence, as he'd introduced himself, shoehorned himself into the driver's seat and fired up the sports car. Everybody pushed. The Syndic, who had come to supervise, leaned down to help in the pushing. But she was high-centred from front to back, and the little thin wheels just flipped gravel through the open doors of the church.

"No problem," said the Syndic, using his favourite two words. "We shall lift the little car."

He grabbed a corner of the front chromium fender and nodded to other parts of the car that were solidly anchored enough not to come off in men's hands. Each of the crew grabbed a portion where indicated. Clarence was still in his seat.

When they glanced at him he said, "Do you mean I have to get out and WALK?"

Looking back, I can recognize that as the moment when Clarence

29

inserted himself into the heart of San Sebastian in a way I could never quite manage. Everybody laughed: it was a shout, a rage of laughter; and this is the land where laughter ranks with song as a truly important and serious matter of life.

They shouted that he must stay in the seat. They insisted. When he tried to get out the Syndic pressed him back into the red-leather bucket seat with his hands on both Clarence's shoulders.

Thus was the car lifted out of the gravel, Clarence and all, and thumped down on firm ground. He promptly took everybody for a ride, one by one, starting with the Syndic, whom he scared out of seven years' growth with his cornering.

Angel watched with his heart, I thought. I doubt this world had often shown him anything he wanted so much as a ride in this strange toy automobile with its snorty voice. I wished that Clarence had noticed him, but he didn't.

After he'd given rides to all the lifters, most of whom insisted he do things ever more dangerous at ever higher speeds, he came back to the Syndic and myself and asked where he might find somebody to cash a hundred-dollar traveller's cheque.

The Syndic sent him to Pretty Little One. The Syndic, I was beginning to notice, sent almost everybody with problems, with ideas, with complaints or with financial questions, to The Pretty Little One. "She is one who understands so much," he would say. "Very intelligent."

It is the very essence of success for any politician to surround himself with intelligent people, and I often wished I could improve his own self-image by telling him that he was walking in the footsteps of great men by not pretending to know what he did not know. But it is a tricky thing to the prideful. Most people are grievously insulted to be called ignorant, never having heard Will Rogers say that we are all ignorant, just about different things. So I never got to tell the Syndic.

I left my old heap at the square and went to Pretty Little One's with Clarence because my ancient newspaperman's curiosity and my newly acquired suspicions were both aroused. Why does a man with a reserve Indian accent have golden hair, and how does he pay for cars like a classic TD?

"You are welcome to ride but don't ask to drive," he said.

"Why would I want to drive a car that's the size and colour of a package of Dentyne gum?"

"Because every man wants to drive a cream puff. I'm just saying no to you now so it won't seem so impolite later on. No. I regret to say, sir, no. You could dance with my wife, if I had a wife at the moment, but you can't drive Cream Puff."

He double-clutched for a right-angled street corner, never touching the brake and doing it all rather deftly. "One reason I can't let anybody else drive her is that Morris Garage chose to make her gears out of glass. Just one miss and the teeth can all come up in your lap."

"Young man, I drove one of these when Christ wore three-cornered pants."

"As far as from Ontario to Mexico?"

"Well, all right. I spent most of my life in Detroit iron. But I did take a few turns around the town in one of these once, and it made me wonder what the hell was wrong with people who spent their money on a car that wouldn't carry anything and cooked your right foot until it blistered."

"In my case I can tell you. Us Indians just can't be trusted with money. We are notoriously improvident. Our gene pool didn't have any bankers in it. This machine is severance pay from a North Sea diving job, also pension funds from the diving company, also four years Registered Retirement Savings Plan contributions, which I cashed out. Twenty-one thousand and enough left over to keep me in beans and tortillas here for a month or so."

"All that proves to me is that you owned twenty-some thousand dollars more than you needed."

He continued as though he hadn't heard me. "Maybe I should have stuck with diving for another year or two. I could have bought one of these in the Concours class."

"What's that, to us ham-and-eggers?"

"You don't drive Concours TDs into gravel piles. You don't even drive them where it's dusty or raining. You move one of them from one exhibition to another in big vans filled with nitrogen. When you cross deserts, the computer raises humidity, and in the coastal regions it reduces moisture content inside the van. Mine is only cream puff, and it's all right for me to drive it almost as if it was a real car."

"Happy days, when you go into retirement with only a cream-puff sports car to support you."

"You've read the book, haven't you? Never trust a drunken Indian.

Now, tell me about The Pretty Little One. Is she truly young and pretty?"

"The opposite," I said.

I wondered what grief or pain had actually driven him across a continent and into San Sebastian de Hidalgo. The place for a good-looking young man with a sports car was a tourist town, not here among a bunch of old farts. In my mind, I was storing interesting notes for the journal when we turned in to Pretty Little One's place under the sign, "TOURISTS WELCOME; HERE SPEAK MUCH ENGLISH AND SOME SPANISH."

There was, as usual, a whirlpool of activity that she was encouraging by beating her arms and shouting occasionally. One crew of men was building a coconut palm–frond roof on the porch of one of her little rental cabins. Others were digging a trench for no obvious purpose.

A Mexican-built Ford farm tractor was attached to a coconut palm stump, which the driver was about to drag out of the ground. He revved the unmuffled motor a few times. The little front wheels lifted a few centimetres off the ground and thumped back again.

"Too high on his drawbar," said Clarence. Maybe Clarence was a know-it-all. I hoped not. They're usually tiresome people; useful, but tiresome to be around.

I introduced him to Pretty Little One, who looked him over in a friendly manner, but with alertness, like somebody making up her mind whether to buy a dog for a pet. Pretty Little One she was not, but you wondered if a pretty girl was hiding under the blankets of fat. Now and then you thought you saw a young beauty peeping out of those black eyes.

Clarence explained that his money was in traveller's cheques and that he needed about a hundred dollars American in pesos until the city banks opened the next Monday.

"I will ask Arturo. I am sure he will oblige you."

She went to her husband, Arturo, and took a fat wallet from him. He got out of his rocking chair long enough for her to reach into his hip pocket. It was likely to be the most strenuous exercise Arturo would have that day. Arturo was always the calm centre of the swirl of activity at Pretty Little One's. He occupied a position similar to that of the Queen in Canada. Everything was done in his name. He reigned, but did not rule.

No one could doubt who ruled at this establishment. Sometimes I thought she might be ruling the whole town. So much of the decision-making in San Sebastian was done in this cluttered yard, with its tourist cabins that were never finished and its restaurant that opened and closed at times never announced.

Unhesitatingly she counted out 190-some thousand pesos into Clarence's hand, calling out the notes one by one as she passed them over. To make the count exact she added big metal pesos, heavy as lead, in denominations of five hundreds, tens and even singles.

I spoke English, in a casual tone. "Don't be deceived by how fast she made the calculation, Clarence. When you work it out on your pocket calculator you will find she paid you exactly today's bank rate, keeping out precisely 1¼ per cent, which is her commission. We're going to pickle her brain when she dies and send it to the professors at Harvard."

The man on the tractor kept the engine barking as his machine bucked up and down. A palm is not a true tree but a monstrously large piece of grass, and each palm frond has its own tube running down the trunk and forming its own root. The roots are, therefore, a vast disk, and to pull them out involves taking a fair nick out of the face of our planet.

"Wait a bit, Dark Horseman," said Pretty Little One to the driver, "I'll get them to dig around the outside of the root some more."

"That's a funny name," said Clarence.

"It's one of our names for Satan," she said. "Everybody in Mexico has a nickname. That's the Devil's."

"What is Mac's, then?"

"I don't have one," I said. When she looked at me, I realized that I did but nobody had told me. She was laughing.

"He is Wolf Man. You see those pale eyes, the hair on his muzzle? Watch also how he paces back and forth when he is thinking—restless, like a wolf."

Well, it was better than being called Double Wide because I was fat.

"Mr. Clarence also has a nickname, Pretty Little One."

"Truly?" she said, and Clarence also said, "Truly?"

"Truly. He is called The White Indian."

"You are Indian, Mr. Clarence?"

"Indian, also Mexican. I had a great-grandfather who ran a pack train to the gold fields in British Columbia. His name was Juan

33

Gómez, but he changed it in Canada and called himself for the place in Durango he came from. There were three lakes there, so he called himself Juan de Tres Lagos. After awhile the descendants forgot how to spell Tres Lagos and now it's the name I have, Trelegis. So I have come back to see my ancestor's home."

"The state of Nayarit is far from the state of Durango. They do not have maps in Canada?"

"Come off it, Pretty Little One," I said. "Half the people in this village think that Canada is part of Los Angeles."

She laughed and hugged me. "Clearly," she said. "Clearly, Wolf Man. Come, let us have a beer to welcome one more Mexican home."

She waddled off to the concrete-block building that had the Coca-Cola sign on it. It was a restaurant, bar and soft drink stand, to the extent it wasn't being used as a warehouse, toolshed and bedroom for the cook. The beer she brought us was, I noticed, half-size bottles of Pacifico. It was a cheap round for her. The White Indian traded his for a Coke. She drank nothing.

"Arturo will not want to join us. Arturo has a very delicate stomach, which is upset by beer." We arranged ourselves around a tin table that another beer company had provided for the establishment.

Seeing the tractor operator standing idle while the other workmen pawed around the ground with their rusty, broken hoes, she called him over also for a Pacifico. Dark Horseman parked the machine and came over to engage with Clarence and me in those ornate Mexican forms of introduction. His name was Jésus Davila Camacho, which I registered in my notebook that night, but it was for the notebook only—he is forever fixed in my memory as Dark Horseman, or sometimes Satan.

He was a big, heavy man with arms like telephone poles. He had a moustache of which to be proud. In San Sebastian anyone was proud to have a moustache, women most of all. It distanced them from Indians who, it was said, couldn't grow good ones. He was probably almost pure Indian himself, but no matter, he had a moustache. I thought there was an uneasy stillness in the man, a sudden quality. But I may be disremembering. He was, in fact, handsome, healthy and muscled like a lion. But for so vigorous a man, he was, this day at least, quiet. That's all. Very quiet.

He and Clarence talked baseball until it was time for a second beer. This time we all bought our own, and they were larger beers.

"So your great-grandfather's name was Juan and he came from Durango," Pretty Little One said. She had the ability to fire a question as a newspaperman can, as a command rather than a request, a method of eliciting a response even from somebody who doesn't want to make one. It has always surprised me, the human impulse to answer a question instead of saying, "None of your business." She had learned that somewhere.

"Not exactly," said White Indian. "John was the name he took in Canada. His original first name was Dorothy but in Canada people made fun of that name."

"Ah. A man named Dorothy. In Durango was a very important man named Dorothy. Have you heard of Doroteo Arango?"

"No."

"But you have heard of Francisco Villa? Pancho Villa? That was his true name. Doroteo Arango. You have read of him?"

"Some," said Clarence.

"Let me tell you a story about Francisco Villa. When he was a general, he came to a poor man in the hill country one day. He said, 'Come with me, I need soldiers.' The poor man said he could not. 'I have responsibilities, General. I have a wife and child to support.' Villa said 'Introduce me.' When he met the wife and baby he shot them both. 'Now,' he said, 'you have no more responsibilities. Come with me. I need soldiers.' That was Pancho Villa. Is that not true, Arturo?"

Arturo pressed his head forward and back, making a crease at the back of his neck; his second burst of activity this day.

"As Arturo will tell you, Villa was a crazy man. He was truly Mexican. Crazy. We are a people too much in love with death. We fuck skeletons."

"Then why is he a hero to the Mexican people?" I said.

"A stupid question, Wolf Man. A revolution needs men like Villa. Needs them desperately. Must have them. That is why we are grateful to God that He sent us General Francisco Villa when the revolution needed him, the murderous bastard. If we had depended upon the delicate people like Francisco Madero all would have been lost. Try the palm again, Dark Horseman."

She said it all without breaking stride or changing tone. As Dark Horseman walked away she said to us, "Now, friends, do you know that man?"

35

"Why would we?" I said.

"There is something of Pancho Villa in the Dark Horseman."

"He is a man who drives a tractor," I said.

"Ask him, one day, to tell you how he killed the man who murdered his father."

"How was that done?"

"He will tell you. All men tell far more than they need to tell. He will tell you. It is the nature of a man to talk too much." For once, she did not turn to Arturo for confirmation, although I'm sure he would have agreed. He never disagreed.

White Indian also rented one of the little concrete-block cabins. Three others were empty, given over to cockroaches and lizards. San Sebastian's tourist trade was never brisk. One other, she reported, had been rented this day by a professor and his wife, who were interested in birds, whales and something called the ecology. "He talks a lot. She is smarter." What else was new?

There were ever a few earnest seekers after truth drifting into San Sebastian and fleeing with the dawn when they discovered that nobody here wanted to share their insights. Once they learned that the only evening meals in the village were those eaten by the noseeums, the ecologists usually fled to Cancun or other tourist centres where they could be among people with appropriate concern for comfort as well as Brazilian rain forests.

The professor would be tiresome and his wife sloppy and noisy, and my notes on them could wait to see if they lasted more than forty-eight hours. If they didn't, they would be merely two names from Pretty Little One's register.

About him, I was right. He turned up while we were on our third beer, our hostess now well into a profit position after having invested one free Pacifico and one Coke in us. The professor spoke to us earnestly about estuarine protection. He was weedy, and you expected to see him carry a clipboard.

There is a brand of pretentious academic with whom I had been thrown into contact for far too long by circumstances not of my choosing, the circumstances being that I was a small-town editor and that meant bumping up against every damn type of human that exists. One of my reasons for retiring was to be rid of such people, and one of the compelling reasons for coming to Mexico was that I would not have to suffer their acquaintanceship south of the Rio Grande. I don't know why I was so optimistic, but I was.

I nodded when we were introduced and thought our mutual incompatibility might be apparent to him, but it wasn't. He remained confident that my interest in him, and any thoughts he might care to share, was intense.

I was wrong, wrong, wrong about the wife. She had violet eyes with large pupils, in which I drowned. So did Clarence, who rose to pull out a chair for her and catch a breath of her perfume. Even Arturo lurched out of his chair and made a bow before resuming his life's work of rocking back and forth.

All her bones were small and delicate and there was to her skin a translucent quality. She was a flower. You feared to take her in your rude hands but, oh, you also longed to do so, to awaken the sexual creature that lay within, to introduce her to pleasures and passions of which she knew not. As the professor prattled on I wondered, as I had many times before, why it is that the assholes of this world so frequently marry the prettiest women and catch the most trout.

Not to my surprise, both Pretty Little One and Consuela, who had emerged from the restaurant kitchen, detested her. Do not ask me why. God can testify she did not offend them. Phoebe Nell spoke little and was offensive to none.

The professor had bought the first secondhand Mexican-built Beetle he saw in a Guadalajara used-car lot. He had violated one old and simple rule—that of common sense. He had been sold a lemon. In its second day after purchase, the Volkswagen had lost a battery, one gear and a tire.

Jon had a special talent, common among bureaucrats, for turning small problems into big ones. From San Diego, the nest out of which he and his wife had recently tumbled, he could have driven here in his own car in four easy days. Instead, he used one day to book a plane and another to get tickets, go to the airport and fly to Guadalajara. He then spent a day in Guadelajara recuperating from jet lag, a malady to which he thought himself prone. Next day he bought the shabby old Beetle with the engine that sounded like a bagful of hammers, and two days later he completed the one-day trip to San Sebastian.

He had thus accomplished a four-day task in six days, at extra risk and expense. He insisted his was the rational approach, pointing out that, in addition to a degree in sociology, he had also studied political economics and sometimes lectured on the subject. No doubt he did. His disciples are everywhere.

He went on to explain that when he left Mexico he would resell the car, doubtless at a profit. It didn't seem worthwhile to point out that it is seldom easy, in any country, to buy a used car from a dealer at one price and then, a month or so later, sell it back to him at a higher price. This was particularly the case if you bought the first heap that hit your shins when you walked onto the lot.

But he was inoculated against all forms of worry, which proves, I suppose, the value of higher education.

He held a doctorate and had published several papers. This, he was confident, would impress Mexican policemen. Also, he was chairman of an ecological study group in Southern California, and—as he put it—this gave him political clout.

Perhaps most important, he said, both statuswise and overallwise, was that he was in Mexico on a grant from the Widdemeyer Foundation.

"I don't think many Mexican policemen will have heard of the Widdemeyer Foundation," I said.

"Possibly not. Many Californians haven't either. It's a rather small, closely held fund which our university doesn't talk about much." And not many American taxpayers will know how much they're paying you for a sabbatical leave or whatever it is that brings you here, I thought. But I didn't say it. I had not come to Mexico to acquaint idiots with their condition. I had come to listen and that included listening even to California dingbats.

He was sublimely confident that the village mechanic, known as the village blacksmith until the day before yesterday, would be able to repair his automobile. As for government interference, he was equally sure there would be none, the Mexican president having spoken so fervently about the need for more ecologists such as himself to serve humanity.

Thank God the professor was an American. I need not expect a call from the Canadian consul in Guadalajara saying, "I wonder if we could call on you for assistance. There's a fellow citizen in jail here who says you can help him."

After a few pointless inquiries about the nonexistent environmental movement in San Sebastian de Hidalgo, he left us. It was time for his meditation period, he said.

"Jon likes to stand on his head in the corner at least once a day;

then he sleeps," said Phoebe Nell.

"Picasso did it once a day all his life," said her husband. "He said it fed blood to portions of the brain which were otherwise not well supplied."

"Fascinating!" said Clarence. "When I went to school our teacher told us Picasso did it as a stunt to get his picture into *Life* magazine. I never heard the other explanation until now."

The professor considered prolonging the discussion but appeared to think better of it, a wise decision such as he didn't often make. Phoebe Nell seemed vaguely disturbed. There was a faint shadow in those violet eyes. Her pliant mouth came open and her little pink tongue lay for an instant against the bottom of her upper front teeth. Something was not fitting the pattern to which she was accustomed.

She walked away with Clarence's lustful gaze clinging to her simple cotton dress like cigarette smoke.

"Your motor is running, Clarence."

"Out of my class. Too delicate. Too much married, too. She couldn't manage adultery unless she had his permission."

 I was tempted to say that with those two it was the bland leading the bland, but let it pass. It was, after all, stuff for my notebook.

Not for the first time since I came to San Sebastian, I wondered if the Mexican republic was ever host to gringos who had their bubble well centred. The professor's elevator didn't go to the top floor. Clarence was in love with eighteen hundred pounds of old machinery that had a top speed of seventy-five miles an hour and seats as hard as the pews in a Presbyterian church. Wilbur was kissing cousin to the Wizard of Oz. Little Margaret killed dogs on the street for the glory of God.

I turned for enlightenment to the sanest person in the village, Pretty Little One, who said, "You know, Wolf Man, how it is with some men who look weak and frail and foolish? In time of trouble, they are the men who shine. They are the brave. The leaders. They emerge from the bud into a great fruit."

"You are suggesting your professor is that type?"

"No," she said. "He is an example of the opposite."

I started to laugh, but at that moment the earth shook beneath our feet. The tractor had flipped on its back and Dark Horseman's two sandals were lying empty in the dust while a dark stain began spreading from beneath the machine. I puked on the tin tabletop.

CHAPTER 5

THE CLUMSY GOAT FIESTA

[The Andalusians of the army of Cortés] distinguished themselves by their quick wit and resourcefulness and a certain swaggering gallantry, as well as by their irresponsible ways and their refusal to accept the official version of anything as the gospel truth.
—William Lytle Schurz, *This New World*

Every one of us has a dark beast of terror we keep chained in the dungeon of our soul. Mine happens to be vehicle accidents. Like most newspapermen, I've seen plenty of deaths—men shot, on purpose and by accident, drownings, and most of the rest.

In our town, the sheriff used to issue engraved invitations to attend hangings, and I have seen a couple of those, also. They were surgically clean, compared to what happens on the streets. No deaths ever chilled my soul like traffic fatalities; the injuries are so grotesque. One of the first I attended as a cub reporter involved a high-school girl whose face had been sliced off as she went through a broken windshield. I almost stepped on it, a complete face, two inches thick, like a Halloween mask, lying on the pavement. I saw many more that bad, later.

The one constant is that people's shoes fly off. They are always scattered about the scene, shoes with the laces still tightly knotted, flung off the foot by the last spasm of life. When the tractor flipped and I saw the empty shoes, I knew Dark Horseman was underneath, dead or dying, and that the damn thing was too heavy for any of us to lift in time. So I was as useless as the proverbial tits on a bull when Clarence, who still had his wits about him, started running towards the tractor and calling out, "Get some poles! Get something to pry with!"

I just tossed my cookies—projectile vomiting, they call it, when kids do it—and then I sat there, hopelessly, uselessly. Pretty Little

One sat there too, but for a different reason. She said, "Don't worry about him. He was born to be shot. Think about my tractor. I borrowed it from the Escobar family."

As Clarence approached one side of the tractor, Dark Horseman walked around it from the other. More dramatic, in a different sense, than the Devil coming out of the smoke cloud in Faust. He had a Raleigh cigarette package in his hand and was tapping one on his fingernail before lighting it.

"You're all right?" said Clarence.

"Why not?" said Dark Horseman. He put the cigarette in his mouth and lit up with a little plastic-stemmed match. There was not a tremor in his hand and his voice, as usual, was deep and calm. He had Paul Robeson's voice.

Probably without conscious thought, he had thrown himself to the right and downward as the tractor came backwards, although exactly how he got out of there neither he nor any other man might ever know. It must have been a convulsive leap to make his shoes fly off that way.

He saw the shoes on the ground now, went over and pulled them on.

"I admire your style," said Clarence.

Dark Horseman blew out smoke, eyed him through the cloud and shrugged.

"There they go, young men in their maleness," Pretty Little One said to me in a quiet voice. "Just wait awhile and watch The Dark Horseman. In an hour or two, he'll be crying and asking for his mother. At this moment, he has to appear casual, as if he'd just dropped a cigarette package on the ground."

"He does it pretty well. I'm looking at his hands. There is no shake."

"He knows you are looking for a shake in his hands, because he knows you, too, have the maleness thought. He thinks everybody in Mexico is waiting, looking for a shake in his hands. In fact, the 85 million other Mexicans are not noticing him at all, but he can't believe that. So he won't let his hands shake. Boys in this country train for this from the age of ten on. What he is, in fact, is a clumsy goat."

She walked over to the tractor and bent down to look at it, as well as a woman built like a culvert pipe can bend. You could see her calculating the cost of the smashed exhaust pipe, the hood, the controls and the lost gas and oil to the nearest $100 potmetal coin.

41

When I was so small I was hardly worth keeping, somebody gave me a kaleidoscope for Christmas, and I remember that what fascinated me was how rapidly the patterns changed. With one turn, a brilliant coloured pattern occurred but click, one more turn and everything was rearranged and a new pattern was before me.

Now it was happening at Pretty Little One's canteen. Before the tractor reared back and shook the earth, it was a workaday weekday afternoon. A few workmen shovelling, chipping, carrying and shouting at one another; Arturo in his rocking chair, sea birds crying, fishermen walking past carrying little canoe anchors or netting, children darting around like fish in a tide pool and, just to supply enough noise, somebody in a Datsun pickup truck shouting over a loudspeaker that he had exquisite dresses for sale, cheap.

The thump rearranged that kaleidoscope instantly, although briefly, into sombre colours and shadows. Some, like myself, froze and were useless and others, like White Indian, moved as men should in an emergency. But this pattern, too, lasted but a moment. Once it was determined that Dark Horseman was unhurt, there was another click, a silent one, and there was bright light, colour and laughter all around us.

Fishermen came running from the nearby beach, and men raced over from nearby houses. Within minutes, or so it seemed, two men with tractors roared into the yard from nearby fields. They pulled the capsized machine back on its feet, but nobody was much interested in the obvious damage it showed. There would be another time to think about that.

Having found no tragedy, everybody came to the natural conclusion that it must be a comedy. It had to be operatic.

They teased Dark Horseman without mercy. You don't turn tractors on their back, Satan; they aren't like women, they don't breed that way. Somebody produced half a bottle of brandy and offered him a pull. Another raced away to the beer parlour and came back with a case of beer.

Pretty Little One, never a person to fail to face realities, saw that a fiesta had begun and contributed three dozen beer. Consuela brought the ghetto blaster from the kitchen, set it on the tin table and turned it to maximum volume. Within five minutes the Syndic had arrived, bearing a fresh bottle of Bacardi. Within ten minutes, three or four wives and children had joined us.

Children always came with wives. In San Sebastian there were parties for men, which were usual, and parties for men and wives with children, which were occasional, but there were never parties for just men and their wives. A woman would be almost as unlikely to attend without her children as she would be to attend without clothes on.

A knot of workmen at one corner of the yard tossed money into a common fund and sent one of their number off to the Valenzuela family, who were known to have killed a pig at four o'clock that morning. He returned within minutes with platters of crackling and other pork portions, and with two of the Valenzuela boys, who were supposed to be hoeing corn that afternoon.

Consuela gave Coca-Cola to the kids, further eroding their white, even teeth while maintaining her nation's position as the second-biggest consumer of Coke in the world, and then, before I had time to think, pulled me off my chair and made me dance the cumbia with her. Because I didn't dance much better than Dark Horseman drove tractor, this added to the general fun. Some clapped their hands to encourage me. Others joined in the dance.

I narrowly missed treading a three-year-old child to death; he had staggered happily into our dance arena with a piece of pork crackling in one hand. Consuela swept him up on her big, strong arm, placed him on her hip and kept dancing while he shrieked with joy and smeared his face with pork fat.

It was time I contributed to the party. I conscripted Clarence to drive me to the one grocery in town where liquor was sold. It wasn't easy. The professor wasn't back, but Phoebe Nell was, and she was dancing opposite The White Indian, not with the vigour and joy of the Mexicans but, as you might expect, with that compelling delicacy she had.

She smiled amicably when I stole him, and went off to look for her husband again. One got the impression that Phoebe Nell had not spoken sharp words or exerted herself to anger or any sudden actions for many years. Perhaps she never had.

I intended to buy Bacardi, which sold for about the same price as the Coke you mixed with it, but, above the mutter of the Cream Puff's exhaust, I could hear the noise of the party and remembered what fun I'd been having. Did I want to do anything on the cheap today? Should I not spend, as the saying goes, like a drunken gringo?

I bought no cheap liquor but had Clarence drive me to the house, where I picked up my last bottle of Glenfiddich Highland Malt. He raised his eyebrows when he saw it; Clarence had acquainted himself with more of the better things of life than antique cars.

"They say it's habit-forming," I said. "I wouldn't know. I was never able to afford enough of the stuff to find out."

When we returned to the party, people were standing in a ring, clapping hands, while Dark Horseman and Consuela danced. They were doing what we call the Mexican Hat Dance; people in San Sebastian called it the Dance of the Common People.

Like so many warm, rich and lovely things here, it exalted simple things. It was the dance of a rooster and a hen, nothing more—he, proud, strutting, bold and very male; and she, attracted, but wise in her teasing. Dark Horseman, each time rejected, strutted and stamped his feet; while Consuela smiled, her gold-filled front tooth shining in the afternoon sun. The instant he turned and she was under his gaze, the smile vanished; her eyes were downcast, demure, and she delicately danced away, as if unaware of the magnificent mate who awaited her.

Dark Horseman was a heavy man, but he was catty-footed. He had tiny feet that seemed to float above the ground. It was all a great blaze of colour, passion and sound, with little boys and girls on the out-skirts of the crowd doing imitations. I was sorry when it ended with his bestowing a triumphant kiss upon her, behind one of those sombreros that measure a metre across the brim.

She danced with Clarence next, but who could follow an act like Dark Horseman's? The crowd applauded anyway. Mexicans seem capable of being gracious with gringos who try to dance their dances or talk their language; they are not afflicted with that terrible snobbery of the French, who reject any strangers who exhibit the slightest imperfections of grammar or accent.

One of the Valenzuelas had a guitar and sang. Two of the fisher-men became insulting to one another and wanted to fight, but were separated. The travelling dress-salesman left his truck and joined us, a bottle of tequila in his hand.

Clarence and I were leaning against the crippled tractor. I was sip-ping the malt. It was hard to forgive him for mixing it with Coke, but I tried. My God, in the Highlands you're a rogue if you so much as add water. Thinking some more about it, I came to the conclusion that White Indian had been drinking his Coke straight after pouring the world's finest barley bree on the palm roots. But I have known many alcoholics, and I know how to forgive them.

Yes, he confessed. "I try to let a year or two go by between drinks." He might have said more, but we found ourselves, suddenly, unexpectedly, in the presence of the silent boy Angel. He had a bucket and a rag, and he wanted to wash Cream Puff.

Clarence spoke English, so he could express himself without being understood. "Wash Cream Puff in a mud puddle? Kid, I wouldn't even drink your water here. I wouldn't even sleep with your sister."

"That's insulting, Clarence. You had no business saying that."

"I spoke English and I spoke pleasantly."

"No boy deserves to be insulted in any language for trying to earn his crust. You may have been poor on the reserve sometime yourself, Clarence."

"All right," he said. "Sometimes I just don't got class, as we drunken Indians like to say. But Mac, think about it for a minute. I have fought off kids with greasy, gritty rags at every service station this side of the American border. They are the worst road hazard in Mexico. They kill more motorists with dirty windshields than the Inquisition took down here."

"No child trying to work deserves insults, whether he understands them or not. You tell him in Spanish to get clean water from Consuela and do it."

"I was always taught to respect age," said Clarence. He spoke to the boy in Spanish, explaining how he wanted the car washed. We three all walked over together to Cream Puff, and Consuela brought water with lots of soapsuds in it.

"What's your price for the job, Fragment?" said Clarence, using the nickname he had learned from Consuela.

The usual answer, which infuriates gringos, is, "Whatever it is worth to you." However, the boy answered straight and true.

"I would like you to take me for a ride in this car," he said, solemn, unsmiling.

"That's all?"

The kid tried to retain his dignity. He wanted to say a simple yes and nothing more. But the truth popped out of his mouth. "I would like to be taken for a ride where other people can see me in your car."

"You are classy, kid," said Clarence.

45

Fragment was still wiping and polishing an hour later, warning the older boys not to lay so much as a finger tip on Cream Puff and, in the case of the younger, heedless toddlers, managing to coax, wheedle and jolly them away from trouble with a knack you can learn only by living among many, many small children. More than I had lived among. I have always found kids a bit of a pain in the ass, including my own when they were small, but the boy named Angel did seem to be a little different.

When night pounced upon the village and tried to smother it, nobody noticed at Pretty Little One's place. Some of the original participants had left after the first hour, but now, some three hours after the accident, two more tractors stacked with party people trundled down the street, the news having just penetrated to outlying villages.

A couple of the fishermen had left to visit the whorehouse at Santander, having been unsuccessful in urging the rest of us to join them. The loss of them was made up by new arrivals.

Consuela's party time seemed to have ended. She was in the little kitchen, serving up meat fried over charcoal, and a rich turtle soup.

I noticed that the establishment was selling food and drink again and suspected that when the party wore out (probably after 9:00 P.M., the village's official bedtime, except for those visiting the whorehouse) Pretty Little One's generosity in donating the first few cases of beer would be fully compensated, and perhaps the tractor repairs as well.

"You aren't having any beer?" I said.

"In Mexico we say there are three kinds of a fool: a man who rides without a bridle, a man who dances with his own wife and a patron who drinks with his employees."

"Very neat."

"Besides, I like beer in the heat of the day. Have some soup, real sea turtle."

It was soon after seven that Dark Horseman began shaking, as she had predicted.

"Go sit with him, White Indian," I said. "He seems to like you."

"No," she said, "Leave him."

"You mean he doesn't want company . . . ?"

"Dark Horseman has witches in his head. He is dangerous when he shakes."

White Indian snorted. "Your noses, Pretty Little One!"

"I have spoken. You can listen or not."

White Indian decided not to. He went over to Dark Horseman, who was shaking and crying. He didn't touch him, or speak to him. He sat beside him. I remembered Ken Chow, sitting beside me in his restaurant, just sitting, as a friend should. When I left, half an hour later, they were still sitting together. Dark Horseman shook, put his head in his hands, stared wildly about him from time to time and cried some more. He gave no indication that he knew White Indian was beside him.

I went home through the dark streets humming "Song of the North" to myself and reflecting that for the first time in many months, maybe many years, I was happy. Simply, elementally happy. Nothing great or important had happened to me, and as for my barley water, it was all gone and I might not see any more for months or perhaps forever. Nothing really mattered; nothing does when you are happy. I was happy about everything, about nothing. I knew the world was a good place and I was grateful to be in it.

A block from the house I stopped humming and began singing "Song of the North." I stood in the centre of the street and sang out the English version:

> and for a tender while
> I kissed the smile
> Upon her face

People lingering in their doorways before going to bed for the night smiled and clapped their hands.

As I unlocked the big iron door that opens into my patio, I was finishing the song.

> The mission bell's chiming
> And I mustn't stay
> South of the border
> Down Mexico way.

The neighbour, Juan Diego, lying in a hammock under his palm trees, picked up on the tune and sang the Spanish back to me. It's one of the rare songs whose English version is more sentimental than the Spanish.

For a flirt of a girl I lost my head
For a flirt by the name of Marieta

"Good night, Juan Diego," I called.

"Good night, Wolf Man," he called back. "The people said that you got drunk, but I do not think so. I think you are just happy."

I wouldn't make notes that night, but they were in my head. Tomorrow would do. As any newspaperman knows, the good stories write themselves. Why I thought I had discovered anything important I couldn't at that moment have told you.

Then I remembered I'd left my old car at the plaza. The devil with it. Tomorrow would do. I clanged shut the iron pedestrian gate behind me and switched off the automatic yard lights, which the owners had installed to ward off the burglars that San Sebastian didn't have. I would sleep well this night.

I remembered when Mother read me bedtime stories, in the days before I could read myself. A little boy in one story was so tired at the end of a happy, scampering day that "He fell asleep before his rosy cheek touched the pillow." My rosy cheeks were courtesy of people who operated a pot still in Scotland, people of whom Mother would not have approved, but I was planning to go to sleep that way.

I switched on the living-room light. There was a large man with a pistol facing me and, over in my favourite chair, another, a small olive-skinned man with eyes like a lizard's. "Your neighbours don't know we are here," said the lizard man. "You should not make any noise. We wouldn't like that."

CHAPTER 6

THE TINY PERFECT POLICEMAN

Poor Mexico, so far from God and so close to the United States.
—Attributed to, among others, José de la Cruz Porfirio Díaz, president of Mexico (1877–80, 1884–1911)

"You don't mind if I ask who you are?" I said. I wasn't sure I wanted to know.

The man with the lizard eyes conveyed some signal to the big man with the gun, who stuck it back in the waistband of his trousers. He seemed disappointed that he wasn't going to be allowed to fire it.

"We must apologize for coming in on you this way," said the Syndic. I hadn't seen him. The blue shine on the big automatic pistol had filled just about my entire horizon. The Syndic had been in a dark corner of the room, elbows on his knees, twirling his hat around in his hand by the brim.

"You will apologize for nothing," said the lizard man.

I was reminded of what I had been told before but I had forgotten. There was no typical Mexican. If there was a universal characteristic of these people, it seemed to be courtesy; yet here was a man with none. Some psychic surgeon had excised it from his personality, leaving nothing much but the taste of metal.

"Sit down," he said. I sat.

"I don't know who you are or why you're here," I said.

"Ah. The English tradition. We have not been properly introduced." He spoke English, perhaps as well as I do. It occurred to me there might be a reason for his using it. Neither his palooka nor the Syndic would know what we were saying.

"I simply want to know who you are and why you're here."

"What a coincidence. Precisely the questions I had to ask of you.

49

However, I have my answers. You are a policeman, operating within Mexico without the approval of the Mexican government or the knowledge of our own drug enforcement agencies. Those questions having been answered for me, the only one I'm left to ask is, can you give me any good reason that you should not be expelled from Mexico?"

"Yes. More than one. I am not a policeman. I am a retired newspaperman. I have broken no Mexican laws. I am behaving myself and you have no reason and no right to expel me."

He was lighting a cigarette, something he did neatly. He was a neat man—neat clothing, neat and well-polished shoes, a small, well-trimmed moustache. Not the sort of man you'd expect to be smoking Raleighs. They should have been Turkish ovals, and I should have been Agatha Christie, who could see merit in people like him.

"You are, then, standing upon your rights. How is your balance?"

I didn't answer.

"Listen to me, because I am only going to tell this to you one time. We Mexicans are a quaint lot. We can't make telephones work, our trains don't run on time, and there isn't a storekeeper in the country who can make change. You can all see that, you gringos. What you don't see is that we have not lost an ability to take instant and effective action. Unlike you people, we have not given over the streets of our cities to the criminals."

"I suggest we haven't either."

He waved a dismissal. The thin smoke of the stubby little cigarette followed the movement of his delicate little hand. "I attended the FBI school in Quantico. We did not dare to walk the streets of Washington by night, except in groups of three. And we were all trained policemen.

"You have lost the control of the streets of your cities. Yet you have the unparalleled audacity to come to Mexico and teach us about police work. As for expelling you, we have arranged that in the Mexican constitution. Section 33. A few words on paper, nothing more, saying that you should be expelled for the good of the republic. No appeals. No lawyers. No bleatings in the press and no protest parades."

By this time I realized that the perfect little man was reacting to invasion of his turf. This calmed me enough to also notice that his heart, to the extent he had one, had overtaken his head. There was a

50

thin red flush extending from one cheekbone to the other across a classic Greek nose, and his lips were coming away from his white, even teeth. It's when the emotions take over that you can sometimes win a point or two, and why not try?

"Neither of us is doing anything improper in San Sebastian," I said.

"I will decide that."

A mistake, tiny perfect man. You should have bumped your shins on the word *neither* but you didn't. All you heard was another squeal from a rabbit caught in a snare.

I put the card up my sleeve. I might have a chance to play it later. After all, that's what it all was, a game. I couldn't believe that anybody was playing for keeps.

I had lost all fear of the man with the gun. He was doubtless a policeman. There were, by my count, at least six different kinds of policemen in the country, ranging from elderly men who played downtown meter maids to men like my uninvited guest, who was doubtless a federal agent and, beyond that, a specific type of agent—a narc. The man with the gun was of one of the lesser breeds. He could drive a car, obey orders and shoot, but probably not much more.

I had no thoughts for the Syndic and no sympathy for his deep embarrassment in this little scene. If I were a better man I would have been more thoughtful about poor Cuauhtemoc, who had offered me nothing but friendship and good will and who was now being humiliated in front of me. I should have; I regret that I did not, but there it is. I did nothing to relieve the Syndic of his humiliation. Maybe I was a bit scared. I like hunting-guns but have always had an aversion to pistols and the other short kinds.

Alvarez, who finally introduced himself—no Christian name, no matrilineal name, just Alvarez—had a lot of bile to get rid of, and I let him spit it up. When he was through he'd be very tired but purged and quieter.

I couldn't warm to the man, but I could understand him. He was an intelligent and well-educated man who'd been treated too often as a second-class citizen. Traditionally police have not been cherished in this land, and Alvarez was a judicial, a federal and an undercover, making him even more suspect, feared and disliked than the cop on the corner.

And one could guess how often he was gaffed and played in the shallow water by rednecks in the FBI academy. None of this he spoke

51

of; doubtless he thought it was all hidden, but the hard truth poked out from time to time in the perfect English of the perfect little man. "They were tremendously relieved at the academy when I showed up wearing shoes."

Because he was obviously well-read, there was no lunacy of our great drug-prohibition crusade that was unknown to him. He told me, chapter and verse, how opium growers in the mountains of Sinaloa were acclaimed as patriots during the Second World War. They were then replacing Turkey as a source for the morphine and other opium derivatives needed by the American army. The sons and grandsons of the same heroes, growing the same crops, now watched Mexican army regiments sweep through their mountain plantations once a year, burning those crops and seizing anything loose that aroused their cupidity.

The crops were the same, but the world around those simple little farmers in the hills had changed. Whether you were a hero or a criminal was, after all, merely a matter of dates, as Talleyrand said about treason.

Somehow, I doubted Alvarez's concern for the poor Indian peasant with his opium and marijuana crops. Prosperity was the sort of thing Alvarez would be likely to reserve for the deserving, which he was and ignorant peasants were not. He was so vain, so supercilious, so unusually, strangely discourteous. "To the bad manner born," I thought to myself, a nice touch for my notes but not one to reveal at the moment. My fear of him had evaporated. My respect grew, although I would have preferred otherwise.

"You said you were a journalist," he said.

"Never," I said. "Never. I said I was a newspaperman. In my country, a journalist is a reporter who can't hold a job."

"Don't play word games with me. You say you are a journalist. If so, you will be able to tell me what is the biggest agricultural cash crop in the state of British Columbia."

I guessed cattle, or maybe apples.

"The biggest cash crop is marijuana. If you want to burn marijuana plantations, why don't you burn the ones in British Columbia? Why come all the way to Nayarit and Sinaloa to do it?"

I could have told him that his army was doing the burning, not ours or the Americans', but it seemed better to be silent. You don't pull the lid off a pressure cooker until all the steam is gone.

After awhile, he cooled off, and I was able to suggest I make us some coffee. He waved me back into my chair and ordered his constable—chauffeur, bodyguard, whatever he was—to make the coffee. Since the guy wasn't going to shoot anybody tonight, I suppose he might as well have been doing something useful. I pointed out the coffee and cups to him.

When Alvarez started drinking the coffee, which the constable had made too weak and too cold, I said, "My turn to speak?" and he nodded.

"I not only don't have police powers in Mexico. I also don't have them at home. I'm a simple, old, tired-out newspaperman who has a brother-in-law in the RCMP. He asked me to write gossip notes about the people in this area, and that's what I write. Gossipy letters." So far, I hadn't written my first one, but it seemed close enough to the truth to be useful. When that worked, I tried one more trick: "I'm sure Fitzgerald has told you."

When he didn't dispute that, I knew I'd guessed right. Staff Sergeant Fitzgerald was a Mountie stationed in Mexico City to whom I was to send my gossipy notes.

So I had learned two things this night and was rather proud of myself. I had learned that Captain Alvarez knew how inconsequential I was in the great scheme of things before he began berating me and I had learned that I was not the only gossip writer in San Sebastian.

It was a temptation to push my luck and test the name of the other man on him, to say "Clarence and I" or "Wilbur and I" and watch his reaction. But I decided not to push.

The captain was here to let me know where the eagle shat in the region of San Sebastian, and now I knew.

I didn't have to like him to be interested in him. For one thing, I had never before seen an angry man speak so violently for so long without using a single word of profanity. If he had spoken Spanish, this would have been easier to understand: Spanish is a poor sort of language for cursing; it has none of the crackle and lightning flashes and rolling thunder that you can accomplish with English. But he had spoken clear English throughout, excluding both other men in the room from the conversation.

Hoping to include the Syndic and placate Alvarez, I switched to Spanish and told the old southern U.S. sheriff joke about the FBI: "There are three things in this great republic which are vastly overrated: home cooking, home fucking and the FBI."

Alvarez replied in implacable English. "They are excellent policemen. It is the citizens of the United States who have failed them, not they who have failed the citizens."

So, in English, I offered to talk to him about the notes I'd made, and he waved that slender little hand to push away the suggestion. Fitzgerald, he said, would show him my notes, if they contained anything of interest.

Then why, I said to myself, are you here breaking into my house, waving guns in my face and embarrassing the village syndic, who is a decent fellow-citizen of yours?

I don't know the answer to that question even now. Perhaps it was to demonstrate to me that he was a dangerous man to insult. I could have settled for guessing that. When I see a rattlesnake, it doesn't matter to me whether or not it shakes its rattle. I am as repelled one way as the other.

It was long after this joust in the night that I learned how he first got the idea that I was a policeman. It should have been anticipated by anybody who knows that, in a bureaucracy, anything that can go wrong, will.

In Ottawa, someone who had sent their brain out for lunch had misfiled my name so that it appeared that I was somebody, rank unclear, serving on detached duty instead of being somebody's brother-in-law on no duty.

The union movement within the RCMP made the next error. It was called the Association of Seventeen Divisions and had never quite attained legal status, the RCMP Act being a stern Victorian-era document. Union organization work was done by an underground force like the Maquis in France during the German occupation.

Some unionist borrowed and later, undetected, replaced a floppy disk of RCMP members' names and locations. This, complete with my mistaken identification, was used to send out union promotional material, addressed to each serving member, by public mail service. Clearly, the man who borrowed the disk had so little common sense he needed a union to protect his job.

In Mexico, Thailand, Turkey, Afghanistan and half a dozen other places, undercover policemen suddenly found themselves getting junk mail that explicitly described who they were, with name, rank and serial number. It was a wonder nobody got killed.

54

As I was to learn, apparently only the Mexican post office had an unprecedented spasm of efficiency and, following standing orders, passed the letter to me along to their narcs in Mexico City for checking and resealing.

I never did get it. Probably our Mexico City embassy bureaucracy lost it also.

But this was an absurdity that I was to grapple with long afterward. On this night, it was enough that the Syndic and I were humiliated.

At 1:00 A.M., when all the town had long since gone to sleep, Alvarez made a signal to his constable, who went outside. A few minutes later his big, black, obsidian-shiny car rolled up to the gate from whatever part of the neighbourhood they had hidden it.

The captain entered it like a ring being tucked into a purple-plush jewel box, and the car muttered off down the street.

I went to bed. Probably I had not acquitted myself with brilliance, but I hadn't been as stupid and useless as some overpaid people in Ottawa. And Alvarez was an interesting man, even though he did remind me of a kid half my size who whipped me in a fair fight in grade 5.

So I tucked my rosy cheek into the pillow, but it wasn't the same as when I was a little boy and it didn't get any better at 7:00 A.M., when White Indian pounded on the gate and wouldn't go away until I promised to come for a moonlight shoot on birds that night.

Now awake, I pulled out the portable word-processor and wrote a note to my brother-in-law.

RESIGNATION

I don't need this crap. Tell your cottage friends thanks for the house, but I'm going home today with maybe a stopover at Cancun. This whole prohibition nonsense should be cancelled. It is absurd and dangerous. The funny parts are over. The hard boys are taking charge, and one of them is named Captain Alvarez. He is your Number One, just wait and see. But you will never catch him. Find me a new kitten for the house, will you? I will want company when I get home.

Like so many of my best editorials, nobody saw it except me. I left it in the computer until the afternoon, when I started thinking about

White Indian's invitation to the night flight and how such a shoot would have angered The Tiny Perfect Policeman if he knew of it. Shooting birds by moonlight is illegal everywhere, but it is rare good sport, and this was my one chance to do it in Mexico.

I called up my resignation note on the screen and punched a few keys to kill it. I killed it dead.

CHAPTER 7

SHOTS IN THE DARK

My only experience in hunting rail [was when] the birds had little cover. I soon reached the legal limit without missing a shot and still remember that facile experience with distaste. I have never wanted to shoot another rail. . . .

Success, when it comes, must be difficult and uncertain. The effortless taking of game is not hunting, it is slaughter.

—Former U.S. president Jimmy Carter, *An Outdoor Journal*

The importance of night-flighting birds may need explanation in an age when a large, profitable industry of expensive publicists, professional demonstrators and other salaried public nuisances has grown up, charged with trying to stop all hunting and consign all hunters to community-service work gangs. Factual information about hunting is unpopular and becoming scantier.

Therefore few people will know that night-flighting, which is rare and done surreptitiously, is a strange sort of shooting; it is hard shooting and, of course, illegal and approved of by nobody except people like Count Tolstoy, before he became politically correct.

It may be the ultimate test of a shotgunner, a man who excels over a rifleman as a dry-fly fisherman excels over wet-fly fishermen (and everybody else on earth). Anybody can shoot passably with a rifle if he has eye, muscle and breath control. Shotgunning depends on the Taoist philosophy of being in harmony with yourself and with the universe.

Nobody can shoot a shotgun well on a day when he has been fighting with his wife, worrying about a tax audit or losing money on the market. Wingshooting is in the province of universal harmony, which may say more about life and death than the anti–blood sports people can understand.

The other interesting thing is that you know before you shoot whether you are going to hit, and on this night I knew I would hit birds.

We bumped over a dirt track that somebody had cut absent-mindedly through the scrub, and set up on a bean field that lay not far from the ocean, whose swell sent regular whispering sounds to us as it hissed up and down the sands of the beach. We did not, of course, come in Cream Puff. That was a car far too beautiful to be useful for anything. We used my old Chev instead.

We had only one gun, a reliable old Winchester Model 12, which The Pretty Little One owned or borrowed or had some mysterious form of claim upon. Let us just say that she produced it.

The Mexican government does its tireless best to keep firearms from its citizens, for it prefers that only soldiers and policemen have the things. This hugely encourages the people to acquire guns—any old guns for any old use—even if they are too poor to buy ammunition for them.

Angel was the third member of the party. "We don't call you Fragment tonight; your name is Bird Dog," said White Indian.

I had always adhered to the rule that I would never night-flight birds without a dog to find the cripples in the dark, but like many of my Presbyterian strictures, it seemed to have faded under the tropical sun.

The sky had been needlessly exuberant about the loss of the day, but now it was quickly fading, and a few strands of mist hung over the bean field and stitched together the weedy little shrubs of the pastureland beside it.

A cowboy, half a kilometre or more distant, was singing as he took the Zebu cattle into their night corral. His voice came clear through the twilight air, pitched to a mournful tone to salute the death of the day.

You could hear the words clearly. The man in the song had been shot and was dying and every drop of blood that fell from him turned to a rose, which he wanted to give to his lady love. Her beauty was greater than his roses; nevertheless, he lamented that he did not have more blood in his heart with which to make more roses to throw at her feet.

"It's a beautiful melody," I said. "But why does he never sing about the next part, when he marries her and turns her into a barefoot slave woman, and then, because she's starting to look old, goes out and finds himself a second front?"

"No worse than my father," said White Indian. We had switched to English. "He beat me and my mother regularly for as long as I can remember."

"Is he where your blond hair comes from?"

"That, and a capacity to stand pain. He was a half, but white was the half he preferred. He married my mother, who was pure Cree, because he needed somebody to look down on, I guess. My mother was a saint. Simple as that. A saint with a great, unbreakable spirit. There is never a day I don't remember her."

"How did it all end—the beatings from your father?"

"I got big enough to fight him, and once I got him down I never let him get on his feet again. I ran him off the place.

"After I made my first big money in the oil patch, I built a new house for Mother, and she said it wasn't right to keep him out of it, so I let him come back. But he knew the first time he ever put a foot wrong he would be either dead or back on Skid Road, and that one suited me just as well as the other. So he hung around for a few years and then died as he had lived, meanly and shabbily. I wouldn't go to his funeral. There are a few things I wouldn't do, even for Mother. Yet there it is. He was my father. He is part of me." Clarence had a gift for looking at himself unsparingly.

"Are you talking about the birds?" said Fragment.

"In a way," I said, going back to Spanish. "They'll be here soon."

"Will it be possible for me to shoot the gun?"

We both looked at him. Angel had a little boy's face, out of which there peeped, with disturbing frequency, the face of a fully grown man. But his body was small and he looked closer to nine than eleven.

It's the intestinal parasites that eat them up. He probably harboured about a dozen kinds in his body, all of them sharing his tortillas with him. The neighbours told me he had been found eating earth at one time. It's a sign of vitamin deficiency, but the kids who eat earth usually end up with the worst of the many amoebas.

"That gun would knock you into the next field, Fragment," said White Indian. "But another year, when we go hunting together, yes, for certain."

The boy nodded. He was beginning to treat White Indian like the father he didn't have.

He wore thin cotton pants and a torn shirt, nothing more. As night came down on us and the air chilled, he began shivering.

"You are cold?" I said.

"There is not much cold," he said.

"But you are. Wear my jacket."

"Thanks," he said, in the tone of voice that means no, thank you.

You don't argue with that. I kept my jacket. He kept his pride. He kept shivering.

All the sounds of day had gone, including the song of the cowboy, and we waited for the cries of the ducks. They are fulvous tree ducks, an intermediate stage between duck and goose that favours the goose side. They fly in flocks, making wild and foolish cries that the Mexicans must have had in mind when they named them peepeecheenee. There are two varieties, and each is just as gooselike and crazy as the other. You can never be sure what they will do next; they don't know themselves.

This night, the collective foolishness of White Indian and me coincided with that of the peepeecheenee, and when the full moon was just heaving itself upward from the Mother Mountains they came in on us and we began shooting.

"You first, Dad," he said.

"Age before beauty," I said.

At night, shooting time is a fraction of a second that has been whittled to a point. There is, sometimes, a rustle of wings if the air is still. There are the cries of the birds, but these are less reliable for shooting because they come and go; there is a ventriloquial quality to them in that the near may seem far and the far near. What you may see for an instant in the moonlit sky directly overhead is one glimpse of dark wings opening or closing, like a single pulse from a dark star. In that breathless moment you mount the gun, aim and fire. At least you may be sure the bird isn't out of range; if it can be seen in moonlight it can be hit.

On a still night the noise of the gun is shocking. You expect game wardens from two counties away. Flame makes a big orange flower at the end of the gun, pyrotechnics you never see when shooting in the daylight hours. Before the gun leaves your shoulder the birds are past, and you wait to hear a thump on the ground, which is the only thing that will tell you if you hit.

There were two thumps. I had fired into a dense flock although I'd only seen one bird. That meant one would probably be crippled and wouldn't be found in the dark. It's one of the things you have to forget about when you don't have a dog.

Angel scampered into the beans, and when he came back we could see his white teeth before we could see his face. He had both birds, a live one and a dead one.

"Nice bird-dogging, kid," said White Indian, offering just the degree of praise that avoided condescension. Angel handed him the dead bird, and White Indian passed it over to me. I had never shot peepeecheenee before, but I had seen them in an ancient Egyptian painting that shows hunters getting tree ducks by throwing curved sticks at them.

"Kill the other bird," said White Indian.

"Will it not keep fresher if we leave it alive until we get home?" said the boy.

"Kill the bird, Fragment."

Angel wrung the bird's neck and we laid the two kills together on the ground next to the palm trunk.

When the next flight came over, White Indian also took two, but he did it with picked birds, reloading by slapping the trombone tube on the gun faster that any man I'd ever watched before. He was a know-it-all, a do-it-all. It all came, I suspected, from being the child of a strong mother and a useless father, a pattern that has created the men who fill history books. Oddly enough, I also liked Clarence, which is something I can't say of the few other great men I've known.

We had our fifth bird in hand before the thought came to me, as it often has before in my lifetime: What in the name of all that's holy am I doing here? I was a stranger in a strange land, using an illegal shotgun, shooting birds out of season and without a licence, and doing it all by night, as burglars do. Also, what we were doing could hardly be better advertised. In this calm air, the gun blasts must have been heard two, three or more kilometres away. Finally, be it noted, the gun we had was old but precious to any Mexican. A couple of enterprising bandits could hardly find an easier task than to creep up on a couple of men and a boy, knock us on the head and go quietly into the night with our gun.

"We have company," said White Indian.

The pops weren't loud, but they were explosions. They came from a bobbing light about half a kilometre away. Somebody was walking through the bean field, holding a torch or wearing a headlamp. The light wavered, switched back and forth and kept moving towards us. There was no machine. It was a man walking. There were more explosions.

"Somebody is throwing firecrackers into the bean field to scare away the ducks," said Fragment.

"I don't know what effect he's having on the ducks, but he has sure scared the hell out of me," I said. "Let's get going, White Indian."

"There's more birds where these came from."

"Clarence, our ass is out a mile. We don't have licences, we don't have a gun permit, we don't have a local guide, and may I remind you we never got around to finding out who owns this field and getting his permission."

"When was the last time you met anyone around here who cared about any of those things?"

We kept arguing until the man with the bobbing light was so close he could hear us talking. A retreat would have been undignified. Vanity, vanity, all is vanity, said the prophet, and it gets you killed sometimes. So we waited while he walked up, looking into the bright krypton lamp on his forehead.

"Good evening," he said.

Why, I wondered, wasn't I more surprised to find it was Dark Horseman?

"Good," he said, "good," looking at our little pile of birds. He handed Fragment half a dozen small firecrackers, which the boy put in his shirt pocket. Dark Horseman had in his other hand one of the guns Noah hung over the mantelpiece on the Ark.

It was a muzzleloader, caplock, and when he passed it to me I saw the dragon on the side lock. It was one of the old Hudson's Bay Company trade muskets made for the triangle route of China-British Columbia-Hawaii. This one had aged in the salt sea air and was much chewed down by rust. Its appearance had not been improved by painting the whole thing, lock, stock and barrel, with orange enamel house paint.

Dark Horseman offered to load the gun and to let me shoot it. He carried powder in a tiny pickle bottle and had some number 4 shot in another, and there was wadding he had stamped out of cardboard.

My curiosity was rewarded when the night-flight of peepeecheenee came over and the gun knocked me back a century or so. The thing couldn't carry enough powder for a good kick, but it hung fire so long that you thought the snap of the cap was the main charge, and I had started pulling it away from my shoulder when the main event came on stage. It gave me a bruise on the right cheek and everybody else a great laugh. Laughter was the universal salve in San Sebastian. If it was possible to laugh at any fact or misfortune, that was the balm applied.

For all that, it was a beautiful old gun. It came to the shoulder so easily. Mounting the Winchester afterward was like trying to shoot with a hockey stick. I told Horseman that, but he said that, frankly, he'd be just as happy with a gun a century or so newer. Where he obtained this one and why he was chasing ducks out of somebody else's bean field we didn't get around to asking. I should have, but I'm unprofessional.

More birds came in, and we passed the Winchester to Dark Horseman. Unlike White Indian, he wasn't much of a shot. There were many passes before he got a bird down, and while Fragment was racing away into the night to find it, we all agreed it was maybe time to pack it in, for the moon was high and the air was cold. But before moving, Dark Horseman lit a fire to warm us, using the thin sticks of a mesquite-type bush apparently rich in turpentine. We all got around the fire, pushing the child to the front because he was shivering continuously.

"Angel," said White Indian, "I want you to look after this jacket of mine. It's a good one, and I'm going for wood and don't want it torn by the thorns. So you look after it for me. Yes?" He put the jacket around the child, who nodded his head gravely just once.

From a fire it was a short step to suggesting that we clean two or three birds and barbecue them before going home. They would be tougher than sin, but having been taken illegally, would have their own special flavour. Besides, I found to my surprise that White Indian had a spill of salt wrapped in newspaper in his breast pocket. The kid was ecstatic and, quite forgetting about the precious jacket, raced off into the dark thorn bush, still wearing it.

First he came back with the pockets full of limes from a tree that a farmer or God had carelessly planted in the pasture. From a corner at the far end of our field, he found a plantation of chilies—Tail of the Rat, they were called; one of the hottest of the ninety varieties grown in Mexico. Then he was gone for almost twenty minutes, and I was beginning to worry about him when he came back from another far field with a watermelon, tunking its side with his knuckles to show us that it was just ripe enough to be sweet without being mushy.

Dark Horseman went off somewhere else and returned with ears of corn to bake in the coals of our fire.

I sometimes think of that night as being the Second Fiesta.

Like the first, the party at Pretty Little One's, it was spontaneous and arranged with extraordinary deftness. Within half an hour, here in the middle of the night in the dead centre of nowhere, we had assembled all the main ingredients of Mexican cooking—meat for barbecue, lime juice, chilies and sweet watermelon. Also corn, which originated down here somewhere and became the world's third largest cereal crop; corn, the mystic goddess of this land. It happens to be the only domestic food crop on earth that would disappear within a single year if not tended by humans.

What a rich land this was, and how easily one could live from it. Why, then, if they could create a meal out of moonbeams, couldn't people here make their damn toilets flush? Why couldn't they scrape a road level with a bulldozer or make change in the corner store?

We plucked, gutted and split the birds and barbecued them in the Argentine style, spread on sticks and placed upright before the hot coals. The corn charred but seemed sweet that night as we talked, as the tree ducks kept sweeping in on the bean field, yelping and yipping. Little Angel chewed duck as if it were the first meat he had eaten that month. Who knows, it could have been.

Duck fat was smeared over White Indian's precious jacket. He and I both noticed it at the same time, looked at one another and grinned.

Before he could finish his watermelon, The Fragment fell asleep. He just toppled over. I put my jacket on him, over White Indian's, and we built the fire higher. We were both reminded how very small he was. He slept like the dead.

"He is like the brother that died beside me," said Dark Horseman.

"Was that the one who fell under the tractor wheels?" I said. Consuela had told me some version of the story.

"No, that was a nephew and it was in California. We were wetbacks, working day and night to pay off our coyote who smuggled us across and still have enough left to bring something home. He was about thirteen or fourteen. He just fell asleep and went under the wheels. Next day the farmer reported us, anonymously, to Immigration and we were all picked up and shipped out so fast he never had to pay us our wages."

He spoke without rancour, without emotion. Satan knew the world was cold and cruel. He could not change it, but he could survive in it. That was his triumph.

"The brother who died beside me was harder. Much harder." He looked to Fragment to assure himself that the child was sleeping and would not hear.

"Our pueblo was in Sonora, in the desert. We were hungry when my mother got a job as a maid at a hacienda. But the first day she was there, she put a china plate on a propane stove and it broke. My mother was a very simple woman, a village woman. She had never seen china. She did not know it would break over flame. But the mistress, who had been about to pay her a week's wages in advance, took them back to pay for the plate. So we still had nothing to eat.

"My mother sent me and my brother back to our pueblo to borrow cornmeal from my uncle, but it was night when we set out and there came one of those terrible snow winds from the north. The Texans call them Blue Northers.

"We saw the lights of another hacienda and went there. We thought they might let us sleep with the cattle, but they set the dogs on us and we ran back into the desert and got behind some bushes. I covered my little brother with my body as well as I could, but in the morning my little brother was dead. He was very small, like that boy. He had no reserve of strength, as people say."

"A sad story," I said.

"Sad for me. Not for my brother. Because that morning I knew, I knew absolutely, that my little brother was already with the Virgin of Guadalupe and that she was never going to let him be cold or hungry or frightened again. A wonderful thing, the faith of a child. Do you remember what it was like?"

He had packed his brother's body to the pueblo, and because nobody could afford wood for a coffin, they had buried the little boy wrapped in a blanket. However, he said, the priest performed the ceremony free. The mother was brought home for the funeral, but that, too, cost her a day's wages.

"Pretty Little One says there is the smell of death about you, Satan," said White Indian. I couldn't have said that, but he could. I don't know why, but he could say it.

65

"She talks a lot, that one. But I know what she talks of. It is the time I killed Barracuda."

Barracuda, he told us, was a very big man, very large, very important, who had made money far too fast for an honest man.

"I went to his house in Cuernavaca. It was a day, I had learned, that almost all his bodyguards were away, and I was right; he answered the door himself. He was an old man. He had been reading. He had an Excelsior in his left hand and his glasses were pushed up on his forehead.

"I said, 'Do you know me?' and he said, 'I beg your pardon, I'm afraid I don't.'

"I said, 'Oh well, you probably wouldn't remember me. I was only nine years old when you came to our house and murdered my father. Now I am eighteen, and I have come here to murder you.'

"He knew how to die like a Mexican, that old grandfather. He looked at my face, nodded his head and said, 'Yes. Yes, I see the family resemblance now. Your father would be proud of you today.'

"I was beginning to shake and I knew if I didn't shoot quickly I would not shoot, so I brought out the big pistol and fired, and the whole top of his head came away. When I walked away, very calmly, one woman was screaming, his daughter, I think, and another woman had run and knelt down and taken Barracuda's head in her lap, bloody as it was.

"I saw her bent over, and do you know who I saw? I did not see the tiles, the wrought iron, the marble. I saw my mother, bending over my father in our dusty yard among the chickens and the pigs. It was the same woman I saw. My mother.

"I wanted to say to her, 'Do not grieve for us, Mother. We men are not worth it, with our silly, prideful and wicked ways. Stop your tears, Mother.' I may have said something like that. I don't know. I began to shake and I remember nothing more. But they tell me that I tried to kill her, too. I fired all the rest of the magazine, they say, but I only hit her lightly once or twice. Who knows?"

"What business was your father in with Barracuda?" said White Indian.

"Of that I know nothing, of course. I was only a child when my father was shot down. And I had never known him truly because he was hardly ever at home. My mother supported our family. He just visited, now and then."

66

He poked the fire and watched the sparks dance.

"What my father was really doesn't matter. It is not a part of my story. He was my father. He was me and I am him. That is enough."

"A funny thing you should say that," said White Indian.

"Life can be hard," I said. There are times you must say something, no matter how banal.

Dark Horseman shrugged. "We suffer. Then we die."

Blackness was creeping in upon our fire from its edges and the moon was high and small and far away. The night now seemed very cold. We started home. Fragment never awakened when White Indian picked him up, but I noticed in the last light of the fire that the man he would become no longer looked out of his face; the face was again that of a little boy. He wrapped his arms around White Indian's neck as we walked to my car, which wouldn't start. Dark Horseman, strong as Paul Bunyan's blue ox, pushed it. The engine fired and we drove back to the village, speaking no more, each living with his own memories.

CHAPTER 8

A PRESENCE IN SAN SEBASTIAN

Age appears best in four things—old wood to burn, old wine to drink, old friends to trust, old authors to read.—Alonso of Aragon

Staff Sergeant H. P. Fitzgerald
Royal Canadian Mounted Police
Canadian Embassy
Mexico City

Dear Mr. Fitzgerald:

Am sending this from a fax rental office in Guadalajara to your private fax number in Mexico City. This, I was told, is a secure way of sending information to you.

What I have is not much information. As for security, I suppose it libels a few people, but people in this country don't seem to have taken up the habit of suing every time they break a fingernail on the Rice Krispies box, so that probably doesn't matter much either.

My brother-in-law told me that I was to write you long, chatty notes from time to time, saying nothing more than what I was observing in San Sebastian de Hidalgo. He said I was not to try to be a policeman—it was too late for me; I'd never make it.

The instruction to not try to be a policeman has been reinforced by a colleague of yours, Captain Alvarez of the federal police narcotics division, and I suppose you will be going over my material with him, assuming it is worth going over. He indicated he had no interest in my talking to him directly about my observations. He indicated, in fact, that it wouldn't bother him if I dropped dead. My nickname for him is The Tiny Perfect Policeman.

68

However, I am grateful to be told to write at length. I was editor, publisher, and full and complete dictator of half a dozen newspapers in Ontario, but was never able to grant myself freedom from the Procrustean bed. Now, at long last, I can be prolix, if I haven't lost the capacity for such error.

First, this place:

San Sebastian is a cluster of small and rather dirty two- and three-room buildings, holding one another up on narrow, dusty streets beside a lagoon. It has a church, a first aid station where bloody rags from the last childbirth can sometimes be found on the floors, and a post office that operates out of somebody's living room. When a letter for you arrives the postmaster sends it to your house with his little boy, who blows a whistle outside your gate until you come and take it, so I suppose it's fair to say that Mexican mails work much better than the Canadian mails do.

Of course, you may not hear the whistle. San Sebastian, although small, is not quiet. We seldom hear even the restful sound of the ocean beating upon the reef called the Drum, which is only a kilometre or two from my house. The dominant sounds are the shouts of children, music from ghetto blasters, the barking of dogs and the crowing of fighting cocks.

The priest summons people to prayer with a loud-speaker whose raucous tones reach far, far beyond the village limits. I can't quite reconcile this with the law forbidding him to wear his robes outside the church door. Personally, I'd rather let him wear robes on the street and stop the 6:00 A.M. loud-speaker, but then it wasn't my revolution.

All farm tractors are unmuffled and sound like Vickers machine guns, and full-size explosions are by no means uncommon, because conspicuous consumption in this village takes the form of fireworks. They are exploded all day, and sometimes at two and three in the morning, for almost all the many fiestas. On New Year's Eve, in addition, every citizen runs outdoors at midnight and fires the pistol he is not supposed to own into the sky, emptying the whole magazine.

Sometimes a silence falls upon San Sebastian that lasts as long as five seconds. It is like one of those embarrassing moments at a cocktail party when the assembled guests are seized with the notion that somebody is going to make an announcement. When such a silence falls here, the people say it is because an angel is flying overhead. Very few angels fly over San Sebastian.

I know. I live next door to a veterinarian who raises fighting cocks. These birds normally crow at sunrise, but in this pueblo they are more ambitious. They begin crowing at 10:30 P.M., anticipating the dawn. When the sun finally rises, they are too hoarse to utter a croak. Need I mention that all through the night the other roosters of the village, who believe they could have been just as good as the fighting cocks if they'd had a better start in life, are trying to wear out their vocal chords under the moon, while the burros are braying, dogs are fighting and strange creatures are screeching?

A century ago, oceangoing ships anchored off the outer beach and were loaded with coconuts, sun-dried fish and other cargo by men who lightered them out of the lagoon to deep water. San Sebastian was one of the alternate ports, albeit a poor substitute, for San Blas, the great fortified harbour out of which Spain reached for western North America and failed to grasp it. Even San Blas is almost forgotten now. Gringos write "Class of '86" on the cannons at the fort. San Sebastian is even more forgotten, because its lagoon is silted up.

I told you it would be a chatty note. But you're a busy man; I should not trespass too much on your time. Let me review my notes—my list of non-suspects, you might call it.

I write my comments beneath each name; the mundane facts, ages and addresses are added as an appendix to this note.

MARIA DEL CARMEN DÍAZ DE LA RUEDA,
nicknamed Pretty Little One

There is a presence that hangs over San Sebastian, watching all, caring for all, and never forgotten. It is not the Virgin of Guadalupe.

The Pretty Little One forms a sort of reservoir of information and advice for the village. She knows all, sees all and speaks little. She is a keen student of the dollar.

She has what most closely approaches a tourist facility here. There are four concrete-brick cabins, with cold-water taps that sometimes run, and a canteen that sells Coca-Cola, beer and, as whim dictates, meals, some tasty. She also has space for trailers and can locate for her guests just about any desired service—horses to ride, boats to charter in the lagoon, or taxi service to the nearest city.

Everything is conducted in the name of her husband, Arturo,

whose task in life is to hold down a rocking chair so that it doesn't fly off to the moon. If you ever see a rocking chair on the moon, it will be a sign that Arturo got off it for longer than one quick trip to the bathroom. He is as harmless as a lizard on the wall, and just about as good company.

If there is a major drug shipment to be made out of this old, silted-up harbour or the ocean beachfront, I have no doubt that Pretty Little One will know of it. However, she is not likely to speak of it to me, to you, to anyone. She knows how to keep her own counsel.

Of course, your interest is whether she is a major figure in drug operations here.

Certainly she could be. She is intelligent and seems well-read and well informed. However, if Pretty Little One is so smart, why ain't she rich? It's a fair question.

She has held the commanding heights in this pueblo for twenty years or more, but she still tries to do her own tire patching on her old truck. She squeezes every peso until it looks as if a train had run over it, and does not now, and apparently never has, exhibited any sign of affluence.

She has a striking ability to pick up rapidly on any idea. She can listen to a couple of her guests talk about soybean futures on the Chicago Exchange, and leave them quiet and thoughtful as she suggests how to make a fortune out of the Brazilian drought, about which she has heard from some other guest. She vacuums the brain of every person she meets and seems to have a remarkably clear and retentive memory of what she has learned.

However, there are strange gaps in her encyclopedic memory. She was making some rather acute comments the other day on the prospect of Canada, Mexico and the United States forming a common market some day. An itinerant American businessman had spent a night at her establishment, and they had discussed the idea. But in the course of talking to me about it a few days later, it became apparent that she could not clearly distinguish between Alaska and Canada.

In any case, whatever her undeniable astuteness and all-around wisdom, somehow she ends up with little money.

I think I can understand that, though gringo friends of hers in this pueblo cannot. Pretty Little One lacks capital, and without capital, thousand-dollar ideas can never become million-dollar ideas. She could have capital. She could borrow. No one has a higher reputation here for business acumen. But there is another lack in her: she can talk confidence but she doesn't have it.

For all her knowledge of finance, she cannot understand money. She is rather like a Canadian scarred by the Great Depression, believing that a penny saved is a penny earned instead of one-tenth of a penny lost. Given her peasant impulse to hide money under a mattress, she probably failed to take advantage of the 75 and 80 per cent bank interest rates that accompanied the inflation, so any savings she may have had probably disappeared like fairy gold turning to dust at dawn.

An indefatigable worker she is, but she is also one who would miss out on a million-dollar deal while searching for a dime she had dropped under the counter.

I made it my business to learn more about Pretty Little One than she thinks I know. When two sets of parents led her to the altar to marry Arturo and become his means of support, she was one of prettiest creatures San Sebastian ever produced. Now and then, in her eyes and in her expressions, the beautiful woman inside peeps out and you are struck, just for the moment, with the thought of what a ravishing creature she was.

Within six months of the marriage, she ran away to Mexico City with the man who drove the Coke truck. I have seen pictures of him. He was a thin man of modest appearance, and I am told he had much to be modest about. I will never understand women's choice in lovers. Never. At any rate, he was the great passion of her life. Within a fortnight he was dead.

So much of this country seems like a continuing grand opera that one expects Pretty Little One's lover to have died in some combat of cosmic proportions and been borne to Valhalla by the Rhine Maidens. No such thing. He stepped in front of a bus on Insurgentes Boulevard in Mexico City and was declared dead at the scene.

She came back to San Sebastian bearing his child, the lusty, busty, delightful girl named Consuela. From the day she returned, Pretty Little One devoted herself to the care and feeding of Arturo, the making of money and the accumulation of many kilos of fat.

She and I have an hour together most Sunday mornings during which we drink some beer. My beer.

We do it Sundays because that is the day she comes around to sell me Watchtower Bible tracts. She is a devoted Jehovah's Witness, although she tells me she hopes Consuela, when she eventually marries, will have a full Roman Catholic ceremony because it is, after all, so beautiful.

Being nine parts atheist, I have enjoyed some heavy debates with her over our Sunday-morning beers, but never quite like those involving Clarence, The White Indian, who often shows up on these occasions and drinks coffee by the bucket. The White Indian even pulled out a Bible one day and began pointing out pivotal passages to her. Whom did the children of Adam and Eve marry? Why did an all-merciful God put little children to death just because they had made fun of an old man with a bald head?

She wouldn't even look at the pages. "God is not mocked," she said. "God is merciful. God waits for you, knowing, quietly, that you will some day accept Jesus in your heart."

White Indian, who is a bit of a smartass, is completely frustrated by such an argument and often goes off in a pout.

Obviously, Pretty Little One has the sophistication, the circle of acquaintances and the will and determination needed to run a major drug operation. But she doesn't know that she has all these qualities, and if she is your Number One in San Sebastian, well, I am from Missouri, Mr. Fitzgerald.

CLARENCE TRELEGIS,
nicknamed The White Indian

On his father's side, his despised father's side, White Indian is descended from a Mexican packer who went to the Cariboo gold rush in British Columbia in the 1860s. His mother, whom he worships, was pure Cree, he says.

I mention the Indian aspect because it is a factor in Mexico as well as in Canada. As you know, this country is mestizo, a blending of Caucasian, black and native Indian bloods, and this is true of more than 90 per cent of the Mexicans. However, in special ways, they disavow their predominantly Indian heritage. Pretty Little One confided in me her regret that her attractive daughter has no hair on her face or on her legs and arms, the lack of which makes made her seem more Indian.

White Indian was listening at the time she said this, and I wondered how it felt for him. When you're in a dominant majority, it's easy to forget the constant put-downs that minorities experience. For Clarence, even here, there was no escape from the tag *Indian*. *Indian*, good man in the bush, poor man in town; *Indian*, always Saturday-night rich; *Indian*, can't handle his liquor. He was impassive, as they usually are. It doesn't mean they don't hear.

So I suppose I should confess to sympathy for White Indian, though he has a less than delightful personality. He has an insufferable contempt for everyone who is less intelligent and adept than himself, and, in truth, most of the people on this earth are not as intelligent or adept as White Indian. Some combination of genes produced a specimen of unusual health, vigour, resilience and general intelligence. If he had some sense, he'd be perfect.

It is his pleasure to seek out the difficult, such as fighting oil-well fires or diving into the North Sea for the oil companies. Once he has mastered the trick of anything difficult, he walks away from it contemptuously, letting it be known that what is difficult for ordinary men is boring to him.

White Indian is the man who bats a thousand and then tells the talent scout to go pee up a rope because his real interest is in catching smallmouth bass or playing jazz.

He has told me nothing about why he is here on the coast in the state of Nayarit instead of over on the other side of the Mother Mountains in the state of Durango, looking for the birthplace of John of the Three Lakes, his great- or great-great-grandfather.

He could be a major player in a drug operation here. My hunch is that he is working for you, either as a half-assed amateur, like me, or, more probably, as a sworn member of the Force. He did let slip once that he dove for you people in Sheet Harbour, Nova Scotia, at one time to retrieve a cache of drugs sunk there by a delivery ship.

JÉSUS DAVILA CAMACHO,
nicknamed Dark Horseman, Satan

A big, powerful man with a violent history. He is probably epileptic or schizophrenic, but except when in such a state has a nature best described as sweet.

He comes out of hungry Mexico. He is probably the sole survivor of eleven children. There is possibly one other, a sister, who may be still working as a prostitute in Campeche on the Gulf of Mexico shores.

Dark Horseman works for Pretty Little One or anybody else who will pay the minimum wage. He comes from the high desert country on the other side of the Mother Mountains and was once smuggled into the United States by coyotes to work as a wetback. Like most experiences of his life, that one was tragic.

You should find Davila in newspaper files quite easily. He is the man who assassinated the gangster they called The Barracuda in Cuernavaca some six, seven or eight years ago.

He was captured after the murder, and since Mexico puts people in jail for twenty-five years for murder, and won't consider pleas for early release until about twenty-four of those years have gone by, it seems to my simple country-newspaper mind that he must have been pardoned in exchange for playing double agent in this narcotics business in San Sebastian. You won't confirm or deny this, but I am not asking you to, either. It just seems obvious enough to bear noting.

The friendship that has developed between him and The White Indian I take to be further proof of my contention. Again, it doesn't matter if I am right or wrong. I am writing a chatty note.

Before closing Dark Horseman's file, it should be noted that he is far too poor, far too clearly destined to lifelong poverty, for there to be any serious consideration of him as a drug lord.

HENRY TERWILLIGER III,
nicknamed The Drunk

Within his hearing, he is also nicknamed Pinocchio. He is long and gangly and given to sudden, jerky movements such as puppets have.

He is married to a woman named Grace. She is a saint. I need say no more about her.

While I don't have the facilities for checking here, I have no doubt that your people will find that Henry is what he says he is, third-generation Detroit automobile family with an estate at Grosse Pointe. He says he spends fifty weeks in Mexico and two weeks at Grosse Pointe, which is about one week too long.

The Drunk is devoted to the U.S. Constitution, the Bible and the Republican Party, not necessarily in that order of preference.

"People say my views are simplistic," he told me once. "But I say times like these cry out for bold men with simple thoughts. There is absolutely nothing about protest marches and flag burnings than can't be simply solved by sending them all to heaven."

Henry can also prove that the United States did not lose the Vietnam War, but won it. However, that takes half an hour and involves charts. Most of us agree to join the Republican Party when he approaches: it's easier that way, even if you aren't a U.S. citizen and cannot vote Republican.

He has a large and handsome estate with many servants. He is given to throwing popcorn parties for kids, being staunch in the belief that there is no such thing as a bad child. Only when they reach their teens do they become prey to drugs and sex, traps set for them by the Kremlin.

The people here like him, in part because their kids like him and they trust their children's judgement; in part because he never preaches to them about the Bolshevik menace, believing that they are so far sunk unto socialistic depravities as to be beyond redemption.

My conversations with him indicate that neither he nor his father has ever done a hand's turn of work in their lifetime. This explains the devotion to free enterprise, granddad's free enterprise having sustained the family for so long. However, the thought of him being capable of arranging narcotics transshipments, dealing with the heavily muscled men I suppose to be involved in that trade, is not very credible. Besides, Grace, who is twice as smart as he is, wouldn't let him do it.

WILBUR OSHASKI,
nicknamed The Pole

The Pole flew Liberators over Europe for far too long. He finally created a nervous breakdown for himself, which brought him before a board that offered him the choice of serving on the ground or taking an honourable discharge. "Sir," he said, "if I can't fly any more, I would rather give up my commission." They put him back flying.

"I thought it was the right pitch to give them," he told me here. "They usually take talk like that seriously. I couldn't tell them the truth, which was that, for Christ's sake, I was just fed up with having Germans shooting at me while all those fat patriots were sitting in bombproof bunkers in Surrey and Kent and telling us to get in there and hit 'em hard." Wilbur flew out the war. He came home to the U.S. Midwest with a couple of medals, but like any good veteran he doesn't talk about them.

After making a bundle in the farm machinery business, he came down here and married a Mexican woman, a Mayan from the South. She is as quiet as Wilbur is noisy, and they are the perfectly matched pair. There are no children, and they are too old to create any now.

For most of his life after the war, Wilbur was an ideal cocktail-party man, replete with jokes, witticisms and a barefoot charm. However, for the last ten or maybe twenty years, his needle has stuck in the same groove, and the same melodic phrase plays over and over again until you think you might have a split in your own skull.

He settled here in 1960 and seems to have everything he wants to get from this world—privacy, the right to indulge in his foolishness, and a wife whom he truly loves and who must love him.

If he is involved in one of North America's largest drug movements, I cannot imagine whence he summoned the energy or ambition, or, for that matter, why he wants a few million dollars' reward for such exertion. He tells me he can't spend what he has, and it is true, his tastes are simple; he really doesn't need much money to fulfil them.

OTHER LOCAL MEXICANS

Pretty Little One excepted, it is hard to suspect any Mexican in San Sebastian of being a kingpin in the drug trade.

There are a couple well placed for it. One is Antonio Ochoa Bajaras, who had a duty-exempt manufacturing plant in the Frontier Zone near Nogales and made a heap of money. He has enough to buy into a drug ring, but all he seems to do here is tend his garden. He has a young family, a boy and a girl, from a second marriage, he himself being close to sixty years of age.

He takes little part in village life, being, in truth, a lone representative of the wealthy class. His children go to private schools and will go on to American universities while he and his wife commute to the big cities for social and cultural refreshment.

The fact that a man has a million American dollars doesn't stop some of them from trying desperately for a second and third million, so it could be that Mr. Ochoa is Number One. All I can say is, the evidence is zero.

Another natural suspect is the Syndic, our mayor. He could be concealing a grand design to make millions on drugs, ship it out of the country and retire to Aspen, Colorado.

I just don't think so.

I am sorry to be so unlike a policeman, but then, I am not a policeman.

It's just hard for me to associate Mexicans whom I have observed here with high-level crime. My reasons may not seem logical but to me they are real.

(I realize you know more about the Mexican drug lords than I will ever learn, but indulge me; let me make my point.)

The tradition here seems to be that Mexican bandits flaunt their power. They reward their friends, destroy their enemies and ignore those policemen they are not hiring.

In San Sebastian, nobody is flaunting. There is no peacock screeching and, with their impulse to male display, if there was a peacock here he would screech.

What do ordinary people in this village think about the drug trade?

Their reaction is to sing ballads about the drug lords, as they did about Pancho Villa and other cruel and violent Mexicans.

I visited Mazatlán awhile ago. It is in Sinaloa, the next state north. In the nightclub the balladeer was singing about Manuel Salcido Uzeta, who is called Crazy Pig.

> They say this man is very bad
> Sirs, I don't believe it.
> He is legendary, he is valiant
> And because of this they fear him
> But at the bottom of his soul
> He is a sincere friend.

Crazy Pig is in hiding now, but they still sing about him.

They also sing about Shaggy, the nickname of Rafael Caro Quintero, who has been arrested in Costa Rica and is now jailed in Mexico City. Shaggy is credited with walking into a Mexican federal police office with four bodyguards, each carrying AK 47s, and saying to the commander, "What is your choice? Silver or lead?" The commander chose silver.

He is supposed to have been involved in the torture and murder of an American Drug Enforcement Administration man in Guadalajara. The ballad about him goes:

> Born in Sinaloa
> The sort not born every day
> And that do not surrender
> For killing a policeman.
> Today he is arraigned
> They say they want to judge him
> The Americans, over in their lairs
> They take him to make our souls sweat.

I guess any man who walks around festooned in gold chains and kills people will get a ballad written about him here. It's the same as Hollywood glorifying wretched little hoodlums like Al Capone.

But there is, perhaps, a better reason than selling songs or movies for these people to admire the drug lords. They say to themselves that no man who is hated and hunted by two national governments could possibly be all bad. I can understand that kind of thinking.

I take it you are trying to pick up a more discreet gringo drug baron, born to a different tradition, and I wonder if your source isn't one of the established Mexican drug operators. I realize you won't confirm or deny.

Marian Marjorie Dodds,
nicknamed Little Margaret

Boston Brahmin family. She got cross-threaded sexually and had a lesbian love affair for which all the rest of her life has been one long atonement. This is hardly the place for grief and remorse on that issue. The husband and wife who run the pharmacy in town are both males, and the husband and wife who run the clothing store are both females.

Little Margaret is fat, forty and frumpy. She means well with such intensity that people like me run away and hide in the woods when we see her coming. She loves God, all the saints, whales, macramé, Schweitzer and, when she can't think of anything specific, all mankind.

A constant doer of good deeds, a constant pain in the arse, but a good creature who deserves a harp in the choir of angels when she passes over the Great Divide.

If Little Margaret is in charge of this drug shipment it should be allowed to proceed, because with the profits she will feed half the children of the Sahel for two years.

JON JOHANSSEN
AND HIS WIFE, PHOEBE NELL
no nicknames

Jon the Professor is like Little Margaret. He favours good deeds being done on behalf of the poor, the weak, the witless and a few of the undeserving. However, Little Margaret thinks this can be accomplished by prayer, personal sacrifice and the intercession of saints. Jon's view is similar but different. He favours the creation of committees and study groups and sees approaches to government as being more important than approaches to the Almighty.

He, too, claims to have the ear of the powerful, but they are not saints; they are politicians and prominent environmentalists. What Little Margaret leaves to the infinite wisdom and mercy of God the professor has identified as a government responsibility.

He is here on a grant from the Widdemeyer Foundation. As far as I can discover, he has been engaged in such projects, hanging on the tit of one grant or another, for the past ten years. As he says, he may never get around to teaching any more. I find him a nit, but a harmless nit. He has spent the past week arranging for a game preserve to be established between the municipal dump and the oceanfront beach.

Since he doesn't speak enough Spanish to shout "Fire" in a smoke-filled room and make himself understood, I personally doubt that he has so thoroughly convinced the Spanish-speaking municipal authorities in Santander of the benefits of game preserves. However, he believes that he has, and, to an academic, a belief is every bit as good as the real thing.

His wife, Phoebe Nell, does not appear to be an intellectual giant but she makes up for it with grace and charm; more, in fact—she has a rare and compellingly delicate beauty. I probably should record that she does have a nickname, applied by Consuela and her mother, who for some reason do not like Phoebe Nell. Maybe it's because you can see the delicate blue veins through the translucent white skin of her forearms. They call her The Cunt.

ALL THE OTHER PEOPLE

There is a steady trickle of people through San Sebastian. Gringo tourists come into the pueblo, find there is no restaurant in the terms that they understand that word, and flee in panic and disgust. Some earnest whale-viewers and bird watchers also come, and they too leave for surroundings more chichi.

There are always a few weedy young men peddling marijuana, insisting that theirs comes from the Mother Mountains where all the best is grown. LSD makes its way into the pueblo. The oldest boy of the Montero family was fed LSD unknowingly by some teen-agers and has been left mentally crippled; he now has an attention span that cannot exceed twenty seconds. I suppose there are things to be said for prohibiting drugs; I wish possibility was one of them.

People here blame the drug problem on the Americans, who, they say, have introduced the unnatural appetite for drugs into their country. This is a bit like the claim that child molesting is unknown in the village. It is called "the Mexico City thing." When things are going wrong, it is convenient to have foreigners to blame. For the same reason, Washington blames the Mexicans for the trade: if people down here didn't grow it, there wouldn't be any for hoodlums in New York and Los Angeles to use. One claim is about as absurd as the other, but both claims are making a very large amount of money for a great number of people.

However, Mr. Fitzgerald, I must tell you that large amounts of money are not visible in San Sebastian. What people here have they earned one peso at a time, and most of them haven't many pesos.

What I can gather is that White Indian and Dark Horseman play on our team and may be watching each other. The rest, dear Staff Sergeant Fitzgerald, is silence.

I append a list of all characters for checking to ascertain the accuracy of what I say about them. Did The Pole fly Liberators half a century ago and was The Drunk third-generation rich? In detective stories, this is where earnest, plodding Lieutenant Columbo solves the mystery. There is some small but significant factor that does not check out. Well, if so, the police of three nations can accumulate the information fast enough and, supposedly, move rapidly enough to make use of what I send them.

My conviction is that a major player in the great world of drug prohibition is a larger, grander figure than any appearing before me. There should be a magnetic quality. Compass needles would turn towards him as towards a mountain of iron ore.

END OF MAIN REPORT

I sent a lot more dull data and waited with the faint hope that Fitzgerald might satisfy some of my aroused curiosity and respond to one or two of my guesses.

He responded promptly to the fax, but Fitzgerald was not a chatty man. He transmitted a single word, printed, in capital letters:

RECEIVED

CHAPTER 9

THE GLORIOUS DEATH OF THE GUZMÁN FAMILY ROOSTER

The little cockroach, the little cockroach
He is not able to walk
Because he has no, because he has no
Marijuana joint to smoke.
—"The Cockroach," popular old Mexican folk
song, composer unknown

It was a typical Sunday in San Sebastian, but that was not startling. Every Sunday I'd seen here was the same. There was a little less work done than on the other six days of the week, and a little more noise made because there were more people at home to make it. The same hot, yellow sun stood above us and the shadows of the trees and the houses were marked in the dust as sharply as if cut out with scissors.

Pretty Little One had propelled her 120 kilos through the town to bring me Watchtower Bible Society tracts and drink my Dos Equis fine Monterrey ale.

White Indian snorted up in Cream Puff and joined in the religious debating society but not in the ale drinking. He made himself strong black coffee. I noticed little drops of sweat on his forehead when he looked at our bottles. It was one of the times when I felt sorry for him. Nothing on earth that you eat or drink should be important enough to make you sweat blood, and I counted myself lucky that I wasn't him. Next he would start arguing with Pretty Little One about things she held sacred, and my sympathy would, I knew, evaporate fast enough.

"It is good to see you still sober, White Indian," she said.

In San Sebastian the people either spoke so wrapped in courtesies and indirections that a gringo could scarcely glimpse the real mean-

83

ing of what they said, or else they were so blunt that you were staggered by what hit you. There didn't seem to be any middle ground.

"What has my sobriety got to do with the price of tea in China?" he said.

"I know that expression. I had a doctor from Peoria in Illinois who used to use it. It is a dismissal of important matters. You should not dismiss important matters, Mr. Clarence."

"Then tell me, who cares if I get drunk or not?"

"You have a responsibility to that child who follows you everywhere, The Fragment. After all, you have become to him like a father."

"God be my witness, I didn't ask for that."

"What has asking got to do with anything?" She sucked up the last of her first bottle of beer, and I found another cold one to tuck into her hand. She swallowed some. "You must realize that the boy has tremendous resentment of his natural father."

"I thought the father was caught in a storm and drowned on the reef."

"That is right. He drowned when the boy was only four. At first, the boy thought that his father had died because he had been a bad boy and a bad son. But later on, he thought that he had not been all that bad and he became very resentful of his father's dying and leaving him. The mind of a child is not like the mind of you or me, White Indian. To him, you are a father. You owe him a father's duty."

"Why, when I have given things to people, do I have a debt to them?" said Clarence.

"You have been in this country long enough not to have to ask a question like that," she said. "Drink your coffee and let the word of God enter your heart."

Typical of White Indian, he launched into religious argument, declaring that modern scholars have found proof that the Virgin Mary was a Greek prostitute and that the father of Jesus Christ was a Roman soldier.

"A sad thing, that a man should be still so ignorant on his thirty-eighth birthday," she said. "By that age, most men have left childish rebellions behind them."

She had gaffed him. His jaw dropped. "How would you know that today is my 38th birthday?" he said.

She pressed a forefinger to her temple. She was gifted with second sight. She was also, I realized, gifted with White Indian's passport, which he had displayed when registering at her bungalows, but he had forgotten that. Smartass was on his ass, and I enjoyed it in a quiet, gentlemanly way by merely saying, "I, on the other hand, didn't know. Many happy returns, Clarence."

By the time his memory caught up and overtook his surprise, he had already lost the trick. He had also lost the momentum of his argument. He went back for more coffee.

We turned our conversation to government, the weather and other things men can't do anything about except talk, and half an hour or more must have passed before we became aware that little Fragment was sitting outside my big iron gate. He had probably spoken my name once or twice through the latch hole but, getting no answer, had seated himself outside, on the ground, with the limitless patience that occupies so much of the poor people's time.

When the truck that sells drinking water came honking by, I opened the gate and found him there. He had two immense coconuts in their thick green husks, and they were about as big as he could pack, one under each arm.

He passed them to me. They were birthday presents for Mr. Clarence and there was also a letter for him, if I would be so good. He had a folded piece of blue-lined paper in his shirt pocket. It was a wonder it didn't fall out, because the shirt was almost falling off Fragment. This was not a school day and he was not clad in his one and only good-shirt-and-pants combination.

He would have left, but I insisted he come in and say happy birthday to Mr. Clarence and drink a Coke with us. He allowed that such was a good idea. He handed his paper to Clarence, silently, and silently went to the back of the yard to whack off the tops of the cocos with an old machete.

I brought out some glasses and he poured the milky white juice into them, proud of himself. I, not proud of myself because I was out of Coca-Cola, sent him to the nearest grocery to buy a few bottles.

Neither Clarence nor I asked why Fragment knew about the birthday, and Pretty Little One was uncommunicative on the subject. Clarence read the birthday note, shook his head and read it a second time.

He passed it across to her.

"Read that," he said.

She glanced at it. "A bold, strong hand," she said.

I could see from my chair. It was bold writing, but only because it was written all in capital letters. Fragment was in grade 5 but his writing was what we would expect of a kid in grade 2. Except, that is, for the content.

Pretty Little One refused to read the letter. It was, she said, a private affair. I had no such compunction. In the newspaper business you learn to take information where you can get it.

In reproducing his note in English translation, I have removed his misspellings and tidied up the grammar but leave his run-in printed words—my tribute to village education in rural Mexico.

DEAR MR.CLARENCE IT WEIGHS UPON ME HEAVILY THAT PEOPLESAY YOU WILLSOON LEA VE OUR PUEBLO AND GO FAR AWAY TO CANADA. ONTHIS YOUR BIRTH DAY LET ME ASK YOU IN THIS LETTER. WHEN YOU ARE SO FARAWAY IN THAT PLACE WILL YOU PLEASESTOP SOMETIME AND THINK OF ME, YOUR FRIEND FOREVER ANGEL FLORES PARDO DE LA SEGOVIA

"You should have a tennis ball in your throat, White Indian," I said.

"Spanish can be a very strong language," said Pretty Little One. I would have suspected that she wrote it, but the the scrawled letters were too awkward. It was Angel's handwriting—I recognized it—and what it said came unaltered from the heart, mind and hand of a child.

When the boy came back with the Cokes White Indian said, "Fragment, it's time you drove the Cream Puff." He threw him the key. "Go out and fire it up and I'll come out and join you. We won't race it. The Syndic told me the other day that people are complaining that I drive around the village too fast."

"Truly?" said Fragment.

"Of course, truly. Go. Warm up the motor."

Sydney Carton couldn't have done better while going to the guillotine and saying that this was a far, far better thing than he had ever done. Clarence, however, chipped off some of the nobility by turning to us after Fragment had scurried out through the gate and saying, "I have lost my mind and now I am going to lose my Cream Puff."

He got in the passenger side and retained enough composure to say nothing, but his face was stiff. I wondered if White Indian had ever had the same solicitude for any of the three wives he'd had.

They went down the street faster than I expected. Clearly, this wasn't the kid's first turn behind the wheel. He'd been given lessons somewhere. Probably White Indian had taken him out on the salt flats somewhere, where there were no other vehicles or people or anything harder than a mesquite bush to be hit. No doubt he'd hoped that would do. But how could it satisfy Fragment, to drive where no one could see him or be brought to believe it?

They were back five minutes later, White Indian holding a dead rooster in his hand.

"The Guzmán family's," he said, displaying the corpse. It had long silver feathers and looked to be three-quarters fighting cock. One eye remained open and had retained the light of wicked intent.

"The most expensive bird in the flock," I said. "Always the way, isn't it?"

"That's what I figured when I went to pay the blood money," he said. "Everybody says Mrs. Guzmán is so tight you couldn't drive a poppy seed up her ass with a mallet. But she had seen the whole thing and she was laughing so hard the tears were running down her face and dripping off her chin. 'He went out to fight you,' she said. 'He thought your car was another rooster. How magnificent! He didn't have much of a life, but you gave him a glorious death.'

"She wouldn't take a peso. All she insisted on was that I have to eat the rooster, which I guess is a punishment. Plumpness and tenderness are things this bird was never good at."

"And now?" said the child.

White Indian sighed and got out of Cream Puff. "Ten minutes exactly," he said. "Go with God, kid." The boy's heart and the little car lept together, and in an instant he was accelerating around the corner of the street running her up through the gears not badly at all.

"Maleness, the sickness of all Mexican men," observed Pretty Little One, who had come to the patio gate to watch. She took her tracts and her thoughts down the street to seek converts or, perhaps, to get Mrs. Guzmán to retell the story of how the rooster fought the MG. Stories such as those were prized in San Sebastian, much as rock hounds thrill to finding fire agates.

There was no point trying to take the anxious Clarence off the street, so I went into the patio and brought him out his coffee to drink there. That was when Mr. Ochoa came trotting up to us, crying out that he had lost his mind and probably his daughter. Fragment had taken her away in that devilish toy. Everybody had seen how Clarence defied all the laws of physics in it. It should have been nicknamed "the Russian roulette machine."

"He said you'd be waiting for him here," Mr. Ochoa said to White Indian. "All I want you to do is to tell me that she will be safe with him."

It was no time to discuss the Guzmán family rooster, which lay crumpled against my door. White Indian answered soberly, calmly. I was proud of him. "Your daughter is safe as in the vest pocket of God," he said.

"I hope so. I pray so. I must have been out of my mind."

We all listened for snorts from the MG's exhaust, but that was silly. Both the priest and a rug salesman were using loud-speakers simultaneously, and no sound so ordinary as a car with a muffler could rise above their desciptions of heaven and broadloom.

Mr. Ochoa would have to wait for his daughter the way men waited for returning bomber crews in England during the big war. Either she would come back or she would not. The decision was not in his hands.

"There is something disarming about that little Indian waif," he said. "He came to me, not to my daughter. Of course she knew about it and expected him, but that is the normal duplicity of her sex. After all, she is thirteen, only two years from a Mexican girl's most important birthday.

"He made a little bow and introduced himself and said he hoped he might have my permission to take my daughter for a ride in the car, with her approval, of course. You don't expect that from little poor ones. And then I looked in my daughter's eyes and I was lost. I didn't see her pigtails or the smear of dirt on her face, I saw the light in her eyes. Here was her first cavalier, her first among the tens and the hundreds, and was I going to say no and send him away like a beggar boy? No. I could not. I said five minutes. I must have been mad. Was I? Am I mad?"

"No man can have daughters and remain completely sane," I said. "But you are as sane as most of us. Come with me and have a rum and Coke."

"With your permission, I cannot leave the street."

"I will bring it to you."

When I came back he and White Indian were sitting on the big cement front step, each lost in his own dark apprehensions. I assumed they had introduced themselves, but I was wrong, because Mr. Ochoa began talking about Mexico's Indian problem. He wouldn't have done that had he known Clarence's nickname.

"He is very dark, that boy, very dark, very poor, very Indian."

"You are all Indian here, in different degrees, are you not?" I said.

"It is our great unsolvable national problem. Politically, nobody can speak it, but privately we all know it. It is the Indian who holds Mexico back. Sufficient unto the day. Think not of tomorrow. That, and our terrible passion for mediocrity. The Mexican never wants to do any job better than just good enough. We aspire to the second rate."

"You are hard on yourselves, on your own people," I said.

"I have to be. After all, what do we try to do well?" said Mr. Ochoa. "Only a few particular things. Art, music, dancing, soccer, architecture and the ritual killing of bulls. In those, we aim for perfection and come close many times. In our industrial life, our economic life, our political life we cheerfully accept second or third rate. That, sir, is the Indian in the Mexican character."

The White Indian seemed to be hearing nothing. I suppose when you've lived with this from childhood it becomes only an irritant, like a stone in your shoe. Or maybe the other kind of irritant, which brings on cancer.

"But your Spanish ancestors came mostly from Andelusia, which was horribly poor then and is now horribly poor," I said.

"Yes. You know history. I knew you would, Mr. Macko." The Ochoa family did not use nicknames and were presumed not to have them.

"It was history that was in my head when the poor little one came to the door with his rags fluttering like flags in a wind. Do you know what I thought of, Mr. Macko?"

"I must say that I do not."

"I thought of Juárez, whom you will know. Benito Juárez. He probably looked like that little boy at one time.

"What a strange nation we are. We complain of the Indian, yet there stands Benito Juárez, towering above every other president we have ever had. Father Hidalgo, Obregon, they were merely firebrands, easily ignited, quickly extinguished. The father of Mexico, our George Washington and our Abraham Lincoln combined, was Benito Juárez, and what you may not know is that he was a pure Zapotec Indian. There wasn't a drop of European blood in him. And our second-greatest was Lázaro Cárdenas, and he, too, was Indian. A Tarascan from Michoacán. How strange, how inexplicable."

"General Sherman may haave been right," remarked Clarence. "The only good Indian is a dead Indian."

People here had invisible wires that stuck out of their psyches and brushed against obstacles, like the old-fashioned curb alarms we used to put on car fenders. Mr. Ochoa's wires had just made contact. He did not know what he had said wrong, but he knew he was where he should not be in this conversation, and he fell silent.

To fill the quiet moment I said, "So the boy Angel reminds you of him?"

"Yes. Who knows what genius is in that little dark head?"

"It won't do much good in there unless you get him out of these village baby-sitting classes they call schools and apprentice him to a real school, as Juárez was. Why don't you give up a couple of bottles of expensive French wine and help him out?"

Of course, I said no such thing. I had been here long enough to learn to blunt such natural combativeness. All I said was, "A pity that child cannot go to a great school, as Juárez was taught by the Franciscans."

Maybe it's better, speaking that way. Mr. Ochoa looked me in the face. "I can feel what you are saying, Mr. Macko," he said.

He spun around when the drone of the TD's engine could be heard one street up. The car was coming very fast—apparently Fragment was going to make another circuit of town. But no, Clarence had been teaching him far too much. As the kid entered the intersection he bent down, grabbed the flyoff brake, locked both back wheels and cramped the steering wheel hard right at the same time.

With the wheels locked, Cream Puff skidded, and as our street came into his sights, the kid dropped the brake handle, tromped the accelerator and straightened out the car for a fast run straight at the three of us. The manoeuvre was not well done—he fishtailed a bit— but the amazing thing was that a boy of eleven could do it all.

One of the men beside me whimpered. If it was White Indian, it was for his car; if Mr. Ochoa, for an only daughter. I shouted, "Bravo!" What the hell good is a sports car if you can't show off in it?

One of my favourite memories will always be the image of two little brown faces with brilliant slashes of white teeth seen through the windshield, two kids laughing for the sheer joy of living, or for the joy of still being alive, if that's the way to say it.

Fragment left all the brakes alone and rowed his gears to slow the Cream Puff. A few metres from us he even double-clutched and got down into bull low, which, in addition to being brittle as rock candy, was also unsynchronized.

The little car muttered to a stop ten centimetres north of White Indian's knee. The kid switched off and raced around to the far side to open the door for his lady, a large thirteen-year-old who would never acknowledge a child as small as Angel were it not for his exceptional, exciting magic coach.

She swivelled her hips sideways, poked her legs out knees first, tightly clenched together as if holding a birth control pill between them, then put two little feet on the ground and in one smooth, swift action came out of the car and was standing, straight as a cedar stick. At home, women go to night classes to learn how to get out of small cars gracefully. Here was a child who knew it all at thirteen after a single experience.

The young lady inclined her head graciously to acknowledge her squire, nodded her head just once for propriety's sake towards her father, and walked away down the street to home and the envy of all her friends. The father, pathetic in his relief, followed her at a respectful distance. As he went I heard him say, "Thank you, God, for the use of your vest pocket."

White Indian, whose emotions were almost always invisible, just said to Fragment, "You are sympathetic, you two. You and that car." He took a deep breath, called on whatever gods he recognized for strength and went further.

"Go ahead, Angel. Take the car again. Take your mother for a ride."

"I went to my mother first. She would not come."

"She need not be afraid. You are driving well."

"My mother says she has nothing to wear."

I wondered if Clarence remembered the day Fragment boasted about his mother owning a veil so fine it could be drawn through her wedding ring. That had been when his father was alive, he said. He did not say what had happened to the veil since.

"Oh, well," said Clarence. "Oh, well. Another day she shall come. You and I will talk to her another day."

The new Juárez thanked him gravely and started for his home. He had to collect coconut husks for the fire. They had no stove; the mother cooked on a grate made of scrap-steel reinforcing rods in their backyard, where a single hibiscus grew.

CHAPTER 10

FIESTA GRINGO

If I were dictator of the world—and please, Mr. Printer, set this in larger type—I WOULD SHOOT ALL IDLERS AT SIGHT.
—Sir Henri Deterding, founder of Shell Oil

A couple more weeks wore out. I ate often at Pretty Little One's barbecue meat place and flirted cheerfully with Consuela. Often as not, White Indian joined me, originally, I think, because he was making a play for Consuela, which had her mother's full approval. Later he turned his attention to Phoebe Nell, which had nobody's approval, not even mine. It doesn't really matter to me, I suppose, if somebody wants to sleep with the wife of a dumb, trendy professor, but the woman had an innocence about her that shouldn't have been disturbed.

She was, as far as I could see, quite unconscious of what it did to male glands when she sat wrapped in a snow-white terry-cloth robe and let her little blue-veined foot move up and down, up and down, while those violet eyes with the big black pupils looked with an expression of utter trust into the eyes of whatever male confronted her.

The professor didn't deserve protection against cuckoldry. He was a pompous ass whose days were spent on needless problems he himself had arranged. The failure of the Beetle's brake system was such a project. It began with trying to make the local blacksmith and welder sober enough to pay attention for a few minutes; it extended into trips to town for parts and endless phone calls to Guadalajara for more parts. The waste of time never seemed to bother him; time, like research grants, was apparently a limitless reservoir, ever available to him. Neither was he upset when the wrong parts arrived or the black-

93

smith turned the right parts into wrong parts by virtue of having become drunk again.

Every such setback was an occasion for readjusted planning, new interfaces, reviews, reviews of what went wrong with the last review, and flow charts drawn on eight-by-fourteen letter-quality paper. He had the soul of a bureaucrat. Even with his personal affairs, it did not matter so much if no good came of them all, provided everything had been done with sufficient paper and planning.

Where White Indian went, The Fragment was usually not far behind. He polished Cream Puff once a day, twice if it was driven more than a few blocks.

Whenever the opportunity presented itself, he tucked himself into the bucket seat on the passenger side and rode proudly beside White Indian through the streets and the country lanes. Usually he nodded to friends but did not wave.

White Indian and I went to Fragment's house one day, the boy being away at the school. I wondered how they survived when the rains came. The palm thatch, dripping with those small, deadly scorpions that kill a baby or two every year in the village, was rotting and the sky showed through. The walls of wattle sticks, daubed with mud, also had holes. Inside the portal (there was no door) there was one room with a bed for the mother, another for the son, and a picture of the Virgin of Guadalupe, which had been bleached by so many suns that only the blue colours remained.

The mother probably had beauty once, but it was now long gone. She was probably thirty but would scarcely pass for forty, even with a following wind.

Like her son, she was grave, courteous and reserved; also, as he sometimes was, she seemed unutterably weary. Probably the intestinal parasites tore at her also. It was a thing about this pueblo I would never become reconciled to—the worms start eating you before you die.

We had heard from someone other than Angel that she had care of a horse, which was for rent. Horses interest me even less than Chamber of Commerce people, but a jog around the fields wouldn't hurt and it would have been a graceful way to put some money in the mud-walled shack.

"With regret, I must tell you the horse is dead."

We asked what had happened.

94

"We had him tied up over there"—she gestured—"but there were no rains. Nothing grew. He starved to death."

The slow and terrible death of the horse beside their house seemed to have made no deep imprint on her mind or her heart.

When we left she turned up the battery radio, her only companion while the boy was in school. In their neighbourhood there seemed to be little visiting house to house.

> The day on which you were born
> Were born all the flowers
> And above your baptismal font
> The nightingales sang.

"What are you smiling at?" said White Indian.

"I was thinking about old Henry Terwilliger complaining to me about too much laughter and song."

"What did you say?"

"I said, well, I suppose you could look at it that way."

"Maybe you are trying too hard to understand things here," he said.

He was being ambiguous again. Just what did Clarence know about matters here? It seemed obvious to me that he was some kind of police agent, if for no other reason than that he chummed around so much with Dark Horseman, who just had to be out of prison on a ticket of leave provided by the Mexican narcotics police.

But I never spoke, even indirectly, about my own little hobby. The old newspaper instinct to respect confidence still operated and he, too, kept his counsel well, although just one time he slipped and referred to Alvarez as The Tiny Perfect Prick.

There was no reason for him to know Alvarez or to have formed any opinion about his personality. Always it's in the little careless remark that you find your story.

What nagged me was that I couldn't identify which of my innocuous remarks was the revealing one. After sending my long chatty note to Fitzgerald in Mexico City I came to the conclusion, a second time, that I was wasting everybody's time with such stuff. In the whole dispatch, there was scarcely one solid fact or one item properly researched.

My brother-in-law, I decided, had found me a rent-free house in Mexico and offered me an excuse for accepting it. I would continue accepting it but would leave police work where it belonged, with White Indian, Dark Horseman, Alvarez and whomever else was here looking for the great mover and shaker of the drug trade.

No sooner had I decided on this than my sister sent me a long, chatty note. It had, I noticed, been opened and resealed by somebody on the way to my door, and I didn't think it was the post boy who did it.

"Mac, you old dog, you're sounding more like your old self. I just can't tell you how much Harry and I enjoyed your nice, chatty letter. You have a rare gift—I guess it's newspapering, is it?—of saying so much in so few words. Wish we could meet some of the people you're meeting; they sound like fun. Write us some more, please."

At this point she drew a little round, smiling face. She then rambled on with reports on the state of my empty house, what my kids were doing and what hers were, the ordinary sisterly comments that come in a sisterly note.

Now what in the name of Sam Hill had I told Harry that excited him? I had no awareness of having said something important. Like Clarence using the term Tiny Perfect Prick I had said something significant without knowing it.

I went back to the computer and read my notes and could see nothing. I kept picking at it. It was like trying to dislodge a sliver from a corncob that had stuck in the back teeth. It was there, but I couldn't get it loose.

All I could do was not resign, my second non-resignation since coming here, and in the spirit of something or other, I went to the Syndic and suggested he tell Alvarez that I might introduce him to all of the gringo community if he wanted to come to a party being given by the Terwilligers.

This made the Syndic extremely nervous, as anything to do with his superiors did. Since the meeting in my house that night, we had remained friendly, even close, but my association with police work had become a non-fact and was never mentioned. Now I was bringing it back where daylight struck it.

"Since we both know what this is about, Syndic, I can talk openly to you. Who is this big, important man who is arranging the drug shipment?"

He winced. I was being frank and open with him, the one thing about gringos he found distasteful. Nothing, I realized, repelled him more than the American who, bankrupt of all capacity for indirection and circumvention, says, "Let us be frank with one another."

"There are no big, important people here, unless they are gringos," he said. "The people who would handle such a shipment here are small men, sir, poor men, men trying to earn just a little extra money to feed their families and romp with a mistress, perhaps. I keep telling the captain, we do not get people of great importance in this village."

"And the captain is not impressed when you tell him that. . . ."

"We have a saying about men like the captain. Strong, ugly and with authority."

"I wouldn't call him ugly."

"I refer to his manners."

"Do you know what Pretty Little One said about Captain Alvarez?"

"No."

"She told me once, 'He is too pure; it corrodes his soul. Alvarez is like bright new metal; it rusts in the salt air more rapidly than older, dirtier pieces of metal.' "

"She is a very astute woman. She would have made a good syndic."

So it was arranged for Alvarez to come to the party as a representative of a firm in the export business. The Syndic, invited by Grace, also came.

He had chanced upon an English-language greeting card display somewhere at some time, and he brought her a card as well as flowers for the occasion of her birthday. The card had a huge purple lily embossed on its front, and the English words "Our Thoughts Are with You in Your Time of Sorrow."

"How beautiful," said Grace, and pressed his hand a second time. "How could you have known that the lily is my favourite flower?"

She was called O'Grace for the purposes of the party. A big green cardboard shamrock on her dress said so. Henry had decided to combine his wife's birthday celebration with that of the patron saint of Ireland, the date of which was far distant from this day, but that didn't matter. Everybody had an O and an apostrophe in front of their names on the big lapel tag. These hero badges were not usual at parties in San Sebastian, but then it was a very small place.

The local people's parties seemed to just happen. Even if they were planned, almost everything went wrong. Whoever was barbecuing the pig got drunk, and the poor little creature was reduced to a lump of charcoal. Some young lady in the kitchen put chili powder instead of coffee in the urn, which would prove the best and funniest thing to happen all night. Somehow, things always worked out. Guests scurried back to their own kitchens and found coffee powder that was noticeably less awful than chili powder. Running through all the disorganization there was a strong current of general fun.

Gringo parties were different. They were relentlessly organized and remorselessly detailed. As with so much he did down here, the white Anglo-Saxon North American was determined to prove the virtue of programming.

In the big gringo colonies at Ajijic, Chapala and Tlaquepaque the planning of a gringo fiesta could occupy weeks and ruin the peace and quiet of every husband, guest and grocery-store owner in the community. Guest lists were as carefully scrutinized as for parties at the White House in Washington, often with more stringent rules of eligibility applied.

In San Sebastian the gringo colony was small, there was not a party every second night, and those that were held did not run at the same manic level. But nobody was left in any doubt that this was a serious business and deserved serious attention.

The Syndic made his hesitant way to the barbecue, where Henry—in a green tam and a green apron, silently, seriously, as one conducting a religious rite—was cooking hamburgers. A zone of quiet lay around him. The whole garden party was quiet, except for the kitchen, where the Mexican staff were making coffee, salads and turkey sandwiches, teasing one another with engaging personal lies, and breaking out almost as regularly as surf on the beach into roars of laughter and singing.

The Syndic, having been served a hamburger stacked so high that no mortal man could eat the thing without spilling ketchup and pickle down his shirtfront, was gazing at it wanly and wondering what he could do with it, in politeness.

None of the locals would like any of the food they would be served this day at the Terwilligers', but this was no reflection upon the hosts. People in San Sebastian disliked and deeply distrusted any food that they themselves had not been fed before age six.

It wasn't only gringo food they detested. They would have no part of the cooking of Veracruz, Tampico or Monterrey. They were among the last people on the planet into whom the cooks of Canton had not sunk a taproot and never could.

So it was no surprise to see the Syndic making his way towards the noise in the kitchen where he might, perhaps, find a few Tail of the Rat chilies to slip into the hamburger. Once there, he stayed. It was a familiar pattern.

I told myself that I envied him because he was where the fun was. Then I told myself that I was offended for him, because the mayor of a town should be a guest of honour and sit at the head of any table. Finally, I told myself that I was just another damn snob, a snob from old Orange Ontario, a damn snob like the damn snobs from Cleveland, Toronto or Podunk Junction.

Pretty Little One arrived arrayed in a hectare or more of brilliantly coloured print with flowers in her hair. Arturo, she regretted, was having one of his poor days and didn't feel well enough to come.

"Exactly what is the matter with Arturo?" White Indian asked, blandly.

She chose to treat the question seriously. "We do not know. The doctors can find nothing. But, as you can see, he has no energy."

"Oh."

"And how are you, Wolf Man, sober as ever?"

I told her it was the difference in the Cauacasian metabolic system, something I was almost beginning to believe. Of the Mexicans I had met, I could drink any six under the table without losing my speech or my legs; at least, I could have in those days, when I began my days by brushing my teeth with whiskey. Alcohol and milk, it seemed, were two things their systems couldn't handle. Milk made them feel sick and six drinks of anything stronger than beer laid them flat. Of course, it didn't stop any of them from trying more alcohol, although all the adults had given up on milk.

"If I may, I have some business with the lady," said Henry Terwilliger III, well-known local chef and drunkard, who had so far this day fulfilled only half his mandate. He had legal documents in his hand.

She took them and poked them in the sash of her dress.

"Read them," he said. "Read them."

She took them out, glanced at them and folded the papers again. "Yes, yes. The watermelon contract. It is as we said."

"You're a difficult woman to do business with. I like things signed and sealed."

"I, on the other hand, prefer Jew deals, honour between two men and no paper at all."

"Do me a favour. Check it."

"Arturo will check it," she said. "At some other time."

My notes from that afternoon are still beside me. I wrote them in my own mysterious shorthand on the back of a green cardboard shamrock. I see them now for what they are, memorials to wasted time.

NOTES

Terwilliger and Pretty Little One. Papers. Business deal. PLO—White Indian.

1. Why she refuse read contract and dismiss as unimportant?
2. If important, why Henry make public before myself and White Indian, early in day, still sober? Attempt to demonstrate that deal exists, in front witnesses? Why?
3. Confronted PLO. Says deal is $5000 (US) watermelon shipment Nogales, her share 3.75%. No hesitation talking.
4. Why HT III fool around $5000 deal? Hobby? Check to Fitz in M. City.
6. BS. People million-dollar drug deals don't write contracts and discuss front of strangers. Clarence right. He walked away. Don't bother Fitz.

Although my research wasn't going to illuminate my name in the law courts, this was, for all its excesses, a party to enjoy. As night bestrode us, the quiet yellow lights of the yard lit themselves and shone on the hibiscus beds, the bougainvillea, the ample foliage of the mango trees. The lights in the big house shone through handsome iron grillwork that had been wrought by an artist. He chose to call himself a common welder, but he was an artist and could turn iron and steel into poetry with his torch. His works, bought for the standard ten American dollars a day, were among the items that made the Terwilliger place an estate. The other things included art works indoors that had cost not tens but thousands of U.S. dollars. There is something to be said for having lots of money, even if it's old, tired money.

The locals were the loudest and sounded the happiest, but the gringo guests also became freer in the tongue. To move among them was a smorgasbord of small talk, in which you didn't have to participate to enjoy.

100

Little Margaret had cut out the Syndic from his party of locals and was instructing him on his duty to join in a worthy cause. Politicians of any country become so accustomed to this sort of thing that they can appear to be giving their petitioner their entire and undivided attention, even though their thoughts are on fornication or something else worthwhile.

The Syndic's eyes had that intensity as he stared into Little Margaret's, and I could guess he was dismissing everything she said. The burden of her plea was that in the name of peace, order and good government the Syndic should ban rock music. Teen-agers all over the village were listening to it.

"What's wrong with rock?" said Clarence, who had joined us.

"Why, everybody knows that," she said. It was part of Little Margaret's exasperating charm that she was constantly surprised that there were still people in the world who did not believe exactly what she believed.

"I am one who doesn't know," he said.

She switched to English to answer him. "Why, because it's Satanism. All you have to do is play one of those tapes backward. You will hear, 'This is the Devil speaking. This is the Devil speaking.' The voice is very clear."

"That's strange. You'd think the Devil would know that this is a Spanish-speaking country."

She never broke stride. "My dear man, the children here are listening to English-language recordings."

"You can be sure the Syndic will take care of it," I said, and left him to her. It was unkind, I suppose, but if he didn't want this sort of thing he shouldn't have put himself forward as the champion of the people.

"People say my views are simplistic," shouted Henry. "I say that these are times which simply cry out for simplistic solutions."

I recognized the phrase. He was offering one of his favourite solutions to the problems in his nation, where the world's two finest documents, the Constitution and the Republican Party platform, were constantly being sullied.

Henry advocated that barbed wire be run six strands deep around the entire perimeter of the state of North Dakota. All the lefties and pinkos were to be put inside the wire, and any who tried to get out were to be machine-gunned.

His audience of one was a stray tourist, a young postwar West German who had never heard of such ideas but, being a guest, remained polite and attentive.

I went to the kitchen. Pretty Little One had apparently contracted with the Terwilligers to cater the party, and Consuela was among the day's kitchen staff. When I arrived somebody had just succeeded in smashing one of Grace's teacups, and the usual laughter was the result. Sometimes, I thought, this laughter is morbid. These people laugh to drive away realities.

But Consuela's laughter seemed genuine enough. "It was Angela. The tray in her hand, she backed up against the lime squeezer and thought some man was goosing her. Proooh." She flung up her hand to demonstrate the teacup flying.

"It's worth smashing a few dishes to hear laughter like that," said Grace. She'd have said the same if the cup had been her Spode.

"Grace, you're one person in this town who never needed a nickname," I said.

"Now, aren't you an old sweetie," she said.

I wondered why Grace had married Henry Terwilliger III and, having done so, had stayed with him. Speaking of such types, I wondered where Professor Jon was, and asked her.

"They arrived fashionably late. They always do. He insists on having an entrance before a lot of other people in a way they will notice and remember. So I said to hell with him and I left them standing at the door. They could damn well wait there until they put down roots, as far as I was concerned. Then a neat little guy with a tiny moustache arrived and took them away. If Jon doesn't come back, I won't mind. I get tired of people who strike poses."

"Good for you."

"Henry has his faults," she said. "I know them all. But one thing I can say for Henry. He never poses. What you see in Henry is what there is."

I swam around slowly in the dancing waves of local cocktail-party chatter. The weather in the United States never ceased to fascinate them, partly because they exaggerated everything they heard about it on their shortwave radios. The streets of Cleveland had been blocked for two days with snow. Helicopters were flying food into Denver after an ice storm. Five thousand were homeless in L.A. after a rainstorm. They seemed to take a particular delight in such stories, concluding, I suppose, that they reflected well upon their good judgement in deciding to come to Mexico.

When asked if I had heard such reports I had a standard answer. "You only got part of the news broadcast. It is much worse up there than you think."

If they asked for new details I said my own radio had started squealing at the interesting parts and I only knew that it was a total emergency. It was the proper thing to say. It was a party. I had been asked to participate. I was participating.

Wilbur came over and grabbed my arm fiercely.

"Don't give me away," he said. "That's all I ask."

"How can I give you away?"

"Henry. I caught him in one of his silent moments and said, 'Henry, has it ever occurred to you that the Syndic might be a Communist?' That was all I said. 'Has it ever occurred to you?'

"He became very serious and said, 'You never know, do you? Often, they're the quiet ones.' "

"You should ease off, Wilbur. People can get hurt with jokes like that."

"Speaking of jokes, this being a St. Patrick's party, have you heard the one about Pat and Mike?" He told the one about Pat and Mike and laughed immoderately at the punch line. I had heard it before, in high school, and didn't laugh much even then, but I laughed here, because Wilbur wanted me to. Guadalupe raised a smile.

I thought that wives must have a hard time hearing their husbands' jokes for the thousandth time, particularly loyal wives like Lupe. As I write this, it occurs to me that I am not making an original contribution to sociologic thought. However, the fact is that to some of us ideas come late in life. Lupe saw some sympathy in my face and stayed to chat, softly and a little sadly, while he sped off bearing jokes to other people.

"We don't get invited to parties so often now. I suspect it's Wilbur's personality."

Apparently half an hour before he had listened while the West German spoke proudly of the great city of Berlin, then made his own unique contribution to international good will by saying, "I've been to Berlin quite a few times and I always liked it whenever I saw it. It was always on fire."

Her face was tired as she told it and more tired when she revealed that her husband was about to start a new project, something intricate and useless. "It makes him happy."

"And you, Lupe, how are things with you?" She made the gesture of equivocation, hand forward, palm down, rocking the wrist back and forth. It was a delicate hand and she was a charming woman. Most of us men, it seems, get wives who are better than we deserve.

I was reminded of this again when Professor Jon showed up, without Phoebe Nell. He explained that they had run into a Mr. Alvarez at the door, and he seemed to know a lot about Volkswagens, so Phoebe Nell had taken him over to the trailer park where they were keeping theirs. So The Tiny Perfect Policeman didn't need me for introductions. Well, I supposed not. After all, his English was perfect.

The professor, having gathered enough people around him for it to be worth his while to lecture, informed everybody that he had spotted kids from the village shooting at storks with their slingshots.

"Maybe they were hungry and wanted to eat them," I said.

"They're an endangered species. This coast is the only part of the Western Hemisphere where there are storks."

"I don't think storks are much endangered by kids with slingshots," I said, "Goliath, yes. Slingshots play hell with giants. But not storks, I don't think."

The professor was not amused. He talked largely about other small matters.

I listened instead to a song from the kitchen.

> Ai, ai, ai, ai
> Sing and do not cry
> Because I sing to cheer us up
> Warm hearts, beautiful sky.

Before long, Consuela came bustling out of the kitchen, bearing hot black coffee and Kahlua to pour into it. White Indian took the coffee with no Kahlua. He had told me once that he didn't keep attending Alcoholics Anonymous but he followed one of their rules. "One day at a time is all you can stay away from alcohol."

"Your adored one isn't here yet?" said Consuela to him.

"What adored one?"

"The Cunt."

"Why do some people have no courtesy?" he said.

She shrugged. "Who can say? Probably for the same reason that some have no brains." She flounced away.

"Clarence," I said. "Have some sense, man. Grab that girl. Appreciate the fact that she's interested enough to be jealous. And as for Phoebe Nell, don't go whoring after strange goddesses in your heart. Phoebe Nell is not the kind to be interested that you have a black belt in judo." I never uttered a word, of course.

When she did appear, she was a goddess still, but for the first time I saw her faintly flustered. Her delicate hair was just faintly disarrayed, her face flushed a trifle and the pupils of her violet eyes wide. I wondered if The Tiny Perfect Policeman had tried making a pass. Well, Snow White, there are some things you'll have to learn in this world.

Alvarez was, as always, as neat and as full of love and compassion as any three-tined pitchfork.

I took him over to Henry and introduced him as a Mexico City man who was in the export trade.

"There is no bigger export from this region than heroin and cocaine," said Pretty Little One, who stood nearby. "Far more important than watermelons."

Now what, sly one, is that statement all about?

Alvarez didn't turn a hair. "There is absolutely nothing about the drug trade that could not be solved by shooting a few pushers and users in the town square every day at noon," he said. "In a fairly short time, there wouldn't be any drug trade. The drug trade grows in societies which have lost the political will to police themselves."

"Just what I was about to tell our West German friend about permitting television crews into a war zone," said Henry, who was now beginning to slur his words. "That is what the United States did wrong in Vietnam. We let the TV crews in and everybody at home became discontented. Maggie Thatcher knew what to do."

"What did she do?" I said.

"The Falkland Islands. Any television reporter found in the war zone was given a drumhead court martial and ordered shot, sentence to be executed at the rising of the court. So there was no time for nonsense about appeals and applications to the president for clemency."

The German tourist was learning a lot. "At home, we never heard about the British shooting the newsmen," he said.

"There is a lot that doesn't get into the newspapers," said Henry, darkly.

Grace, who had come up to meet the captain, said, "Henry, there is something I want you to do for me, if you don't mind."

"Of course, my dear. What is that?"

"I want you to stop talking for five minutes."

He shut up. Thinking of how much this American social custom would interest the Syndic, I looked around the room for him, but he had departed.

What I saw instead was White Indian falling off the wagon.

He was beside Phoebe Nell, who had apparently asked him what tequila was all about and, probably with scarcely a thought, he was demonstrating. He licked a mound of salt from the web of his thumb and forefinger, took a shot glass, tossed his head back and poured the tequila straight down his throat, then picked up a lime and sucked it. It's a pretty little ritual for a uniquely fine type of alcohol, but it scarcely deserved the attention she gave it. She looked on him as if he were Christ turning water into wine, which was, in a way, exactly what he was doing.

Almost immediately he reached for another. I suppose that's what it's like. They go not a day at a time but minutes at a time and then just plain forget. It was Mescal, one of the best of the old traditionals, every bottle sold with a dead maguey cactus worm curled up in the bottom as proof that it was the right stuff. The saying is, "Mescal helps when things are good and when things are not good."

The party picked up pace even while the early guests were leaving. Perhaps that's the reason some were leaving. The Pretty Little One offered the excuse that she didn't want to leave poor Arturo alone doing all the work, and the West German went for reasons of his own.

The professor found Phoebe Nell recounting to White Indian the story of an old movie that she found unusually interesting. It was one in which Lon Chaney grew fangs and turned into a wolf when the moon was full, and she wondered if there might be something to those stories, or were they all make-believe. White Indian listened to all this with his whole body. Even the professor caught the smell of lust, for once; he took his wife's wrist and they departed.

White Indian, I noticed, already had the alcohol stigmata that afflicts some people. A bright band of red ran from cheekbone to cheekbone across his broad face. He hunched over as if expecting attack from somewhere, but his voice was normal when he spoke to me, even if the words weren't.

"Hello, Wolf Man baby. Are you on the job tonight, baby?"

Alvarez said cold and formal words of thanks and started for the Street of the Child Heroes. As he neared it, the big car appeared, driven by his policeman-chauffeur. Where the car had been hidden I don't know, nor how he summoned it. He must have had a beeper hidden on him. You were reminded of the story that Queen Victoria never looked for a chair when she wanted to sit; she just sat, confident that a servant would slip a chair under her in time.

I guess this was an example of that capacity for instant and effective action he so favoured, like favouring the shooting of a dozen drug addicts in the town square for noontime entertainment.

On the veranda Henry Terwilliger was talking to a man and wife whose names I never did remember. I called them The Winnebago Twins because that is what they came in and that is what they left in the next morning.

"There are suspicions about the syndic of this town," he said. "I say no more, but some say there's a link with the Commies."

I went in for one last coffee with Consuela, who kept singing while she poured. Grace came to join us. Then we heard Wilbur, finishing up one more joke for one more set of listeners. It must have been a joke about Indians but we only got the last line: ". . . Or, my dear boy, you can go back to the Indian reservation, where you won't be noticed."

While Wilbur was laughing at himself, Clarence's voice broke in. "Funny story, Wilbur baby. Say, Wilbur baby, you ever hear of a decoy?"

"This is a joke?"

"No, Wilbur baby. This is about real life. A decoy is what the Mafia uses, and the drug runners use them. They're somebody different enough to distract attention, baby, you understand. Twin babies are good. A big Great Dane dog will do. Sometimes it's a drunk who keeps doing clown acts."

Guadalupe came out of the kitchen, quietly. She took Wilbur by the elbow and led him towards the street.

"I don't know what the story's about," said Wilbur.

"It's a good story, Wilbur baby. A good joke. You'll appreciate it. The joke is, sometimes decoys get killed stone, stone dead. That's the joke, baby."

"We must be going, Grace," said Guadalupe. "Wilbur's had enough jokes for one day."

Wilbur was looking at White Indian as if seeing him through opaque glass.

"The decoys sometimes get to be dead. A hell of a joke, wouldn't you say, Wilbur baby?"

"I'm going home, Clarence," I said. "How about you?"

He looked at me and was suddenly contrite. "Yes. Yes, time for us to go, Mac. Grace, I apologize if I've been noisy."

"You're always welcome, Clarence. You know, you remind me of our oldest boy. That prejudices me."

His face crumpled like that of a kid about to cry. Was he going to turn out to be a sloppy drunk? I got him out quickly into the black-velvet night.

He left the Cream Puff. "I'm certainly not going to allow her to be driven by somebody in my condition!" He was one of those drunks, it seemed, who got on the rails for awhile, slipped off and then got the wheels back where they should be. I wondered how many days long his ride would be and how many red lights, flares and other danger signals he'd run through.

CHAPTER 11

CARRYING THE BLUE VIRGIN

I had no shoes and wept. Then I met a man who had no feet.
—Arab saying

San Sebastian was noisy, dirty and occasionally quarrelsome by day, but each evening ease and peace came to visit us. At sundown, the angelus bell rang. It should have been a deep, heavy sound, a blessing spoken in a throat of bronze, but San Sebastian's only church was a shabby little building, and its bell was meek and tinny. Usually the woman who rang it switched the bell rope rapidly back and forth, and rather than sounding like an invitation to prayer it sounded like an impatient duchess ringing for the maid to bring more tea.

Also, of course, scarcely anybody heeded it or gave a sign of hearing it. A few old women would hobble over to the little church with rosaries in their thin, worn hands, and now and then they would be joined by a couple of fishermen who, on their way to the darkening ocean, had been reminded that death was their constant companion in their little dugout canoes.

It was not what could be called a religious community, but then, is there now anyplace in the world that is, at least in comparison with generations past? My father, in his boyhood, was forbidden to whistle on Saturdays because he was supposed to be preparing for the Sabbath.

In Mexico the departure from religion had been orchestrated by revolutionary governments since the days of President Juárez, and all sorts of strange results were among us. They say of the Spanish, "Three Spaniards, four opinions." In this village it could be said, "Two people, four marriages."

Most young people, sooner or later, chose to live together and did so. Sometimes they never took any more formal action for their lifetimes. If a union was to be solemnized, often at the birth of the first baby, they had the choice of a state marriage, which the church did not recognize, or a church marriage, which the state rejected. Many people had both kinds. The fourth marriage occurred when the husband took a mistress and produced children by her. (Wives might take lovers, but their affairs did not enjoy the status accorded these second-front unions, and they were forbidden to flaunt their infidelities.)

Although most people here ignored angelus as they did most church rituals, except parades and the other fun kinds, they had a familiar ceremony of peace and comradeship as the night rushed down upon them. It followed supper.

The large meal of each day was eaten at noon, in the fields by men who packed their dinners in stacked blue enamel pots and in the homes by the wives and children from chipped, coarse plates. The staple was refried beans, so called, said Pretty Little One, because the Mexicans never get anything right the first time. They were usually scooped up with tortillas, the flat cornmeal disk that served as fork, spoon and bread combined.

At night there might be a tortilla or two, a tiny scrap of smoked fish and a cup of coffee stiff with sugar, which people spooned into their mouths instead of drinking from the cup.

While at supper, and for half an hour after, families held a sort of quiet communion. Sometimes father, mother and children talked of what they had done that day. Sometimes they spoke of things that troubled them, but more often they talked of things that had amused them, pleased them, or in some way made them anticipate with joy the day that was soon to come. They teased each other gently or spoke with love and respect about their dead. Sometimes families sat in complete silence until it was time for bed. To be a family and to be together was enough.

I would have expected Angel to be with his mother at such a time for this familiar ritual but found him instead on the street outside my wall, kicking his toes in the dirt, alone, as usual. I invited him inside for a Coca-Cola but he said "thanks" and went rapidly down the street until his tiny figure was eaten up by the darkness.

He was replaced by another figure, which came out of the darkness towards me. Although he wore faded jeans, an old open cotton work shirt and running shoes, he was nevertheless usually called The Crow because of the black robes he wore in the church.

We exchanged the usual salutations, but when he did not proceed I realized he was paying a call on me, so I invited him through the gate and offered whiskey. He accepted coffee, and we sat together on my patio and heard the first calls of the night birds.

He admired the flowers and the house and refrained from admiring any specific item in the yard or house, reminding me of a hard lesson I had learned. In San Sebastian, to express admiration of something was to ask for it, and one could inflict frightful embarrassment on a poor family by admiring so common a thing as a clay pot or rush chair. You learned such things with much speed.

"With respect, I have something to ask of you," he said.

"It would be my pleasure."

"Concerning the boy Angel, who lives far down this road."

"Yes, the little fellow."

"Little and very dark," said the priest, who was himself fair-skinned and was sometimes called Blondie.

I told him of the time Angel's father had tried to enter the United States, back in the days when entry was comparatively easy for Mexicans, but the border guards had turned him back because his skin was too dark.

"Very hard," said the priest. After a pause he said, "You are a friend of the family, I believe?"

"I would hope so. There isn't much family. The mother and the boy. There seem to be no uncles, no aunts, no cousins."

"Yes," he said. He pulled out a paper packet of cigarettes, offered them, and then lit one himself with the sort of dedicated attention that priests normally give to blessing the wafers and the wine.

"Difficult," he said. "Difficult." He seemed to be speaking to himself and I said nothing but poured more coffee for him.

"You know, of course, of Our Blessed Lady of the Sea."

Of course I did not know of his blessed lady of the sea or any other plaster saint, but he said it innocently. He was an old, gentle and very simple man who truly believed that all the world's people were Roman Catholics; it was just that a few were forgetful or not well enough informed, through no fault of their own.

"She has a special niche in the church. Almost a metre tall. You will have seen her. A carving done by a devout old fisherman who was a

111

master, a genius of wood. Over a century ago he carved it. Originally she was in bare wood, but later the church found money to paint her."

God pity her and her carver if he can see his work from the next world, I thought. The paint is sure to be shiny enamel and the colours will be pink and sky-blue.

"A blue like the sky," he said. "Some of the people call her our Blue Virgin. Very, very beautiful."

The long and the short of the enamelled virgin was that it was a high honour for any boy to be chosen to carry her in the Easter Parade. He had chosen Angel, but Angel wouldn't do it.

He had been on his way to speak to Angel's mother but, seeing me, thought it might be wiser for me to approach her.

"He says it is because of his mother that he cannot carry the virgin; that she would be disturbed and unhappy."

"Is his mother Baptist?" I said. "Mormon? I didn't know."

He poked out the cigarette while almost all of it was left, stabbing as if killing a snake. He was bothered. He was bothered by something I had said and he was not going to tell me what it was. Again, as happened from time to time, I was made conscious that I was a visitor in San Sebastian and not one of its own.

"I apologize, Mr. Macko. I had no right to disturb you with such matters. It is just . . . it is such an honour for the lad. . . . I am so sorry."

"It's quite all right, Father. I'll be glad to say something to the mother."

"No. No. Better not. It was not a good idea that I had." What he had not told me he would now never tell me.

I knew better than to pursue the matter. The more precise my questions became, the vaguer and more contradictory would be his answers. My Spanish, which had until now been perfectly understandable to him, would become ever less comprehensible.

The pattern of evasion was as familiar as it was annoying. Juan Diego, my neighbour across the street, once owed me a handful of pesos. When he didn't have them on the appointed day he hid under the thatch of his roof when he saw me walking down the street. I wanted to shout, "Name of God, Juan Diego, it is nothing. A handful of pesos. Don't pretend you're not there. Just tell me to wait a week." He paid the next week, but until then, he hid whenever I was nearby.

The old Crow rose.

"I thank you so very much for the coffee. It was delicious. You are so gracious, Mr. Macko." If it was delicious, why didn't he drink more?

He gave me his blessing and was gone into the night, hastening off towards the church and the town square, where the brief evening promenade was beginning, the hum of voices and the raucous music of a recorded brass band coming to us across the town.

The first thing I should have done was remember that Easter was a long way off. The second was to talk with the Syndic, with Pretty Little One or with White Indian. The third was to obey my instinct to sleep on the matter.

Naturally, I ignored all my instincts and started down the narrow double-rutted lane that led to Angel's hovel.

The moon was down but the stars glowed like lanterns.

A big shrimper had come in and was anchored on the glassy water. There would be a lot of drunken singing this night.

Angel's home had grown out of the brown earth, and a good wind and rain could have driven it back whence it came. There were no electric lights. Other houses could afford at least a couple of pale, flickering forty-watt bulbs hanging naked from a ceiling, but that was not to be, for his family. But they had money for batteries to play the radio, and it was playing, loudly, as I walked towards the house.

There was laughter from within. The light of an oil lantern shone through the cracks in the walls. A man's voice could be heard. Outside, sitting on their heels, were two crewmen from the shrimper, waiting, like dogs around a bitch in heat. We nodded and said good evening. I pretended to be at the end of my evening promenade, turned and started for home.

On the way home, I saw Angel lying inside a shelter he had built of palm fronds, under a blanket so thin you could read print through it. He pretended not to see me, and I did him the same courtesy.

It must be very hard to be the son of the village whore. How much harder must it be to be the son of the cheapest whore in the village?

In the morning, the shrimper left harbour with black smoke and the hammer of her diesel marking her passage to the ocean. Soon after, Angel came down the street with his books. He had apparently returned home before going to school, and she must have found the time for that familiar miracle of clothing him in pants and a white shirt that were ragged but clean, so stiff with unrinsed laundry soap that they seemed starched.

CHAPTER 12

CHOOSE MEXICAN HELL

When in charge, ponder.
When in doubt, mumble.
When in trouble, delegate.
—James H. Boren, *When in Doubt, Mumble: The*
Bureaucrats' Handbook

"A citizen who tries to approach his government's representatives
while abroad finds himself talking through a hole in a piece of glass to
a discontented civil servant. You may have lost your passport, your
son may have been arrested for smoking pot, or you may be trying to
close a $10 million trade deal. It doesn't matter. She dislikes and dis-
trusts you. I know. I have dealt with many countries' embassies."

In such surly tones begin my notes on a trip to Mexico City, where,
as so often down here, changes were wrought upon me that I did not
expect.

Perhaps it would have been better if I had talked to the 20-odd-
million city residents first and the woman at the Canadian Embassy
last.

Was Sergeant Fitzgerald expecting me?

Well, he was expecting me to drop around if I happened to be in
Mexico City.

Did I have an appointment?

No, I was dropping around.

What was the nature of my business?

"Why don't you just telephone to Sergeant Fitzgerald, give my
name, and ask if he wants to see me?"

She decided, against her instincts, that I was not carrying a bomb or a gun and rang Fitzgerald. The line was busy, and I was asked to wait on one of a long line of chairs set against the far wall of the waiting room.

I was in the company of ten other people, mostly Mexicans. The man in the chair next me was happy to have a chance to practise his English. He had been trying to find out if Canada's immigration laws meant what they said and, if so, what it was they really said, nobody here having yet been able to offer the same answer to that question two times in succession.

"Immigration officers make up immigration laws as they go along," I said.

"Yes," he said. "In all countries they are the same. You have heard, perhaps, that Mexico has a very dense population?"

"Yes, I have."

"Well, let me tell you something, our densest go into the External Affairs Ministry."

I went to the hole in the glass again. Staff Sergeant Fitzgerald's phone was still busy.

When I got back in the chair my companion told me about Mexican hell. I guess it was a place he had been a few times.

A poor lost American soul is told by St. Peter that he must go to hell, but he has a choice: he can go to American hell or Mexican hell.

"What happens in Mexican hell?" he asks.

"They boil you in oil and nail you on a cross and stick a spear in your side."

"And in American hell?"

"Well, they stick a spear in you and nail you to a cross and boil you in oil."

The poor soul shivers and says he might as well take American hell and be among his compatriots.

"Choose Mexican hell," says St. Peter.

"It can't make any difference."

St. Peter says, "Look, I speak to you as a friend. Choose Mexican hell. You know how it is. They won't have the right size nails for the cross. They'll have loaned the spear to somebody who broke it. The oil won't be hot enough."

I went back again to the hole in the glass, where a different woman was on guard against customers. I explained myself all over again, because she came equipped with all the suspicions about my character

115

that the first woman had held. However, she had a different reaction. She told me that Staff Sergeant Fitzgerald had been in Colombia, South America, for a week.

At this point the first woman returned, and they had an argument. After another half hour it was discovered that his local phone number had changed and eventually I was led to his office.

"Why didn't you tell her I wanted to see you?" said Fitzgerald.

"She couldn't seem to get that idea into her head."

"Hysterical tit," he said.

He was a tall, lean, sad man. Probably born with all those hard lines in his face. He had the air of a pastor who has some sad, some bad, some very sad and very bad news for you, and it was a time you would have to be strong. He conveyed that sense even when talking about the weather.

His desktop was decorated with a picture of a wife and a robust teen-age son. On the wall was a plastic bison's head with the RCMP motto curled around it. There was a filing cabinet and a water cooler and not much else except a view of Mexico City's expensive Polanco district.

He explained why I had had a bad time with Alvarez.

A memo had been sent to him by Harry, but by mail instead of secure fax. A new central depot for Canadian External Affairs Department mail had just been established in Charlottetown, Plum Coolee or some other vital nerve centre of government.

Seeing the word *Mexico* on the envelope, the clerk had put it in the South American mail and it had taken two weeks to get back from that continent. The next clerk, who must have seen a map at some time, had put it in the North American basket; but it was waylaid elewhere in the department by a sorter who sent it to Central American Dispatch. On the third try, it reached Fitzgerald, but by that time the wrong signal—the union-generated missive that identified me as a regular police officer, had reached Alvarez.

Fitzgerald's experience with Alvarez had been far worse than mine but, as his expression showed, he expected that sort of thing.

"If somebody plants a bomb on an airliner and sinks it two miles deep in the Atlantic, the Force can solve it. We will get our man, even if he's working the green chain on a sawmill halfway around the world. If it's something like mailing an ordinary extradition order to Manila in less than three months or getting a memo delivered to Mex-

116

ico City, frankly, it's beyond our capacity; we can't cope with things like that."

This had not been one of Fitz's sunnier days in the service of justice, home and country.

Earlier this day he had phoned Ottawa on the open phone system, starting with a Mexican operator who insisted that, if Ottawa was in Ontario, it was part of Greater Los Angeles. She had a sister who lived in Ontario, and downtown L.A. was only a short bus ride from her house. Even when forced to abandon that position, she insisted that Ottawa must be in the United States and that everything in the U.S. was not far from Los Angeles.

When they finally reached the number the phone rang off the wall, and when he tried an alternate number a woman came on the line and said, in English, "This is the French phone."

He introduced himself and said what he wanted.

"I'm sorry, her phone is off; she's out for lunch. It's noon here."

"Are you in the same department?"

"Yes."

"Then you can help me."

"No. This is the French phone. It's reserved for people who speak French."

Although his own command of that language was poor, Fitz tried. "*Eh bien, parlerons en Français.*"

"You're speaking French!" She made it sound like an accusation.

"*Oui, mademoiselle.*"

"I don't speak French!"

"Ah no. But you DO speak English and I speak English so we COULD talk, couldn't we?"

"Not on the French phone."

When he persisted she said, patiently, "I am TRYING to be helpful."

"At that point I knew it was hopeless," Fitzgerald said. "Any time somebody in Ottawa says they're only trying to help you, it's hopeless. I gave up and had a good laugh." It was hard to imagine a laugh disarranging that mournful face, but I suppose anybody can laugh about bureaucracy when he isn't crying.

He took me to lunch—I must have been important enough to rate an expense-account lunch, or he would never have been so profligate—and the ambassador, to whom he introduced me, insisted we take his official car.

"Just take the pennant off the fender," he said. "If you have an accident, let it not be an official accident." He was a good type. Those at the top usually are, if you can ever get past their subordinates.

So we had time for rubbernecking in the city.

When Cortés conquered it with his army of a few hundred ragged men, it was larger, cleaner and better organized than any city of Europe. Today, it is larger than any city of the world, but no longer cleaner or better organized. It's full of smoke and smog and, in the slums, the smell of excrement.

Still, there is no doubt that you are in the Paris of the Western World, and what man can remain unmoved by the sight of the grand Reforma Boulevard, the Zocuala or Chapultapec, where in 1851 the six army cadets they call the Child Heroes wrapped themselves in Mexican flags and jumped to their deaths from the castle walls rather than surrender to the invading American army?

That conspicuous waste of human life plucked at the very heartstrings of Mexicans, and the cadets' names and faces still appear on currency notes: Suarez, Escutia, de la Barrera, de Oca, Marquez and Melgar.

Fitz told me that when Harry Truman decided to honour the dead boys at the Chapultapec shrine, the Mexican soldier on honour guard broke into tears as the American president walked up with his wreath. Fitz reported this with disapproval. If a man wanted to bawl like a woman he had a right to, but he had no business doing it while on duty.

I suggested we go to the restaurant by way of the University of Mexico, the oldest in the Western Hemisphere, and see the murals I had seen just once before.

"They say the Great Wall of China is the last human work you can see when taking a rocket ship away from the Earth. But the last human work that man will remember when leaving earth is the architecture and murals of University of Mexico."

Well, he agreed, they weren't bad. That is pretty extravagant praise, coming from a Canadian; I could tell he thought about them the way I did.

We ate cow intestines and turtle meat in the old Maria Cristina Hotel, off the Reforma Boulevard, where the lobby floor is of tanned bullhides and where beauty and song were all around us.

A waiter, an old chap with flat feet, sat beside us at Kahlua time.

118

He folded a napkin into the shape of a tenth-century court jester's boot, which occupied almost five minutes, then put a hibiscus in it and left us with a short bow, a smile, no words and no requests. We weren't even at one of his tables.

He must have had some good experiences with gringos. Maybe he had a daughter who did brain surgery in Chicago or made speeches in the United Nations. Here, you can never tell at which moment some gentle bit of charm and courtesy will drop into your lap the way a flower drifts down from its vine.

Old Fitz appearing mellower than before, it seemed as good a time as any to bring up the subject of why we were here. So far, it was the one subject we had avoided.

"There are a couple of things I'd like to ask you about, Fitz, if you don't mind."

"I don't mind."

I noticed he didn't promise to answer any. "Well, there's Clarence Trelegis, who we call The White Indian. I figure he's working for you, or for us, if that's proper to say."

"Aye," said Fitzgerald.

"Aye what?"

"Aye, I understand."

"The Dark Horseman just has to be a Mexican agent, or else one of ours. He was released from a life sentence in what they like to call a Social Re-Adaptation Unit. You have to die or spend a thousand years to get out of those places. That has to mean something."

"Aye."

"And although I didn't put it in the memo, for obvious reasons, I believe the perfect suspect is our tiny perfect policeman, Captain Alvarez. He is a policeman, on poor pay, surrounded by millionaire criminals."

"A very astute observation," said Fitz, "which happens to fit all of us."

"Present company excepted," I said.

"Why except me? Are my morals better because I'm white?"

It was hard not to like him, the dour old bastard.

"I don't know why I don't think you're bent, except I figure you believe you were put on earth to suffer."

"Aye."

"Pretty Little One doesn't fit for me. Maybe she does for you but

119

not for me. The pattern isn't right. The same for the other Mexicans. If a Mexican comes into big money he has no way of keeping it secret because he's honour-bound to share it with all his relatives, including the shirttail cousins he didn't even know he had."

"Aye," said Fitzgerald, and ordered two more coffees and Kahluas.

"Okay, I can go on. But I figure you're after a gringo, and there isn't a gringo there who isn't one card short of a full deck. Henry Terwilliger's a third-generation chinless wonder. Peter Pan Wilbur, the professor on the grant, and the Winnebago vagrants—none of them really amount to much. As criminals, that is. They may be all right in other ways."

"It's something I liked in your letter. You have some humour. We need it in this business."

"But you agree?"

"I'm still listening."

"I listed it all in the long, chatty note, and there's been nothing worthwhile since. I wonder, of course, how the people I told you about checked out with Interpol."

"Aye."

"And at home and in the U.S."

"Aye."

"Just for the hell of it, say aye one more time."

"No."

As I said, he was a hard man to dislike.

"One of the reasons I didn't tell your Force to shove this whole thing where the monkey shoved the nuts is that my sister wrote me a letter which said, in ways clear to me, that I had said something important in my first review."

"Your sister doesn't send me letters," said Fitzgerald.

We took a walk through what they call the world's largest flea market, and I bought some magnificent obsidian arrowheads, not one of which was more than six months old. If you used a microscope you would see that the flakes had been picked off with metal, not bird bone. But so what? They were perfect Solutrean points, every bit as good as the ones your ancestors and mine were chipping out a hundred thousand years ago while scratching their fleas and singing their songs in the caves.

There were mariachi bands and Indian women begging while they gave suck to tiny babies. On the street, amid the traffic, a man was gulping naptha, blowing it out his mouth and lighting it into a tall pillar of yellow flame.

"It's like smoking cigarettes," said Fitz. "There's no harm if you don't inhale."

An old man in a sailor cap cranked a barrel organ while munching a taco, which broke and dripped on the pavement. The organ ground out "The Watch on the Rhine."

> Dear Fatherland
> May'st tranquil be
> Thy faithful sons
> Watch over thee.

"How in hell does the nineteenth-century German national anthem wind up in a Mexican flea market?" I said.

"Need to know," said Fitz.

"Need to know what?"

"What we were talking about at the Maria Cristina. You had no need to know the answers to those questions. And here, you've got no need to know the answer to this one. Just enjoy the barrel organ."

> Secure and strong
> True sons of thine
> Stand sentry on
> The noble Rhine.

The old chap didn't have a monkey with a tin cup, but he had a brilliant green parrot on top of the organ, which kept saying in Spanish, "Thanks. Many thanks. Thanks."

Fitz walked up and spoke to the parrot in English. "Hey, bird. Do you know the difference between a Canadian and a canoe?"

The bird tilted his head and looked at Fitz quizzically.

"The Canadian doesn't tip," said Fitz. The old man, who apparently knew English, doubled up laughing.

Fitz threw $10,000 instead of $5,000 in the pot, and the parrot, which knew at least one word of English, shrieked, "Cheapskate! Cheapskate!"

"You know, Fitz," I said, "five thousand here, ten thousand there; after awhile it begins to add up."

"You go next, then."

I bought the entire stock of an old Indian woman's flowers, which she had spread on the sidewalk—so many, I carried them in both arms. I stopped the first pretty girl in a pantsuit who walked down and gave them all to her.

She accepted instantly, happily, and without protestation or any false modesty. She picked a bright bloom, pinned it on my shirt, gathered up the rest and went off down the street with her armload, tossing her lovely hair, swaying her hips, proud as an army with banners. Mexico, Mexico.

We started walking back down Reforma to where we had left the embassy car illegally parked, and Fitz talked about something he apparently thought I should know, or pretended to think I should.

He had spent a month or two studying communications between the embassy and Ottawa RCMP headquarters. Somebody had arrived at the notion that they might be made more reliable.

"So I ended up reporting that the Force had two clear alternatives. We could set up our own communication system with scrambled radios and make some bad friends with External Affairs, or we could use the diplomatic pouch and have stuff lost from time to time because some kid in a mailing room couldn't get the mind above the belt that day.

"I wound up saying, 'A decision is needed, one way or the other.'

"After three months, I started phoning to find out what the commissioner had decided. After another month I asked him directly, by fax. I never did hear from him but one of his flunkies got back to me. The message read, 'The commissioner has accepted your recommendation.' "

Fitz said he was keeping that memo to show to his grandchildren.

"I went out with Alvarez and we got drunk on cheap diplomatic booze," he said.

"Getting drunk with Alvarez would be like making love with a corpse," I said.

He was going to pass it by and say "aye" again, but something made him look at me a second time.

"I heard what you said about him at lunch. You're right in one way. He's a first-class man but he has a rotten disposition. But let me tell you one thing. Even if there is no need for you to know, I'll tell you, Mac. Alvarez has a middle-class wife in a middle-class house. He has two kids, and both of them bag groceries at the Gigantes supermarket in the hours they are not in school."

"Aye," I said.

Fitz didn't laugh. "Don't say 'aye.' Have feelings, Mac. Newspapermen get too cynical. You're not like policemen. We see enough misery and unfairness in this world that it still touches us."

"Touch me, then, because Alvarez has not."

"If you want to hunt up the reports of a U.S. Senate investigating committee some day, you will find it alleged that the Central Intelligence Agency was in bed with a bunch of drug financiers only a few years ago, when they were trying to destabilize President López Portillo. That was down in Guerrero State. I'm not saying it's true. The guy who confessed was under torture, and you can never depend on evidence you get that way.

"But there's a big pile of such evidence about the CIA cozying up to Noriega in Panama and the drug people in the Golden Triangle in northwest Vietnam. Alvarez reads all those reports. How do you suppose it makes him feel?"

"It doesn't touch me much. I'm philosophically opposed to prohibition of heroin, alcohol or any other drug. So I guess I sit it out."

"I can't sit it out and I'm not a philosopher. I'm a policeman. Middle class. I have middle-class kids who have to earn their own money to buy their own dull, boring middle-class clothing. So I understand how Alvarez felt when he was told to back off and let the financiers make millions out of drugs because the gringos wanted things that way. It's all in the point of view, I guess."

"Aye," I said. A little light went on in his eye and he nodded his head in some appreciation. He wasn't insensitive. Different, but not insensitive.

As we were about to part near the Maria Cristina, where, for all the air pollution, the Cup of Gold blossoms tumbled in great profusion over the grey wall, I somewhat maliciously tossed my firecracker in his lap.

"By the way," I said. "Before I go and write more long, chatty notes, Clarence Trelegis, The White Indian, is on a ferocious drunk. He's probably been thrown out of his rented cabin. When I left he was calling his landlady the Venus de Kilo."

"Jesus Cast Iron American Christ! And I'm supposed to be in Bogotá tomorrow!" shouted Fitz.

Sooner or later, everybody says more than they want to say to a newspaperman. I pretended not to notice and shook his hand.

He went over to the embassy car and paid the uniformed man who had guarded it in its illegal parking place. The parking man was playing a sad melody called "Petition of the Soul" on his guitar. He scarcely missed a beat while accepting the $5,000.

I felt too happy, too young and cheerful, to fly back north in a jet with my knees under my chin. I turned in my airline ticket and travelled to San Sebastian on second-class buses. They had tiny little baby goats on the roof, tied by the feet, and tiny little Mexican babies inside the bus, the babies trussed up almost as tightly as the goats with layer upon layer of heavy clothing. I met some wonderful people, old, young and middle-aged, male and female. We told a lot of jokes, sang a lot and ate death-dealing tacos at bus stops, secure in the belief that a happy spirit cannot contract the amoeba.

By the time I got back to San Sebastian it turned out Fitz hadn't gone to Colombia after all. He had come straight to San Sebastian.

He explained that after he left me he had returned to the embassy, cancelled the trip to Bogotá, bought an airline ticket for Tepic and, in righteous rage, telephoned somebody in authority at headquarters who was too busy to talk to him.

Late in the evening, just before he was to leave for his plane, he got the call and opened the conversation by saying, "Are you the dumb son of a whore who's responsible for putting two amateur bird watchers into San Sebastian?"

"I beg your pardon?"

"I said, 'Are you the dumb son of a whore who decided amateurs were good enough to eyeball a drug shipment.' "

"Well, I suppose I am responsible. I'm responsible for everything that goes wrong. I'm the commissioner."

Fitz corrected himself. "I meant to say, 'Are you the dumb son of a whore, sir,' " he said.

The commissioner had not come to head one of the world's more unusual police forces without encountering NCOs and constables like Fitzgerald, and he knew better than to stand on his dignity. He said it didn't matter whether he was the dumbest son of a whore in the world because there was so much competition for the title.

What had come to headquarters, from other sources located in Guadalajara or Colombia, was that somebody on our side had talked wildly in San Sebastian, and the people arranging the shipment were getting nervous.

"I want to know if we have blotted our copybook there."

"I'll get to Alvarez as quick as I can. He's my opposite number. He's a captain. Captain Alvarez."

"Save discussions about your rank and pay for union meetings, and let's stay with the point." It was the commissioner's turn.

"Sorry, sir. Alvarez has been off duty all week. He's in Washington. So if there is trouble, he won't know about it yet; but if anybody on our side has screwed up, God help him when Alvarez finds out."

"That's why I'm concerned. I can tell you the reason there are two bird watchers in San Sebastian instead of one real policeman. Alvarez made it very clear, to us if not to you, that he wanted no foreign police on this job. We asked if we might put a couple of bird watchers in there and he said all right to that, although I understand that got fouled up somehow."

"Yes, the notification to him went astray, sir. He was about as offended as any single human being can get."

The commissioner sighed.

"If it's as bad as the other source indicated, there's not much hope of our finding the top man this time," he said. "There's probably little to do except find the shipment and pick up a few of the little scabby people."

"Screwed, blued and tattooed, sir," said Fitz.

The commissioner sighed once again. "I should have been a cat skinner. That was what Mother always hoped for me. It was steady work."

"Mine wanted me to be a brain surgeon, but I think she'd have been just as happy if I could have got to run a bulldozer," said Fitz.

When they broke the connection, Fitz realized he had not asked the commissioner if the Mexican army was going to make a sweep looking for the drug cache, and, if so, when it would start. It was pointless to try to phone back. It was long past quitting time in Ottawa. Only the top people worked that late in their offices and they turned off the phone bells.

He tried for Alvarez. He was still away. Fitz ran for his plane with his socks wrapped around his toothbrush.

A drug war is just like any other war: a story of failed communications.

CHAPTER 13

"TOO MANY POLICEMEN"

Never believe a political statement until it has been denied.
—Author unknown

As Fitz had anticipated, White Indian had created a great white bliz-zard of problems in San Sebastian. He passed out in the square one morning and was carried home to Pretty Little One's by teen-agers, recruited for the purpose by the Syndic. At his cabin he passed out again while smoking and set his blanket and himself afire.

Consuela found him amid the smoke and thoroughly burned both her hands and forearms rolling him on the floor to put out the fire. At the first aid station, where they treated her second-degree burns, she remarked that White Indian behaved like a pig at times. "But any man deserves to have somebody looking after him when he chooses to get drunk. After all, that's a privilege of men, to get drunk, the stu-pid bastards."

Angel also remained in attendance upon White Indian. Whether or not his own father had been a drinker, The Fragment learned one rule—never interfere with a man while he is drinking. He just ran errands for White Indian and sometimes sat outside the cabin when the man was snoring, waiting for him to devise new chores.

Usually these were trips to the grocery for liquor. White Indian was on tequila. At its best, it is a splendid drink with a delightful, exhilirating aftertaste in the back of the nose. However, as with Scotch, there are many brands, and he was drinking the one the vil-lage people used for starting tractors. There came the night when Pretty Little One was summoned from deep sleep at 2:00 A.M. by policemen, led by the Syndic. In some countries, when police come to the door at 2:00 A.M., it's a bad sign for the occupants, but in San

Sebastian things were seldom structured in ways familiar to other parts of the world.

She appeared at her door in a nightgown, a shawl across her face to keep out the dangerously cold air of the night.

"Syndic!" she said.

He was apologetic, as usual. "It is Mr. Clarence," he said.

"He is dead, I hope?"

"You have humour, Madam. No, he is not dead. Not dead, but in the jail."

"Excellent! I cannot think of a better place for him to be."

"Dear lady, he is yours."

"He is not mine."

"You are his patron."

"I am not his patron."

So it went while all the dogs in town barked about whatever it was that interested them.

White Indian and Dark Horseman had left early that day, clutching money and their genitals, bound for the whorehouse in Santander. Dark Horseman came back to San Sebastian after a brief encounter to report to his new employer, Wilbur, who had some arcane task for him to perform.

White Indian remained in the brothel until all his money was gone. He then hired a taxi to go home in. When the taxi arrived, White Indian said that the bill was entirely the affair of Pretty Little One.

The cabby's main business was driving people to San Sebastian from Santander, then turning around and going back again, for which reason he was called Turnaround John.

Being experienced in such matters, Turnaround John insisted that he was going to be paid in the here and now, not by some third party on some other occasion, and, Pretty Little One's lights all being out, he took his customer to the police station, where Clarence, although weakened by sex and confused by alcohol, defended himself rather ably against three policemen who eventually succeeded in tossing him into the slammer.

"You don't want him to spend the night in jail," said the Syndic to Pretty Little One.

"Clearly, in jail is where I want him."

"But you are not serious, Madam. It is not very much money. It is . . . ?

Turnaround John named his price, $35,000.

"You see," said the Syndic. "The amount is not unreasonable."

"Then let Mr. Clarence out to go to the bank tomorrow morning and take a not unreasonable amount out of his savings account."

"The banker tells me he does not have very much left in that account," said the Syndic. It was a bank where anybody and everybody's accounts were freely discussed with strangers, but the accounts of gringos had a special interest, and many people asked the banker to display their cards. Gringos who were richer and wiser than Clarence did their banking at Santander, where the privacy rules, although not up to the standard of Switzerland or the Bahamas, were stricter.

"Then he should stay in jail and keep the bank money to pay his bill here."

"I am sure you do not mean that when you speak of our friend Mr. Clarence."

"Syndic, you know how it is with men drinking. There are some who lose the legs and not the head, and there are those who lose the head but keep the legs, but whichever it is, they have a presence, a dignity, an ability to keep that essence of reason."

"Yes, I know."

"Well, Mr. Clarence is exactly the opposite."

"He has not driven his car."

"Because I stole the keys and my workmen pushed the car over to The Fragment's house and hid it there under some palm thatch."

"He has not lost his manners among the women of the village. Madam, White Indian is a good man. I like him. It is not right that he is like an animal in a cage, shaking the bars."

"No," said Pretty Little One.

The Syndic sighed. His wife was not the only woman who was unreasonable.

"Then I am obliged."

When she saw him put his hands in the pockets of his faded pants and start pulling out money, her attitude changed.

"I, too, am fond of Mr. Clarence," she said. She stopped at that and waited until he had put all his money in Turnaround John's hand. It was only $28,000, but Turnaround John was a reasonable man. He took it and left.

"I am fond of him and we shall have to do something for him," she continued, to complete what she had been saying.

"Now please," said the Syndic. "Come to the jail before he tears it down. He is a very strong man."

Being reminded of a previous guest who had fallen off the wagon hard enough to shake the earth, she pawed around in her button and notion box where were nestled Norwegian crowns, English shillings, million-peso Bolivian notes and other trashy bits of currency abandoned in her cabins, ones she trusted would some day be honoured by the governments responsible. The only two important coins were a Maria Theresa dollar, still common currency in the Yemen, and a copper medallion commemorating ten years' abstinence of the guest who had belonged to Alcoholics Anonymous.

"This is the passport for alcoholics," she said. "It is the one certificate they recognize. Alcoholics will only listen to other certified true alcoholics."

"But you, Pretty Little One, are not one."

"Many people in San Sebastian are not what they seem to be. Wait for me while I dress."

Down at the jailhouse, where the sleepy guards had been expecting her, Pretty Little One was accorded the usual deference, and she was provided privacy for her discussion with White Indian, who had, up to this point, been shaking the flimsy cell bars and offering to disembowel everybody in sight once they finally gave way.

What she said to him remains unclear. She never told anyone. When he sobered up he couldn't remember. It wasn't the copper AA medallion. He was heard that night at the lockup insisting that he belonged to a class of drunks who were unorganized. Something she said or did cut through the fog of that oldest, most famous, most loved, most hated, most unpredictable of all the drugs.

White Indian followed her out of the cells and down the streets to his cabin like a big dog who'd been scratched behind the ears.

She woke him four hours later, with malice aforethought, and started him sweating it all away with a corroded shovel and a broken pick. That was how Fitzgerald found him, sad, remorseful and sweating so hard that his feet squelched in his shoes.

White Indian saluted him with the shovel. "I am working the Mexican dragline," he said.

What Fitzgerald said next was spoken too low for my informant,

Consuela, to hear, but my guess is that he told White Indian he was lucky that Alvarez was out of the country during these days of wine and wanton.

Even in plain clothes, I would have expected San Sebastian to have recognized Fitzgerald as a policeman as readily as if it had been printed on his back along with the message KICK ME. But in another country, the obvious is not always so clear. There were always stray gringos passing through the village. Pretty Little One attracted strange custom, it seemed.

There had been a blues singer from New Jersey, a mayor from a small town in Italy, a man who dove into small tanks at small circuses and was losing his nerve, and any God's number of examples of the mentally lame, emotionally halt and spiritually blind of our world.

She made it her business to learn a little from each one of them and she had, apparently, a phenomenal memory or else kept notes because she seemed to forget nothing she had heard. On the most arcane of subjects, Pretty Little One would frequently contribute an extraordinary expertise, gained from one of her customers.

But to others in the village, the itinerants came and went so fast there wasn't time to give them their nicknames. Even their faces blurred, one into another, causing old people to remark that all gringos looked the same to them.

Fitz, I suppose, looked the same as a circus tank–diver or any of the others who had been badly strung out. Just another gringo, talking that strange English language, which, when you are unable to make sense of it, sounds like geese in a farmyard, hissing, croaking and gabbling.

He did everything right, as a tourist.

He spent a morning wandering the beach, alone; getting the sun, he said. He rented a boat and an outboard and, with a large lunch packed by Consuela, he toured the byways of the long lagoon of which San Sebastian commanded the mouth. He made a trip into Santander and returned with a serape, a hand-tooled belt and an onyx ashtray—Santander's only concession to tourism, San Sebastian having none.

Pronouncing himself content with his brief vacation he paid his rent, tipped just what was expected, no more and no less, and was leaving for a business appointment in Guadalajara the day I returned.

Pretty Little One introduced him to me as a cement-company representative from Wisconsin. Canadians who want to claim American nationality usually name Wisconsin as their home state; it is the only one where the accent is purely Canadian. He shook my hand in a disinterested way, asked my business and, when I said my home was in Canada, said he had once gone bass fishing in Canada.

When he left I remarked that he seemed a pleasant sort.

"Yes," she said. "But there are too many policemen coming into this village lately."

So much for clever deceptions. Well, if she was prepared to speak plainly, I would also.

"What's going on, a drug shipment?"

When she didn't want to respond to a question, her little black eyes took on a dullness that made them resemble two black currants in a dumpling.

"I take no part in politics," she said. "That is man's work. Although, you know, Wolf Man, there are times I wonder if God was wise to have ordained that men should run the world."

I looked into those eyes expecting a smile, but they were dark and shuttered.

How little of ourselves we reveal to one another. But what the hell, how little we reveal to ourselves.

CHAPTER 14

HIDDEN FURY

Good Fortune is a giddy maid,
Fickle and restless as a fawn;
She smooths your hair, and then the jade
Kisses you quickly and is gone.

But Madam Sorry scorns all this,
She shows no appetite for flitting;
But with a long and fervent kiss
Sits by your bed—and brings her knitting.

—Heinrich Heine

Having been born far from the sea and its sister, the desert, I have never felt at ease with either. Both are subject to moods that come upon them for no apparent reason. Yet both have a fascination I could never completely resist. To me, they are like women who also awe and puzzle me, and it seemed right that on the day of the hidden storm one of the world's loveliest women linked her arm with mine and the odour of sweet violets enclosed us both.

I was walking a few kilometres of the long western beach of Mexico, which begins at the American border and runs to the Guatemalan frontier with only a few headlands and harbours and a town or city or so to interrupt its lonely magnificence, a rim of gold on the western shores of the nation. Our section, the Drum, was in truth no different from a thousand other portions of the national beach except for one thing—it was ours.

Few residents of San Sebastian ever came out to their share of this ocean paradise, perhaps because it was lonely and, except for litter, untouched by mankind.

When a few did come to the beach to play or picnic they came in the largest group possible and, when on the sand, huddled together close enough to tread on each other, trying to press away from them the endless, empty sands on either side.

Gringos were identifiable from afar. They chose to be solitary on these lonely sands and, to the puzzlement of local people, seemed to actually enjoy their isolation from other people. So it was with me, this moody day.

Our sky was blue, with only a few mares' tails in it. The sun beat down and the sands were warm. It was clear air. The headland that thrust its snout out to the south of us and sealed off the next village stood sharp against the sky. It seemed a day destined to pass like almost all other days, dawn at 6:00 A.M., an afternoon sea breeze beginning at 3:00 and ending at 5:00 P.M., and at 6:00 P.M. precisely the blanket of night pulled over our heads while a trillion bright stars shone through its large and small holes.

The ocean's spirit was unlike the sky's. Far away to the west was a hidden storm; some furies had torn at the waters, and the huge waves of that conflict rolled in on our beach. In spite of the sun, which should have turned them a deep blue with a frosting of foam, they came in grey and sullen.

When the ocean moved in this way the waves marched in on the Drum at a slant. If you were venturesome and swam in it, as did some tourists who had nothing better to do with their time, you would be carried down the beach as you swam and have to walk a fair distance back to where you left your clothes, your towel and the other people who left wild oceans to themselves.

I was watching the twist of the water and thinking about the strangeness of waves, winds and women when Phoebe Nell came up behind me and put a delicate little arm through mine.

"You didn't see me." She sounded pleased with herself, like a child playing hide-and-seek with an adult.

"I smelled your perfume."

"Only after I touched you."

"Well, some of us are insensitive clots."

Looking over my shoulder, I could see her little feet had followed my footprints for some time in the damp sand. She wore a dress with a hood. It resembled a monk's and was entirely plain and enchanting.

In my mature years, I can recognize a simple dress like this as being extremely expensive, but for most of my life I thought the more bells and whistles there were on women's clothes the more they cost. I have been wrong about many things like that. I was past fifty before I found out that women didn't wear beautiful clothing to attract men, they did so only to irritate and repel other women.

We walked the beach together beside the sounding sea, and she kept her arm tucked in mine while the hood of her monk's gown tossed back and forth as she talked, sometimes letting the sun glow in her hair and then casting a black shadow on that pale and lovely face.

"I have the impulse to kiss you," I said.

"No. You could not do that. I have never kissed a man."

"Oh, come now. You don't expect me to believe that."

She tossed her head and the hood fell back and the light breeze lifted her golden hair. "It is not what you might think. I do all the things that a normal woman does, except I do not kiss a man."

"Never?"

"I was kissed by an uncle who had bad teeth and bad breath and it was the kind of kiss uncles shouldn't give. After that, I never kissed a man again. That is what is so good about Jon. He can understand that."

Jon, I thought, would not only understand but would prefer anything that was cockamamie.

We walked on and her loose dress blew against me. For a long time she continued her usual quiet silence. It was not shyness, as I once thought, but an essential quiet and peace; she was a still water in the rapid current of life, the clear, deep, still, sweet water of the river of life.

"Why are you here?" she said.

"For the same reason you are, I suppose. I came to listen to the sea and to wonder why it is angered today."

She made a little pout and two creases appeared across her little nose.

"I don't mean here on the beach. I mean here in San Sebastian."

I told her about my wife dying and about a big old house being empty in Canada and she listened, not too intently, I thought.

"And why are you here on this beach today?" I said.

"I am here because Jon has gone to Monterrey for a conference."

"All right. Now that we both know why we are here, let us rejoice in old Mexico. What a lovely land it is. Have you been happier anywhere else?"

The question seemed to puzzle her.

I recited the sort of thing people here would have put to music:

> Come live with me and be my love
> And we will some new pleasures prove
> Of golden sands, and crystal brooks,
> With silken lines, and silver hooks.

"That's pretty," she said. "I saw a movie once where Paul Newman said something like that."

She pressed my arm and I was reminded that it didn't matter if Phoebe Nell was clever because she was so lovely and I turned to look on her pale beauty again while she looked down the long reach of the sand.

As we walked, she talked. It was peculiarly like the performance of Pretty Little One with a new guest; a vast curiosity about how another human being lives, what he does and how he does it. Some people are interested in things, some in people and some in ideas. For Pretty Little One it was ideas that mattered. Phoebe Nell, it seemed, went no further than an interest in people.

I was surprised at the questions on which I stumbled. I didn't know the name, the address or the occupation of the people whose house I lived in. Curiosity is the main baggage a newspaperman carries in his packsack, yet there had been no time when the identity of my hosts had seemed important enough for me to ask about it.

Since I couldn't tell her how I did acquire possession of the place, I had to answer by inventing names and other information. That, I thought, should serve as well as real information.

Then she pressed my arm and pointed. I could see, a kilometre or more ahead, a figure in the surf.

The waves would beat him back to shore but he would advance again each time against the ocean when it receded.

It is irritating to watch this sort of thing at a distance. The stick man moves, like a cartoon figure, but without any understandable pattern. Why does the stick man throw himself against the waves? Why does he assault them, again and again?

The slant of the sea was moving him slowly towards us as we walked towards him, and at last I could determine that he was a fisherman using a surf rod.

"Who can it be?" she asked.

"Only a gringo. The local people fish by swinging line by hand, which they carry coiled around beer cans. Only gringos and wealthy Mexicans from the cities use rods. Also, no Mexican would fish in a sea like this. The waves are boiling with sand. No man can take fish in water as dirty as this."

"It's probably White Indian," she said. "He often fishes off the beach here."

"How would you know who it is?" I said.

"I like to watch what people do. But tell me, why does he fish today if there are no fish in the water?"

"Because he is a man and man is born to dream."

She turned her face to me and smiled with the full lips that had never been kissed, and because I looked at the sand for a time, trying to find a pretty shell to pick up for her, and she turned her face sideways to the rising wind that was lifting dry sand to us, neither of us saw the stick man get knocked over.

He had been moving increasingly far into the surf and fishing waist-deep, backing up when the bigger waves came and lifting himself tippytoe so he kept contact with the bottom. But for all that the experts say, there is no regularity to ocean waves. Even the rule that every seventh wave is biggest is only a folk tale. Waves piggyback on one another and become giants, but they do so unpredictably. It was one of those that must have caught White Indian, because we could no longer see him.

My impulse was to laugh at seeing him get a good ducking, but when he came out of the foam, threw away the surf rod and starting pounding the water, it wasn't funny at all. He was in trouble. Nobody throws away an expensive surf rod unless he is scared, and White Indian was not a man to scare easily.

I left her and began running towards him. But why? He was a kilometre distant and was going to be drowned or back safely on the beach long before I could puff along that far.

Then another figure came out of the sand dunes above the surf line. He was close to the man caught in the undertow.

The new stick man waved his arms—left, left, always left—but if

White Indian could see him he could not understand the signal, and the second man flung off his jacket and ran into the smother of sea and foam to grab White Indian.

They appeared to fight in the waves and often disappeared in the breakers, but after a time they came edging down to the left, as the second stick man wanted, and at last, clutching one another, they were washed in towards the beach and could get their feet on bottom and come staggering to shore, both spewing foaming salt water out of mouth and nose.

When I reached them, they were seated together on the sand dune, still out of breath but now laughing, the usual response to death and disaster narrowly missed.

It was no surprise that the second man was Dark Horseman. Wherever one of this pair was, the other soon showed up. White Indian, however, said he had been surprised to see his friend, and they were both surprised to see us.

"He knew about undertows, but when it came to swimming he was worse than me," said White Indian. "We ended up rescuing one another."

"He is a goat," said Dark Horseman. That is one of those dangerous words in Mexico. When you say it, it had better be to a friend and even then, when you say it, smile.

"I swam better than you, my friend," said White Indian. "My hat floated."

I gathered bits of old crates and other debris to make a fire so they could dry themselves. When I got back with an armful, White Indian was translating Dark Horseman's description of an undertow for Phoebe Nell.

"He says with a sideways sea the water will build up in hills along the beach and then rush back against the waves into the ocean. If you ever get caught in one, swim sideways out of its current and then the waves will wash you ashore. Trouble is, I didn't know that. Trouble with him is, he can't swim. The goat."

He said the word *goat* in Spanish and grabbed the big Mexican's arm.

We started a fire, a pallid, smoky thing of coconut husks and wood so damp that it used up almost all the heat of combustion in expelling moisture. The Horseman fell silent and began looking at Phoebe Nell who, in that strange virgin-queen way she had, seemed completely unaware of her effect on the libido of the human male.

Clarence was also subdued, but if you've gone to look at the opposite side of life and come back, I suppose that's understandable. We talked for a while about the most ordinary of affairs, and Phoebe Nell, who couldn't understand Spanish, poked at the sultry fire with a little stick and let the rising wind play with her hair.

Dark Horseman continued to look her way with an unusual intensity. Through his shirt, which clung to his back, I could see long red scratches. Since the bottom here was pure sand, they must have been souvenirs of a recent passionate encounter. Somebody who kissed as well, I took it. Then he began to shake.

White Indian saw the first tremor.

"We're all right," he told me. "You two go on home. We're all right."

He wanted us out of the way. So did I, if the other man was going to have one of his spells.

"Right you are, Clarence," I said. I grabbed his shoulder and squeezed. She left with me willingly: she was forever so willing, so obliging, so gentle, but this time she did not put her arm in mine as we walked by the angry ocean.

I glanced back once. White Indian sat beside his friend, not speaking, just being there.

White Indian once told me that Dark Horseman's shaking was not his fault because the man had something in him. He used a Cree Indian word and I couldn't understand it. "It's a word that means hidden man," he said. "Dark Horseman has a hidden man who comes out sometimes."

"Schizophrenia," I said.

"Who can understand those funny English words?" said White Indian, who didn't want to talk about the matter any more.

So Phoebe Nell and I left them and walked back to the village, the seas beating beside us, driven by a rage we could not understand but could believe. A sea containing a hidden sea, I thought to myself.

When I looked, once, into her violet eyes during our walk home, the pupils were widely distended. She had been frightened or, in some perverse reaction, exhilarated by what had happened. But her voice was, as always, even, quiet.

"Wherever you see one of those men, you see the other, don't you?" she said.

"They are friends."

"But then why is one of them fishing where there are no fish and why doesn't he even know the other one was nearby? And why is the other one there at all, when he is not interested in fishing?"

"Does it matter? All men are mad. Why should they be exceptions?"

"Some day when I want to kiss a man I will come and look for you," she said.

As so often in San Sebastian, I found myself happy for no particular reason here, by the ocean, beside a beautiful woman who would never be mine.

"I almost forgot to tell you. That funny man, Wilbur Oshaski, wants to see you."

"I didn't know you knew him."

"I didn't know that you knew him so well, either. He seems to have a lot of respect for you."

If Wilbur had so much respect, I didn't know why he didn't take a stroll across town and visit me in the house.

"What is it he does?" she said.

"Well, I guess his main project in life is being Wilbur Oshaski."

"It's a funny name, too. I never knew there was an Irish family in Poland named Oshaski, but that's what he tells me."

I told her that after they made Wilbur they broke the mould, but I don't think she got the point.

At The Pretty Little One's place I expected her to leave me and go back to her cabin. On most days she lay on a canvas-and-aluminum lawn couch beneath a canopy, which kept the sun from her pale skin.

She would wear a well-tailored jumpsuit, usually, and often one little foot would dangle from the cot with a lace-edged satin slipper caught on one toe. She would read, sleep or just rest with her eyes half-opened to the day, comfortable as a house cat and with some of the same remoteness.

Perhaps this day, with its errant winds, made her kitten basket too cold for comfort. She didn't explain why she came with me.

Wilbur seemed surprised to see us together.

He was prowling about in his garden behind the big brick wall, moodily kicking at piles of gravel and peering into holes in the ground.

"Dark Horseman was supposed to be making cement for me here

today," he said. I told him about the events on the beach and suggested that Dark Horseman wasn't likely to be in a condition to work for him or anybody else this day.

Phoebe Nell's eyes grew vaguer. She had a habit of detaching herself from her surroundings. She left us and wandered to the outdoor refrigerator, where she helped herself to a can of Coca-Cola.

Wilbur grew more agitated, as if the undertow had been sent for the purpose of inconveniencing him and his workman.

"Why does that fellow White Indian want to be fooling around fishing on the beach when the water's like this, anyway?" He spoke as if the beach were his own property.

He persisted in urging me to have beer, a ripe mango, some pineapple, coffee or cold boiled shrimp, not one of which I wanted.

Lupe was away. "It turns out it was a slipped disk in her back. She's gone to the specialist." He gave the information as if reciting something he'd memorized.

He was equally detached when exhibiting his blueprint for a kayak-shaped fibreglass boat that could be propelled by paddle, sail, foot pedals and electric outboard motor. He called it the WAMSAK, which he said was short for Water Mode Swiss Army Knife. Normally a project so imaginative and useless would have made Wilbur quiver like a spaniel, but this time the Water Mode Swiss Army Knife didn't pump his adrenaline.

Twice again he complained fretfully about Dark Horseman's absence. When I asked him what it was he wanted to see me about, he couldn't seem to remember asking. At that point Phoebe Nell bade us farewell. I didn't blame her. She wasn't missing any sparkling conversation.

"I wish she wouldn't come around," he said.

"Who? Phoebe Nell?"

"It doesn't look right, when Lupe's away."

So much for the free, untrammelled spirit. It was the kind of talk you'd expect from the old priest of the village.

After awhile I got tired of trying to find where Wilbur's heart and humour were and took my leave also.

"When Lupe comes back, you two should come over and I'll make some mussels *provençal* for you," I said.

"We will," he said. "Yes. For sure. We will. Yes."

"It's a date, then, when she's back?"

"Yes. What fun it'll be." He didn't make it sound like fun at all. Come to think of it, I couldn't remember much laughter or many smiles from Lupe in our recent meetings, either.

I went back to my place under a sky now made darker by driven pewter-coloured clouds. An angry wind, bearing the voices of drowned fishermen, rattled all the palms in San Sebastian.

CHAPTER 15

THE GRAND FIESTA

Let him drink, and forget his poverty, and remember his misery no more.
—The Christian Bible, Prov. #31:7

"Once in a lovely land of song and flowers that was located just beyond the outer limits of probability, there was a little town named San Sebastian. Every year the people of San Sebastian held a great feast day called Fat Tuesday. It was the last day before the religious period of fasting called Lent. At this time all the people of this tiny place set out to prove that they could extract more joy from life than was in it."

If the Force wanted another long, chatty note from me, this was one way to start it, but having read it back to myself, I decided not to treat crime and drugs so lightly when talking to my police friends and I set it aside. Instead of preparing another pointless report, I went dove shooting with White Indian, Dark Horseman and our bird dog, Fragment.

However, calling it up on the word processor when we came home at noon, it seemed a surprisingly accurate and reasoned statement about the village's preparations for the celebration.

Fat Tuesday seemed more important to San Sebastian than Christmas, New Year and even Easter itself, also more important than the patriotic fiestas that celebrate such events as the War of Independence, the Reform, the birth of Juárez or the date Cárdenas seized the foreign oil companies in the 1930s.

Walking over to the plaza at about one o'clock, I encountered Little Margaret, just at the very moment I had been considering how content and happy I was. In time of peace, prepare for war.

I saw her a block away, and something in her purposeful stride warned me to go to ground. She was about to do something for my own good. One of my better reasons for leaving home was that the government kept doing that to me, always at my expense, but in San Sebastian, Little Margaret served the same nagging purpose.

It was one of the reasons she had a thousand acquaintances, all of whom approved of her, but no friends. Her overflowing good will towards humanity had an oppressive quality. Most of us prefer people like ourselves, possessing sins and flaws. I wondered if the vast body of the Holy Roman Catholic Church had expelled her from the nunnery for overperfection. You could easily visualize Little Margaret at at the Vatican with the Pope pleading, "But Little Margaret, I am ALREADY a Roman Catholic."

"Hello, good morning, how is your health?" I said in Spanish, and she answered in Spanish, true to her conviction that all foreigners should speak Spanish whenever possible.

"I am well, thank you, and you?"

"Equally," I lied.

In San Sebastian this was minimal courtesy for people you met on the streets. If your wife was choking on a piece of steak, it wouldn't help to run out and get a passer-by to help you because by the time the normal formalities were exhausted the poor woman would be dead.

Switching back to English, she said, "It's time for your contribution. Ten dollars American would do nicely."

"Contribution to what?"

She looked askance, the old askancer-looker. I had failed a test. I had failed to know something that, being obvious to her, should have been obvious to any non-Satanist.

"It's for Fat Tuesday," she said. "Today is the last day before the Lenten fast."

"Are we all going to eat those white sugar candies shaped like skulls?"

"Of course not. You know perfectly well they're for Day of the Dead. Although I see that the candy shop has a lot of skulls and some candy skeletons too. They must be left over from last November. A little flyblown, but the kids love them."

"That's because they love death and violence."

"And the Lord God, they love him too."

She had enlisted herself in the pre-Easter fund-raising committee formed by the Syndic.

The priest had been delegated to canvass all the village's Catholics, which should have been an overwhelming majority. However, his interests had always been with the poorest people, so what he collected was the smallest of small change.

The Pretty Little One, delegated to canvass Protestants and other malcontents, had extended her mandate and sailed down the main street through the cluster of shops and corner groceries like a pirate ship, all guns blazing. She collected thousands, whereas the priest had been able to find only hundreds. She turned over all her proceeds to him, because, she said, she only understood how to make money; it took the Catholic Church or the government to waste money.

Little Margaret had been delegated to touch the hearts and minds of the gringos, and it was, in all truth, fair enough that we be hit. On this grand fiesta all gringos would be welcome as the flowers of a northern spring. San Sebastian might be short of food at times, but it was never lacked for hospitality.

Little Margaret directed my attention to the effigy hanging from a telephone pole in the plaza.

"That's the Syndic's personal contribution, and it's an expensive one." It was a clothed human figure, made of straw and cunningly wrapped with fireworks. When they were set off, the figure would fizz, flash, rattle and eventually explode, throwing legs, head and all other parts flying out into the crowd.

Yes, I had seen it on other festive occasions.

Skulls, songs, dismemberments, laughter and mariachi bands. Did the Aztecs run the country the same way? Was there music and gaiety and laughing boys courting girls under the pyramids at Teotihuacán while the priests were wrenching the hearts out of the young men and women being sacrificed? Had anything much changed here in two thousand years? Even bribery, so often held up to scorn by the gringo, had an honourable history in this land. Bribery was the first thing Moctezuma tried when he met Cortés.

Looking at the ornate figure above our heads, I wondered how the Syndic could afford such things and came to the conclusion that he could not and was going to be flat broke one of these days. So, for the same reason that I had brought my best Scotch to the Clumsy Goat

Fiesta instead of cheap local rum, I now gave Little Margaret twenty-five American dollars instead of ten.

We did it Mexican style. I slipped five bills out of the American side of my double wallet, folded them and put them into her hands as if slipping her a dirty note. She poked it into a pocket of her jacket just as furtively. If there was one thing the people of the village detested, it was a public display of money, and all of us gringos, even Little Margaret, a Christian and therefore largely insensitive to anybody else's feelings, had learned at least that one lesson.

She went her way and I went mine and all the chiefs of Clan Donald of a thousand years shouted at me that a fool and his money are soon parted.

"She is kind, but extremely persistent," said the Syndic, who had come up beside me.

"She is what we call a pain in the ass, Syndic."

"Oh, surely not," he said.

I persuaded him to come over for a snack at the Amoeba-Free Taco Stand, so named because the young student doctor ran it when he wasn't birthing babies or assisting the old to die. Maybe it was his true avocation, because they were good tacos, but the Syndic assured me that the young doctor's father was a ferociously wealthy man and that the tacos, like the care of the sick, were summer-vacation pranks for the young man.

"Nobody takes a little place like this seriously," he said. He didn't complain. It was a dispassionate observation about the obvious.

We sat on a wrought iron bench beside old Mr. Estrada, at eighty-five the oldest living man in San Sebastian.

He was the region's last certified veteran of the Revolution. As a boy of thirteen, masquerading as a man of sixteen, he had ridden in one of Pancho Villa's cavalry regiments at the final battle of Torreón, on December 22, 1916. What this contributed to the revolutionary cause is less than clear, because by that time the revolutionaries were killing only each other, but he had his veteran's plastic official card to show that he had indeed been one of those Villa called his Golden Ones.

He wore the badge of an oldster, which is a four-day growth of grey beard on his face. I have never been able to learn how they achieve this. There is no day on which an oldster appears clean-shaven, yet neither does the stubble ever mature into a beard. Some sorcery affixes a four-day stubble on their faces as a permanent feature. His face was, typically, a handsome one—strong forehead, straight nose and eyebrows, a firm chin and a sensitive mouth.

After the usual convoluted introductions and inquiries about our health and happiness, he asked the Syndic why there was a soldier on guard in front of the bank.

"The army has moved some troops in to aid the American tourists."

"What aid do they need?"

"Well, perhaps it is a gesture."

"What gesture do they need?" asked Mr. Estrada. "It is true that in the 1920s the revolutionists murdered an American here, but after the Revolution ended the government took out two of the Moreno family's boys and murdered them. That was supposed to make everything even."

The Syndic gave a tiresomely long explanation about army units being set up beside the highways with signs proclaiming that they were present to protect tourists.

"I think," said Mr. Estrada, "the army requires protection from the tourists."

He had been looking towards the bank door, from which now came the rattle of half a dozen shots. They ricocheted off the cement steps of the bank and went whangeee over our heads, chipping leaves off the laurel tree as they passed.

Some saw what happened and were frightened, others saw and hoped for more excitement, and the rest—most of the village—took it for granted that the fireworks had been touched off early.

When the Syndic and I ran over we found the bank manager mopping his forehead, a young militia private with an AK 47 automatic rifle looking sulky and Little Margaret, looking like Little Margaret.

"The lady was coming into the bank," said the manager. "When she passed the guard she put her hand on the top of his gun and pushed it so the muzzle pointed at the ground. I suppose he did not have the safety catch on, and it fired a burst."

"He should have the gun pointed at the ground at all times," said Little Margaret. "They are too careless, these young soldiers, entirely too careless."

By this time a considerable crowd had gathered to admire the chips in the cement steps where the bullets had struck. I could hear young boys speaking with love and awe of the weapon. It is a common type used in the Mexican army, with a protruding magazine. Mexicans, with their passion for never calling anything by its proper name, saw in the curved magazine the knobby shape of a goat's horn, and the guns were known as Goathorn guns.

The Syndic, operating in his capacity as the local police chief, pronounced that the whole matter was a mistake. Regrettable, as mistakes always are, but a matter of no criminal intent or permanent effect.

The militiaman resumed guard duty with the Goathorn gun standing upside-down on his paratrooper boots so that the next accidental firing would remove his foot. Little Margaret went inside with the bank manager to withdraw money from her account. Old Mr. Estrada repeated that the army needed protection from the tourists.

The Syndic and I moved away from the scene of the non-crime.

"Are there a great many women in the United States like Little Margaret?" he said.

"No," I said. "Very few."

His relief, although evident, was brief. His wife appeared on the opposite side of the square, looking about her as a jaguar locating something to kill. No more than a moment could pass before she spotted her appointed lifetime opponent.

I was not the only person on the square who glanced at the Syndic with apprehension and sympathy. It's that way in small towns anywhere—everybody knows everybody else's business. But in the state of Nayarit, where just about everybody lived out of doors, and home was only for sleeping, the relationship was even closer. There wasn't a soul on the plaza that morning who could not detect that the Syndic had, once more, failed a customer while serving a community and that his wife wanted, more than anything else in this world, to have his head on a platter.

He gave a small sigh.

"Wolf Man, I say to you that I never knew what true happiness was until I married and then it was too late."

He shambled across the square to where she was standing, her hands on her hips, glaring at him, wondering what on earth she had ever seen in this man to cause her to marry him.

When they left the tempo picked up again. All the village quivered in anticipation of the celebration, which would begin about dusk. Kids rode around on bicycles decorated with paper streamers. When The White Indian went by in his MG an audible cheer arose. He was to be part of the parade, which was supposed to begin at three o'clock, but which, everybody knew, could not possibly take place before four.

The original plan was that White Indian's MG would provide the throne for Miss San Sebastian. The American custom of beauty queens had penetrated to this part of Mexico, and each village chose one each year, although they were never judged in bathing suits but wore voluminous white skirts that exaggerated the slimness of their waists.

However, it was ruled that she could not ride in the MG because there was no room for a chaperone. MG TDs were so small that a man really needed one for each foot, yet here was a community of adult people who believed that a virgin could be deflowered in one, during a parade, to music, while she was wrapped in clouds of white lace like a cotton-candy stick. The prospect would have fascinated the Morris Garage people. I know it did me.

It was decided that Clarence should chauffeur Mr. Estrada, the war veteran and that, perched on the trunk of the MG, would be Fragment. The boy would have an imitation bullet bandoleer strapped across his chest, carry an air rifle and have a moustache pencilled on his lip, all that was required to represent the most romantic of all revolutionary heroes, the martyred Emiliano Zapata.

No revolutionary leader, not even Che Guevara, has claimed so glamorous a place in the affection of the people as Zapata. He had lived limitlessly far from this village, down in Central Mexico; he had been dead for three-quarters of a century, and not one person in forty in San Sebastian could say exactly who he was or why he was assassinated. None of this mattered. There was just a general agreement that he was both a hero and one of the common people. That was enough. A gentle knight, beyond fear, beyond reproach.

Perhaps that was the basis of this village's Mexican opera. The story of King Arthur's court. Phoebe Nell as Guinevere; Clarence, who worshipped her from afar, as Sir Galahad, and somewhere among us, hidden, Merlin, with his evil laugh.

At the door of the church I met Mrs. Jiménez, Widow of Montero, the white-haired old lady whom the Syndic and I had met the day of the ill-starred cleanup-and-paintup campaign. She stood erect, walked with a cane and bowed to me gravely. I bowed back. Since she bowed gravely to everybody outside the church, I guess it didn't mean much.

In San Sebastian, formality and informality lived happily side by side. Numerous men, women and even teen-agers routinely crossed themselves as they passed before the open doors, through which the altar could be seen. This applied even if they hadn't walked through those doors for many years. It was proper to cross yourself, and therefore it was done. I wondered if Pretty Little One, the ardent missionary of the Watchtower Bible Society, crossed herself when walking across the plaza. Probably she did.

Yet the church itself seemed to be treated as casually as any hot-dog stand in a shopping mall. People wandered in one door and out another, and sat in the pews for a time to rest in the shade instead of in the heat of the sun. Sitting there, they looked incuriously at the priest when he wandered in and out, intent on his own arcane business.

The floor of the church had not been swept for days, and gum wrappers, left by the children who flitted in and out, lay beneath the pews. The current crop of houseflies, which was large, danced in the sunlight that came through the broken window above the plaster Jesus Christ behind the altar. On the street beside the church lay the carcass of a six-foot boa constrictor, which had been in the sun too many hours. A ceremony involving the use of incense would have been welcome.

Being brought up in Orange Ontario, I had been trained to detest the Roman Catholic Church. However, as I got older I became wiser and eventually realized that the Catholics were no more cruel, intolerant or generally detestable than all the other Christians, and as a newspaper publisher I had learned to treat them all the same. My neutrality about both Catholics and the born-again seemed to have become recognized in San Sebastian, and on this day the priest entrusted me with buying all the candy in town with Pretty Little One's loot. There was going to be enough to rot the teeth of every kid in San Sebastian.

Thus I took service with the Scarlet Woman of Rome. By the time I carted in the candy, most of it awful, sticky stuff and the rest sugar skulls that hadn't sold on the Day of the Dead, the plaza was humming. I almost missed the parade. Everything smelled richly of tacos, as well as fried goat meat, roasted corn on the cob and tamales, sold steaming in their corn-husk wrappers. The firecrackers had already begun.

In the square, between the woman who thought she might sell just one more of her plastic buckets and the one who was selling two-dollar frocks for one dollar, I found Consuela and stood beside her to watch the parade.

"They say the young men are going to grab White Indian's car and lift it up and carry it around the square," she said.

"They're all going to die of ruptured hernias," I said.

"For a good cause," she answered.

She spoke so sweetly that I should have suspected something. Only when it was too late did I catch a faint twitch in her eye, but by that time somebody—who, I can never know—had come up behind me and smashed a raw egg on the top of my head.

This was so enjoyed by everybody within sight that it would have been churlish to turn around and see who had done it, so I just scraped the yolk and the albumen out of my thinning hair and said, "I thought that only happened when girls were having a fifteenth birthday." Consuela was convulsed with laughter. She must have arranged it.

Spotting Professor Jon a few shoulders over, I turned to Consuela, pleading. Her look said, oh well, and from her dress she produced an egg for me. I went back out of the line, aimed and fired. It wasn't a bad shot. It went behind one ear, put a small cut on his temple and spread spoiled egg on his designer shirt. He saw me the instant he whirled around, but he would have been hard put to accuse a man so dignified, so innocent of face as a retired Ontario newspaper publisher standing watching a parade with his hands in his pockets. I have spent so much of my working life not laughing at solemn asses in politics and service clubs that it's second nature to me now.

The ten or twenty people who saw me do it had the same gift for circumspection.

"Why, gracious, you have been egged, Jon," I said.

He made a sound in his throat and muttered about juvenility.

"In Canada," I said, "Ukrainians on the Prairies paint eggs for Easter. Down here they throw them at each other. It's a cultural difference, but it's still Easter."

He was not amused. Nothing, as far as I could see, had ever amused the man. To get a joke into his head you would have had to trepan the skull and pump the joke in through the hole with a syringe. Even then, it would have to sit there for a month or two for the grafting process.

He, too, had a problem and a project for me. If it wasn't Little Margaret it was someone else.

He insisted we seize the Syndic and inform him of his duty towards some impoverished Indians whom Jon had discovered camped near the beach while he was bird watching or butterfly chasing or investigating environmental waste.

When I pointed out that the Syndic was in the parade, where he should be, and that the rest of the day would be busy for him, Jon settled for formation of an ad hoc committee, which happened to be one of his favourite kinds. It was decided that he, I and Henry Terwilliger III, The Drunk, would investigate and make recommendations to the Syndic.

So we dragged Henry out of the crowd and rode out to the beach area in his shiny Bronco, Jon's Volkswagen being, as always, in the care of some sidewalk mechanic in Santander who would never, ever, replace all the nuts and bolts he took out of it.

On the beach we found a man, a woman, three very hungry little kids and nothing much else, except the cobs of corn that they had wrested from the nearby fields. They were, clearly, Indians from the mountain country behind us. Who knows how they got to San Sebastian? The woman spoke no Spanish and the man only a broken form of the language. Perhaps somebody had offered them a drive in a truck whose journey had ended near here. They could have been driven out of their fields by troops doing a marijuana sweep. The language barrier was more than we could overcome.

Jon waxed eloquent. Language barriers never bother educated people. They just talk louder. This, he said, was a case requiring the Syndic's intervention, and, if that proved insufficient, the Syndic must call on other people—resource people, he called them—in the municipal government at Santander.

"What these people need is money," said Henry.

That, said Jon, was the worst thing for them and for the Mexican republic. Charity relieved government of its proper responsibility. It perpetuated social injustice.

To this Henry said, biting off each word clearly, "Horse shit. These people don't need committees formed around them. They need help in the here and now."

He reached into his wallet, peeled off twenty or thirty thousand, and gave them to the man, who, primitive Indian though he might be, seemed to have no difficulty in recognizing the stuff.

I hadn't seen this side of Henry before. But, then, I sometimes fail to see the other side of so many people.

Why, for instance, was Henry sporting a love bite, which showed on his neck as his shirt pulled over while he was reaching for his wallet? One could be sure Grace didn't have such passion for Henry so late in the afternoon of their marriage. I recalled the scratches on Dark Horseman's back and wondered if there were some dark, sultry, passionate Latin lady in San Sebastian whom I had signally failed to observe.

As it turned out, Henry was no more in the right this day than Jon. We gave the family a ride into town in the Bronco and, four hours later, the children were all vomiting, having eaten themselves goggle-eyed on junk food and candy, the husband was lying dead drunk in a gutter, and the wife was begging.

In such condition, they offended Captain Alvarez who, exercising his vague but mighty police powers, had the whole family tossed in the town lockup.

When darkness came, I was still thinking about Henry's love bite. Of course, I could be wrong. Maybe he bumped into a sharp Bolshevik. All things come to those who drink.

I saw Grace, dear, gentle, intelligent Grace, and had pleasant words with her. She was going to stay at the street party, she said, until it was time to carry Henry home. "Take Henry home" was the way she phrased it. One of the local farmers, a long, slim fellow with yellow cat's eyes, gravely asked her to dance and gravely, graciously, she said yes and they waltzed away. Grace would have made a great queen, if the country wanted one.

Around the ankles of the thirty or so dancers sped the latest version of dangerous Mexican fireworks, a small erratic rocket that zigzagged among crowds inflicting light burns here and there. Dodging the buzz bombs was part of the normal activity in the square, as was dodging raw eggs, which continued to be smashed in great numbers.

As Grace and her farmer came by I took a hard look at her, one of the only hard looks I had ever given Grace, and was surprised to find that she was quite homely. Her figure was lumpy. She had a big nose and her eyes were fighting for the same seat on the bridge of that nose. But with Grace such things were utterly unimportant.

"She is a lovely woman," I said, speaking to the village plumber, who stood next me, waiting his turn to dance with her.

"With respect, Wolf Man, you are mistaken. She is a lovely woman."

The translation of both lovely woman sentences is identical in English, but in Spanish they can be limitlessly different. I had used the word "is" in its temporary sense, so what I said could be translated as "How lovely she is tonight." He had used the other form of the verb to mean that beauty was Grace's inherent quality. He was saying that she was beautiful when born, was beautiful now and would be beautiful when she got old and died. A wondrous language, Spanish.

When the cat-eyed farmer brought her back, the plumber asked if he might have the honour. The kid banker and another old farmer stood next in the waiting line.

Perhaps I would never understand the people of San Sebastian. When it came to judging the quality of ghetto blasters, designer jeans or electric appliances they could not tell shit from Shinola, but when it came to judging quality in human beings their judgements were unerring, unwavering and often instant. Their eye for quality had a different focus.

On this day I was happy about that. Next time the toilet in my house plugged and I had to depend on the plumber to fix it, I would wish to God that minds here worked differently.

I spotted Fragment and saw he was without firecrackers, so I remembered errands he had run and paid him for them. This enabled him to get his own supply and behave as a San Sebastian kid should—dangerously. Part of the growing-up process in the village was to hold a huge firecracker in your hand, light it and then wait until the very last slice of a second to throw it.

Many little boys who have miscalculated have graduated into adulthood with the end of one or more fingers missing.

So why did I let my little friend do it?

For the same reason that I probably would not have tried to prevent those nitwit students at Nuremberg from scarring each others' faces with swords. In both cases, it's not my country and not my business.

I won't deny that I watched uneasily as Fragment held the deadly fizzing stick and released it only when it was so late that it exploded in the air before it could touch the ground. Well, long live the Revolution.

Dark Horseman floated past and, seeing me, swept his lady around so they stopped before me. I was reminded again how unusually handsome he was, big shoulders, straight posture and a coal-black moustache over dazzling white and perfect teeth. Who said you needed enough food as a child to be healthy?

"Salutations, Satan," I said.

"Salutations, Wolf Man. How glorious is the fiesta!"

I looked around at that dusty, sordid little town square and saw that he was right. There was more human happiness crammed in there than can be found in a long, long search over many lands. "Glorious, for a certainty," I said, and put my hand on the torn shirt old Wilbur had given him. The smile split his face, and the girl he held in his arm, one of the vibrant beauties of the Vallejos family, also smiled. She was wearing a dress the colour of the house-vine flower called Burst of Flame.

He said, "A horse to fill your legs, a fighting cock to fill your hands, a woman to fill your arms. How magnificent, the world God gave to the Mexican people!"

He floated her away, his Burst of Flame flower, and they moved in the millrace of the plaza stream, circling, pausing, glowing, beautiful in the eternity of one moment.

There were more soldiers in the square and men in cheap business suits that didn't fit and a shadow fell that was noticed, perhaps, by nobody except me.

I went home, past the church. The dead snake was gone. Somebody had disposed of the carcass. Probably the Syndic. Dogsbody was the word for him.

It was surprising to find the lights on at the house and the gate unlocked, but it was a lot more surprising to come in and find Phoebe Nell leaning over to drop her breasts into her brassiere. Why had I thought that hers stood up without support? She next put on the top of her snow-white pantsuit and said, "I hope you don't mind. You did give Clarence the key, and this house is so close to the plaza."

Every child is born into our world with a gift, and hers was to have the same restful tone of voice for every occasion. She spoke to me in the same way she had when we walked together on the beach and she wanted to know if it was true that as long as you drank goat's milk you would never get cancer.

White Indian, who came out of the bedroom carrying his shirt in his hands, was less at ease. "We weren't expecting you, Mac."

"No problem," I said. Is there anything else to say?

Phoebe Nell smiled in that vague, lovely way she had and said she really must be getting back to the party, and with that she left, leaving the heavy smell of musk behind her.

White Indian said, "Mac, even though I am not drinking, I have to say it again. Never trust a drunken Indian."

I told him to have a coffee.

While he pulled on his shirt I saw deep scratches on his back. It's a funny old world.

CHAPTER 16

THE PEACE OF GOD

And the Peace of God, which passeth all understanding, shall keep your hearts and minds through Christ Jesus.
—The Christian Bible, Phil. 4:7

Next morning, feeling angry and betrayed (betrayed by whom, for God's sake; was I getting senile?), I got out the wrong side of bed and cooked a nice fat, fresh mackerel, the cheapest fish that swims in these seas but one that I happen to like better than beluga caviar from the Caspian or salmon from Scotland. Eating one usually ensured peace and harmony for any day, but I guess this mackerel was deficient.

If I needed anything to restore my bad temper, it came next—Little Margaret, who lectured me about the cholesterol contained in the southern mackerel and had to be vigorously restrained from running back to her house to get me whatever kind of packaged brown wood chips was the current popular breakfast in the United States.

Her mission here, it turned out, was to find Clarence. "I went to his cabin at Pretty Little One's, but he wasn't there and she seemed vague about where he was when I asked her."

"Was Professor Jon there?"

"No, he had business in Santander today. He is talking to some officials about the stork reserve."

"Did his wife go with him?"

"No. I think she was still asleep in her cabin. Her door was closed and the blinds were down."

"White Indian is probably engaged in some private business," I said. I made her coffee.

"But he was going to take me to the Drum and show me the sea turtles." She talked largely and vaguely—the way she usually talked about anything new and dimly understood—about sea turtles being an endangered species.

I did not tell her that Dark Horseman, White Indian, Fragment and I had relieved a sea turtle of a few of her eggs while she was laying them in the sand, holding our hands beneath her so that she delivered them to us direct. Knowing something of the reproductive habits of reptiles, I felt sure that six fewer eggs on the beach beside the old hut in Nayarit did not mean six fewer adult sea turtles for our next century on this planet.

After we boiled up the eggs, which were like ping-pong balls in soft shells, and not much more flavourful, a great argument developed among us. Dark Horseman, supported by Fragment to the extent that a child is permitted to enter an adult conversation, wanted to take the turtle and eat her, too. White Indian and I prevailed, and when she was through laying and had covered her unstolen eggs with sand, we carried the old lady down to the ocean and let her swim away.

I had not felt all that great about winning the argument. I maybe knew a little bit about sea turtles, but not as much as Dark Horseman and Fragment had learned about hunger. I told Little Margaret where to go to look for the turtles (which weren't there any more), but she got more confused the more directions I gave, so I finally delegated Fragment to take her there. He had been passing on the street, packing home a thin stack of tortillas, for which he had long stood waiting in the scrum at the tortilla factory, where the bicycle chains running the production line always screeched with a uniquely unpleasant sound.

"The turtles are gone, Wolf Man," he said.

I spoke to him in the tone of voice that children in San Sebastian recognize when it comes from an adult. "You will take Little Margaret there so that she can see where the turtles come to lay the eggs. You will do it now, as soon as you have taken the tortillas to your mother."

The two of them drove away in her Volkswagen Rabbit, which still had the plastic wrapping on the front-door panels although Little Margaret had bought it two years before. I guessed she must have been on her third tankful of gas by this time.

Fragment did not take to this car as he took to the MG TD, which proved that he was a man and not a woman, although I guess it would have been indelicate for me to take notice of that fact. I just said,

"Show Little Margaret where the turtles come up on the sand," and he nodded his head, soberly.

I remained at home, cranky. You can be cranky in Mexico too. It's not against any law. Most people my age in San Sebastian got cranky now and then, and nobody thought much of it. It was our privilege. We had lived long enough to earn it.

If I hadn't been cranky, if I had thought a little faster, a little better, there would perhaps have been less blood on the sand. But life is not composed of might-have-beens. As Angel told it later, they drove to the beach near the old, crumbling red-brick hut, and the surf on the reef beat on their ears. It was an uneasy morning. It was far too grey and the seas ran high again for no reason. Again, there was a hidden storm.

They walked the shifting sands beside the uncertain sea while the pelicans, instead of surfing on the updraft of the big waves, flew instead well back from the shore in long, grey patrol lines. The Frigate Binds were also inland, huddled in small circles as sea birds do when a storm nears. None of the crabs came out of their holes in the sand. The light of life was being withdrawn from the beach and the sun shone wanly through thin clouds.

Little Margaret kept talking to the boy, and knowing her, I can find no fault with him for remembering nothing she said to him on the beach. Any kid with brains enough to rattle in a peanut shell can tell when an adult is talking to him for his own good, and a natural insulation against such unwanted advice forms instantly inside the skull. Fragment remembers only that Little Margaret spoke of many things concerning the value of education, always with sincerity. I'll bet she did.

It was proving to be a dull, pointless morning spent with—well, why not be frank—a dull woman on a dull day beside a mournful ocean.

It might all have ended peaceably and pointlessly, as most things do, if she hadn't insisted that they walk back to the car by way of the old red-brick hut, which had been melting into the terrain for a half-century or so. Before being abandoned for some economic reason, it had housed a family, but sun, wind, the occasional rains and time had beat upon it.

He spotted a rift in the sand that he thought might house turtle eggs, so he left her and darted over to investigate. She went on ahead and entered the old structure. He followed after determining that he had seen only a rift in the sand and not a turtle's deposit.

Fragment paused before the empty building. A kid would. We are supposed to have a natural fear of empty buildings that once held people. Ghosts live there. We all know that about empty houses, but adults put the knowledge of it away from their minds. They learn to quench their natural instincts.

So instead of running inside, he knelt and peeked, and saw Dark Horseman pointing a huge blue revolver at Little Margaret.

"Are you going to kill me?" she asked and Dark Horseman answered, "Yes, yes, yes, I must."

Dark Horseman never saw Fragment. Little Margaret had forgotten him. He darted back to the other side of the sand dune and then he began running and hardly ever dropped back into a walk until he reached the paved road that runs from Santander into San Sebastian. That was five kilometres from the beach and Fragment was a puny kid.

His legs grew rubbery and his chest heaved and hurt and when he reached pavement he fell and pressed the gravel of the road's shoulder into his forehead. He wanted to lie there, sleep and forget, but by pressing his face into the sharp crushed gravel of the roadside he knew he would be kept awake to do what he had to do.

As is usual at such times, there wasn't a soul to help him. Not a tractor was in the fields, not a car was on the long, straight paved road.

Just this once in the long history of Mexico, a portion of that vast, old land was bereft of human form and of human face. No songs, no laughter, only the cries of the circling birds above, deploring the coming storm. It was like one of those occasions when an angel flies overhead.

Little Margaret and Dark Horseman were similarly alone in a seemingly empty land, facing each other in the derelict hut.

He had been using a shovel to cover a pit full of the semi-refined heroin commonly known as Mexican Brown. The stuff had the consistency of whole-wheat flour. It was packed into one-kilo plastic bags, heat-sealed against dampness and stamped with marks showed those in the trade how strong it was and who had refined it and when. In the world of illicit narcotics, which is every bit as crazy as the economics of governments, the powder in the pit was worth about twenty million American dollars.

If Dark Horseman had enjoyed even a few more minutes of privacy, he might have thrown sand over the last of the cache and been able to offer Little Margaret some absurd but acceptable explanation of what he was doing. But fate, which looks after all these matters, had not provided him the extra ten minutes.

He didn't hear her approach, and when she spoke to him he grabbed the big .45-calibre revolver as he spun around to face her. By the time he realized that it was just the silly gringo woman who had once been a nun, it was too late for any graceful explanations.

She recognized this almost as quickly as did he, and that was why she had said, "Are you going to kill me?" and he had answered, "Yes, I must," just as little Fragment peeped over the sand dune and saw them.

Little Margaret picked up a package of the Mexican Brown. "Those are drugs," she said.

He jerked the revolver back and forth in front of her.

"Is that why they call you Satan? Because you deal in drugs?"

"Don't talk. Please. No talking."

"And you are about to commit the greater sin of killing me, while God is watching you."

"Enough! Enough!" He was becoming excited. "I can never suffocate again in a prison. You must know that, woman! I cannot let you go the police and, I am sorry, I cannot believe you if you say that you will not."

If Little Margaret's account is to be believed, they walked outside the old building while she said something about two wrongs not making a right. It rings true. It is exactly the fatuous nonsense one could expect from her on such an occasion. What emerges from her account is equally believable. She knew she was going to die.

What amazed her was what has amazed many cancer patients hearing the death sentence from their doctors for the first time. Instead of terror, there was a sense of relief. More, in her case; there was an overwhelming gratitude to her God. In only a minute or two she was going to leave the world with scarcely time to register the pain of the bullet from the gun.

Her mother had died a millimetre at a time in a Boston hospital, long outlasting the capacity of the morphine to kill her pain, a skeletal creature departing life with whimpers and moans. Her father had been carried into infancy by Alzheimer's disease, knowing it all the time and then, beyond that, lapsing into a vegetable state before dying. For some reason, wretched sinner though she was, God, in his infinite compassion, had chosen to be merciful to her.

It was the peace of God, which St. Paul says passes all understanding. She had heard the words a thousand times and liked them without understanding them. Only here, on a sand dune in Mexico, facing a shaking man with a big gun while the waves pounded, only here and at last did she understand the peace of God. She had never felt God's love more strongly. She had never been more at peace with her own soul.

"There is no priest here to whom I can confess," she said.

He waved the gun.

"But you will let me pray? You will do it while I am praying?"

"Yes, yes, yes, woman. Please. Pray. Pray now." He was very agitated.

She pulled at her skirt to be sure that it covered her knees—she had never worn dresses that did not—and started to kneel.

"No, no," he said. "Not there! Not there!"

"What is the matter with there?"

"You are about to kneel on an anthill," he shouted.

Little Margaret had never had a robust sense of humour but one gust of it hit her. "Are we all completely mad? You are about to murder me, and you are concerned about me kneeling on an anthill?" She began to laugh.

"You are right, of course," he said. "Madness. It is all madness." He tucked the big gun back into his torn pants. "I will take my chances with you protecting me from the police. Go with God, Little Margaret."

He turned and walked back to the ruin. She brushed the sand from her skirt and walked towards the beach. When she turned, he was standing in the ruins. Being Little Margaret, she had to live up to that oldest of old Mexican saying: "Man proposes, God disposes, and then the woman rearranges everything." In Spanish it is alliterative.

"You realize, of course, that I must report you to the police. I have to. It's for your own good."

He shook his head. "How God must have loved you, Little Margaret, that he made you mad." He never reached for the gun as she walked away towards the beach.

She should have walked towards her car. She should have driven back to San Sebastian village and friends and safety. This should have been a passable, a tolerable end to it all. But no, she had what Dark Horseman so clearly saw, the divine madness. She forgot about her car and Angel and she walked down the long, empty beach.

She was terribly troubled, because God had left her.

When she was facing the gun, he had come and stood beside her and showed her his infinite mercy and love, but when the danger was over, he left her. She knew that he was very busy and had other matters to attend to, but there was a terrible hurt that he, too, had now left her alone in a world where she had always been lonely.

She went over to where the grey seas were breaking on the dark beach, knelt and prayed as she had never prayed before, but she could not bring her God back to her.

It was the supreme example of somebody doing the wrong thing for the right reason. Everything that the rest of us thought—we, the sane ones—was thereafter distorted by Little Margaret's own particular and unique absurdity.

There are those, including my late wife, who say devotion to God is not an absurdity, but to me devotion to God is the Inquisition, hanging witches at Salem and other barbarities, like the Crusades.

If I had been there I would have whacked Little Margaret on the ass and got her back to her car and to town, but I wasn't there. At that time I was in Wilbur's yard, watching blood dripping from his broken mouth.

At this point, even the man we knew as Satan might have mended all our affairs by fleeing as soon as Little Margaret was out of his sight. There are 85 million people in Mexico and it is the eighth largest nation in the world. There was plenty of room for him to disappear.

But the big man was a simple man and he acted the part of a good, simple soldier. He obeyed the last command he could remember hearing. He resumed covering up the drug cache with his shovel. By the time he was ready to run to some other corner of the country, it was too late. Fragment had found help.

This hadn't been easy for the child. Several farm trucks and one or two cars went past on the highway where he stood and used his thumb, vigorously, the way he had seen it done in the American television movies. This was not in character for a child or man in this country.

Here no hitchhiker lifted an arm or exposed a thumb. One stood, quietly, by the roadside and watched the traffic come. An eye contract with the driver was permissible; even a faint, an almost imperceptible lift of the chin in the direction you wished to be taken.

For a child to do more than this was intolerably bad manners, and each driver who went past was determined to impress that upon Fragment. One of them, Little Joe Salazar, told us later that he had slowed his truck and shouted out the open window, "Compose yourself properly, boy!" before pushing the accelerator and leaving the kid standing there windmilling his arms.

The next vehicle in sight was an army personnel truck, and for this Angel changed his tactics. He hid in the weeds until it was almost upon him and then hurled himself into its path in the roadway.

The driver stood on his brakes and, with only two of four working, skidded sideways, leaving blue smoke in the air. The lurch threw one of the soldiers off the back and he lay on the asphalt moaning with a broken collarbone. The big truck also hit Angel, but it was slowed by then, and the boy held out a hand against it so that he was merely knocked off his feet. He rolled and got up.

This was a time when the rule never to strike a child could not be honoured and the driver was halfway out of the seat, white with anger, when the young lieutenant in the passenger seat reached out and grabbed him.

"No," he said. "There is something serious here."

Big families are Mexico's sorrow, and there are those who say that this country would be wealthy again if there wasn't such a cataract of children being produced every year. Whatever the truth of that, the big family has the advantage that no generation is much out of touch with any other. The lieutenant knew that no boy acted as Angel had except for some powerful reason.

He stepped out and Angel ran to him, wrapped his arms around the young man's waist and sobbed out an almost incoherent story about an American woman who had been murdered or kidnapped by his friend Satan who had a big gun and was digging a grave to bury her in. When he calmed a little and the water could be squeezed out of his story, the lieutenant made a few faultless moves.

The soldier with the broken collarbone was laid in the shade of a palm tree and given water and promises.

The lieutenant was a regular army officer. The ten men in the back of the truck were conscripts. All young men who ever hoped to get a Mexican passport or any other official Mexican government document had to present themselves for six months of military service. Some of them liked the army, a few so much that they stayed in it when their term ended, but most considered it to be drudgery, a task the sooner performed the better.

Another truck with another dozen men pulled in behind the first one, and these men too were brought under command of the young lieutenant. They were moving in that day for a sweep of the beaches. Dark Horseman had been sent out to bury the cache deep before the troops came through.

Although the boy had never seen the packets of Mexican Brown in the hole, for which reason he thought it was a grave, the officer guessed that big blue revolvers and drugs went together.

The two truckloads of soldiers, directed by Angel, drove down the track until they were within a few hundred metres of the hut. The lieutenant then spread his men two or three metres apart and completely encircled the building. They then moved forward.

One shot was fired and a man close to the building went over backwards and said "Mother." This started the rest of the militiamen firing, sometimes at one another.

When the lieutenant had drawn his men back, including the wounded man, it was found that his automatic rifle had been left behind. Also, one of the young recruits had thrown his away near the hut. So Dark Horseman had probably collected two Goathorn guns.

They were assured of this when Dark Horseman fired a short burst and blew up dust around the lieutenant's feet. Perhaps it was a warning, perhaps just another case of bad shooting on his part.

Being regular army, the lieutenant pretended to ignore the shots and the fact that he had wet his pants slightly, and he calmly gave orders for surrounding the hut again. The soldiers were to shoot at nothing, least of all the woman trapped inside. He then shouted for Dark Horseman to come out or, failing that, to send Little Margaret out safely.

Satan called him a goat and told him to piss in his mouth, which is one of the less lovely habits of billygoats. His voice was high and excited. The lieutenant took cover and called Angel over to ask about the man, and Angel told him he was a good man, a very fine man, but he had fits and was very dangerous.

164

One dictum had been drilled into the head of the army officer. Tourists were a sacred trust of the Mexican army, much more important than Mexicans.

He made a round of the perimeter, personally telling each man that not a shot was to be fired unless absolutely necessary to save his own life. Everybody was to maintain a great calmness. Otherwise a gringo woman would be killed.

He left a sergeant in charge and took Angel to Little Margaret's car, where she had fortunately failed to remove the ignition keys, and together they came to San Sebastian to look for Alvarez, who had become, in some strange way, the commandant of an army unit on this day.

It had become an article of faith that Little Margaret was being held hostage in the hut. Once such a belief seizes a group of men, it is almost impossible to dislodge, and every event thereafter supports the error. In this case, it led, quite naturally, to two militiamen telling the lieutenant they had seen a woman's bright dress within the hut; since it was moving, this indicated that she was alive. Others located her footprints approaching the hut but none leaving it. Several reported hearing her crying or calling out faint unintelligible words.

I, who was later to join in this hallucination, had seen such delusion before. In a flood at Hay River in Canada's Northwest Territories, it became a similar article of faith that Indians on an island near the river mouth were facing sure drowning.

The flooded river being too fierce for boats to cross, a rescue helicopter was brought in. It crashed and couldn't fly again; another was dispatched. This one rescued the Indians.

We of the press went on quite a bit, as disaster reporters do, about the calm courage of the Indians in the face of death. The operation continued for some time, until it was discovered that rescued people were paddling back to the island across the raging, impassable Hay River so they could have a second ride in the helicopter, which was in those days a novelty in the North. Never underestimate the power of error.

All the while, Little Margaret, deafened by the rising wind and the surf or else besotted with her own praying, heard and saw nothing while she pursued the God who had held her in the palm of his hand and then, for reasons known only to him, had set her down again in a world she did not understand.

165

Neither did it help matters that in San Sebastian, Angel slipped his leash the instant the lieutenant brought Little Margaret's car to a stop at the village police station and lockup. Although we didn't know it, he begged, borrowed or maybe stole one of the Santa Ana family's bicycles and pumped his way back to where all the action was at the beach.

Fortunately the sergeant had kept calm at the hut, and nobody took a shot at Angel by mistake. They told him to sit over behind a dune and keep his mouth shut. Nobody needed any more broken collarbones or bullets in the chest.

CHAPTER 17

LUCKY WILBUR

True luck consists not in holding the best of the cards at the table: luckiest he who knows just when to rise and go home.
—John Milton Hay, *Pike County Ballads*

The Syndic had led me over to Wilbur's house. He was as sad and sorrowful as any man in public office can be, and for reasons I could not learn from him. He had come to my door in his capacity as our chief of police. He had buckled on a revolver, which lends some people, like John Wayne, great force and dignity; for others, such as the Syndic, it may to do nothing more than cause them to walk on a slant.

"I feel it, Wolf Man," he said. "I want you to know that I feel it."

He kept shaking his head in great sorrow, but I couldn't imagine the cause of it all until I saw the big black car of Captain Alvarez parked in front of Wilbur's gate with the big policeman-chauffeur, the Sergeant, sitting stone-faced behind the wheel.

It was more surprising to find Wilbur sitting in a deck chair opposite Alvarez and bleeding at the mouth where somebody had hit him hard and well.

There were plainclothes federal police—the narcs, I suppose—standing at each side of Wilbur.

The Tiny Perfect Policeman was sitting opposite him with a face that looked like the label on a poison bottle. Alvarez was in full sunlight, and for the first time I realized that he was much older than I had thought. There were papery parchment lines at his mouth and eyes and, in the fold of his hands, between thumb and forefinger, were the deep and crinkled creases by which my mother always said a man's true age could be read. Alvarez was well into his fifties, possibly even, like me, in his sixties.

Or perhaps simple rage had aged the man. Here on Wilbur's patio, next to Wilbur's great and ever-full tub of iced beer and the latest of his foolish passions—this one to drill holes in plastic sewer pipes in the shape of sea horses and make patio lights with them—it was obvious that the majesty of the law that had hit Wilbur in the face.

A more sophisticated man than I would have acknowledged this reality with his first words but I, like the people of San Sebastian, began my conversations in traditional ways.

I said hello, Wilbur said hello. I asked about his health and he said it was good. He asked about mine. I said, equally, thank you. It was one way to escape stunned silence.

"How's Guadalupe?"

"Manila," he said. "There are Healers there. They can find your sickness and draw it out of you."

Oh, Jesus, the old chicken-gut routine. Are things really that hopeless, Wilbur? Aloud I said, "I have heard that it works for some people."

"She's going to be all right. When she left, she was already feeling better. You could see that the pressure had come off her back where the disk has slipped."

"Sit over there," said the captain. He was speaking to the Syndic, who sat over there. It was his clear and hard voice that returned us from the unreality of quacks in Manila to pretended normalities in San Sebastian.

"Mr. Oshaski has a bad memory," said Alvarez. "He can't remember who hired him. He doesn't know where Dark Horseman is, either. Even though he hired him, he doesn't know where his employee is today. The man we also hired. Dark Horseman had two employers, did he not, Mr. Oshaski?"

"You have me and you will do what you want with me."

"How I wish I could," said the captain. "But you are an American. We will put you in a Mexican jail, but you won't stay there. Americans don't like their people being in Mexican jails. They aren't good enough. You will be returned to serve your time in an American jail, where there is plenty of ice cream and current movies to watch."

"I don't know and I don't care," said Wilbur.

"How typically American, to know nothing. Americans knew nothing when Winfield Scott invaded Mexico. They knew nothing about the American ambassador arranging the murder of President Madero. That happy ignorance, which is the prerogative of great powers." A spirit badly corroded, I thought, hopelessly corroded and crusted over. Policemen call it burnout.

"If your memory remains so bad, Mr. Oshaski, perhaps we can bring your wife back from Manila for testimony. She's a Mexican citizen."

"She is a greater Mexican than you can ever hope to be, Captain."

"When is she due back, Wilbur?" I said. Somebody had to say normal, everyday things in this outrageous conversation.

He looked at me straight and started crying. "She isn't ever coming back, Mac. She is dying in a Manila hospital."

The tears ran out of his eyes and smeared his Coke-bottle glasses, and I handed him my handkerchief. What he had told the captain was true. Wilbur no longer cared what happened to him because when Guadalupe died, his life would be over too.

He turned to Alvarez. "Captain. I'll sign a confession here with Mac as a witness if there's any way you can keep it secret from Lupe." He was crying harder now. "She's only got a week or two left, they say. She doesn't need to know, Captain. What good can it do for her to know?"

"You've made your confession in the presence of witnesses," said the policeman. "We didn't need one, anyway. The money you took was marked."

"Please, Captain. What can a week or two matter?"

Alvarez had no time or patience left.

"Put The Women on him," he said, and one of the plainclothesmen brought out a pair of handcuffs, snapped them over Wilbur's wrists and jerked the pudgy old man to his feet.

"Take him out and let him spend a night with the scorpions in the lockup," said Alvarez. "And leave him alone." I noticed the order to not torture. Alvarez was never without full control of his emotions.

Wilbur had regained some of his, also. His face was wet but calmer now when he turned to me.

"What a lucky man I've been, Mac," he said, standing with the silver cuffs glistening on his wrists. "Think of it. I came back from both the raids on Schweinfurt and I married the most wonderful woman in all this world. She loved me. She loved me so much she laughed at my jokes." I heard Dark Horseman again, saw him waltzing up to me in the plaza and saying much the same thing about the luck of being alive in a land like Mexico. It is a country that affects some people that way.

169

CHAPTER 18

THE LAW OF ESCAPE

All my friends are false and all my enemies are real.
—President Porfirio Díaz, who is credited with developing the Law of Escape

The year was 1988, and by this time in Mexico, as well as in the rest of the world, the last hopes for privacy and natural decency were being surrendered to technocrats. Alvarez travelled with a radio phone in his car and a beeper on his belt so that there was no place— bar, bathroom or bedroom—from which he could not be instantly summoned to account for himself by a disembodied voice on a telephone. If Dante could have invented a seventh level of hell, he would have created the modern telephone system.

Thus it happened that the constable at the local lockup was able to make a beeper work in Wilbur's patio and send the Mexican army lieutenant there with all the misinformation that an earnest young man can carry.

Having found Alvarez, the lieutenant told him, somewhat breathless in his excitement, that Dark Horseman was holding Little Margaret hostage and that she had shouted from the old hut but with words that could not be understood. That, of course, accorded with our understanding. Her Spanish was lamentable; she insisted on trying to turn nouns into verbs, and although that works in English it is harder in Spanish.

Of all the people left on Wilbur's patio, I should have been the one to recognize that an idea was snowballing and being pushed down a hill with nobody pausing to ask if it was real or merely a package of ice crystals that would dissolve and be gone if subjected to sunlight.

I was as ready to accept the hostage scenario unquestioningly as everybody else. People say newspapermen are cynical. Maybe they are. But they are also notoriously gullible and from time to time accept the most absurd of stories without pause or thought.

For the first and perhaps the only time, Alvarez deferred to my judgement that Little Margaret was captive, and it was to prove fatal.

There was no doubt of the course the captain would have taken if that annoying gringo woman were not in danger. The army would have poured bullets and, if necessary, grenades into the old hut until not even cockroaches were left alive.

This he could not do. An American woman, a nun of sorts, was in danger and so was his reputation. Wetbacks, the farm labourers who entered the U.S. illegally, might be shot from time to time or die of the heat while imprisoned in boxcars. But such things happened. For an American nun to be shot must not happen. For once, I felt sympathy for Alvarez, who was probably at this moment comparing the lives of Mexican illegal workers with that of a rather silly woman.

Well, what the hell? Who said life was fair?

He sent the lieutenant hotfooting back to the scene to tell the soldiers that any man who fired a needless shot might get shot himself.

Alvarez, the Syndic and I were left to ourselves on the patio. Alvarez began by saying, "We will have to negotiate instead of shooting."

"Does that mean talking to Dark Horseman?" said the Syndic.

"Yes. And hoping that he doesn't shoot the negotiator. I think he would shoot you."

"But it is my duty, I will do it."

"You have no duty except to keep the village clean," said Alvarez, with his usual charm and tact.

My legs and my tongue turned to lead. God be my witness, I have never wanted to be a hero. Alvarez gave me a reprieve. He made the suggestion that others of the village routinely made when faced with difficult questions—ask The Pretty Little One.

"She will have nothing to do with politics," said the Syndic. Politics was an elastic word here. It meant anything that was important, expensive, or dangerous arranged by people associated with government or its agencies.

"Who could blame her?" I said.

The priest?

He was forbidden by law to take part in politics which, by tacit agreement, this seemed to have become.

"There is only one man." said Alvarez. "The White Indian."

Relief came over me like a warm wind. I am ashamed to say so, but would you rather I lie? If the situation were repeated, I would be just as relieved all over again.

We sent the Sergeant to get The White Indian. The Sergeant returned ten minutes later and reported that although Cream Puff was at the cabin door The White Indian was not to be found, nor was Pretty Little One.

The Syndic offered an opinion, hesitantly, as if he were afraid it might fall and break on the patio tiles. Mr. Clarence could perhaps be found in Phoebe Nell's cabin. In the eyes of Alvarez there was a flash of venom strong enough to knock a dog off a gutwagon. My God, dear little Phoebe Nell was hanging a lot of scalps on her belt.

I was perhaps the only one who saw that naked anger, and when Clarence arrived, as full in the face as a satisfied tomcat, Alvarez showed no more expression than any of the porcelain masks made in the style of the flapper era, exquisitely correct and without expression or soul.

"You have no obligation, Clarence," I said, while Alvarez arranged the flowers on my grave for me. Cheap plastic flowers.

"We have to get her," White Indian said. "But why couldn't the silly old cow have passed by on the other side of the street?"

Alvarez answered, "She couldn't resist finding trouble for herself, any more than a dog can resist rolling in rotten fish. Any more than you could resist getting drunk, puking on the walls of the church and explaining to Wilbur how the shrimp boats were going to take a shipment of narcotics out to a mother ship at the horizon." Maybe it was true, but why did he have to say it here and now?

"If he lets her go, will you let him run?" said White Indian.

"You mean, this is only Mexico and the law does not rule in Mexico."

"I mean a deal is a deal, in any hostage taking."

Alvarez considered. "Make your deal," he said.

We were quiet as we drove out to the beach, the Sergeant, Alvarez, the Syndic and I. There had been more shooting after all, luckily with no result. A militiaman had fired for no reason except that tiresome and characteristic belief that it was unmanly to use a safety catch on a gun. Shaking as he was, it was no surprise that he had touched off a burst, and equally unsurprising that Dark Horseman, also shaky by now, had fired from his peephole in the ruin, throwing sand in the soldier's eyes. Satan's shooting had improved since the night we had hunted the birds.

"I am coming over to talk, friend," said White Indian.

"Stay back."

"Just to talk. We can talk, you and I?"

While he spoke, White Indian rose from behind the dune where he lay with Alvarez and me and walked over the crest. I suppose it surprised all of us because it was done so quickly and with such ease, but as I watched him go forward I could see that The White Indian was moving very slowly, like a man walking up to his knees in gravel. He held both his hands down, palms open and forward.

I was grateful that it wasn't me walking across the sand. That, I suppose, was a sign he was closer to being a true policeman than I was. Some police aren't the brightest or shiniest intellects among us but there is an implicit agreement between them and society that when the chips are down they are expected to be prepared to die on the job. He seemed to have absorbed that tradition in a way that I had not. I did not want to go up against a frightened, confused, sick man with a Goathorn gun or two in his hands.

"Stay. Stay. Stay!" came the shrill voice from the hut.

"Let us sit together, friend."

"Stay, stay, stay."

"Don't go any closer," said Alvarez. He had hooked a small radio transmitter and receiver onto White Indian's shirt. It was one of the technical marvels developed for the CIA during the Cold War, like the olive in the martini that was a transmitter for use at cocktail parties.

It was so sensitive we could hear Clarence's breath going in and out.

We had never had a thought about the boy Angel. Now he darted out of his hidey-hole and scampered up to Clarence while the soldiers shouted, "Aiyeee, boy, come back, come back."

On the earphones we could hear Dark Horseman's voice.

"Are you out of your mind, White Indian? Bringing that child out here?"

Clarence was as startled as anyone else when he turned and saw the boy standing right behind him. We heard him whisper harshly, "Get away, Fragment. Get back. Get back."

The boy's voice was choked. He was crying. But we could hear him.

"I am extremely frightened. But I am here."

Clarence, who knew more about the danger and was more frightened, used an insulting expression: "Scram, you little cunt hair."

It was exactly the wrong time for crudeness and insult. We could see the kid's back straighten.

"Everybody in San Sebastian knows that I ran away when Little Margaret was taken . . ."

"You did exactly the right thing. You got help."

The boy's voice continued. "Everybody knows that I ran away, but nobody is ever going to see me run again. I am going up to talk to Dark Horseman and Little Margaret."

The middle-aged army sergeant, who also had earphones, threw them off, stood up above the dune, tossed away his gun and ran forward, shouting, "Brave. Brave boy! Bravest of the brave!"

I wished I could have put out a foot and tripped him. You stupid bastard with your manliness bullshit. That's what it is, all bullshit. Why do you think half the women in Mexico are widows? It's your damnable obsession with manliness.

But I misjudged that militiaman. He knew exactly what he was doing. He had kids of his own. He stunned all of us, including the boy, with his shouts, and once on top of Angel he wrapped his big arms around him, smothered the child's face in his chest and ran with him, squirming, all the way to where Little Margaret's car was parked and where his cries and protests could not further excite The Dark Horseman.

It was done very well and with courage. I was ashamed of my thoughts.

White Indian also walked back to us, and we all lay behind the dune while Dark Horseman let off a few shots at nothing in particular.

"Don't go out again, Clarence," I said. "He's too excited now."

"What about poor old Little Margaret?" he said. "She didn't do anything to deserve this."

"Neither did you."

"An interesting exercise," said Alvarez. "An actual test of whether an adult American has the courage of a small Mexican boy."

He was not without knowledge of human nature, no matter how mechanical his own personality was. Clarence got up and began walking through knee-high gravel again.

"Not American, Canadian," he said as he started.

Then he paused a moment and said, "Not Canadian. Indian."

He called to Dark Horseman. "Just let Little Margaret out, Satan."

"No. No, no. No more prison."

Dark Horseman's voice was far too high, and excited. I remembered, and I'm sure White Indian remembered, how he told us about the shooting of Barracuda's old wife, who had reminded him of his own mother. "And then, they tell me, I tried to kill her too. . . ."

There was some conversation, hard to pick up, between Clarence and the Dark Horseman.

Alvarez talked to the button in Clarence's ear from time to time. Once I heard him say, "Yes, you can tell him that the soldier he shot is only lightly wounded. There won't be any murder charge."

The soldier was dead. I had seen the body lying in the back of one of the trucks that had been brought up from the highway. But by this time I was numbed by it all, by Wilbur, with the silver bracelets locked on his hands; by Dark Horseman, tilted first to the law and then away from it; by the spectacle of the two men talking across the wind-blown coarse grass of the sand dunes in voices too low to be heard without instruments.

Except for Alvarez, we were like children that afternoon. A game had gone too far. It was time to reset the pieces and play it all over again. We wanted a declaration by the adults that what had happened hadn't really happened, that the scoring could be erased by moving all the pieces back to the game's start.

"All right, then," I heard the captain say. "The old woman must be safe. He must be seen to surrender. But you can promise him that there'll be a chance made for him to escape, after he's seen surrendering."

We could see Clarence talking, talking into the rubble of the hut. During a lull in the wind his voice became audible without the electronic aids. "As a friend, as a friend, I say, do this, Dark Horseman."

From the hut a revolver was flung into the air. It fell into the sand. An AK 47 rifle came next, then another and, finally, Satan. He had his hands laced together on the top of his head and he walked straight towards White Indian. At the same time Alvarez walked forward from

175

our position, a soldier with a Goathorn gun on either side of him, and although I thought we were moving too rapidly in a delicate situation, the Syndic and I followed them.

I don't think Clarence heard us coming up behind him. His eyes were on Dark Horseman, who suddenly paused and gave Clarence one terrible look to carry with him in memory through life and most of the way through death.

Alvarez said, soft as a sigh, "Ya."

The soldiers on either side of Clarence emptied their magazines, and the bullets almost cut Dark Horseman in half. Two things remain with me forever: that he made such a small bundle of rags on the ground, that big, beautiful man, and that so much blood came out of him. His sandals flew off.

Alvarez walked up abreast of White Indian and pronounced the usual verdict in such cases in a country where capital punishment was abolished so long ago. "Fugitive from justice. Shot while trying to escape."

No courts, no lawyers, no appeals to presidents for clemency, no newspaper interviews. It was what he had said long ago, the capacity for instant and effective action.

I hoped I was going to be able to remember Dark Horseman the way I saw him in the plaza, with his arms full of woman and his heart full of joy. But somehow I doubted it. The blood was running down a muddy rut towards us.

Clarence turned to Alvarez and said, speaking calmly, almost in conversational tones, "You motherfucker." But he struck as he spoke.

I sometimes think I will never know a man of such varied talents as Clarence. The one he displayed now was an ability for street fighting, which is largely a capacity to never show, in face or turn of eye, what your move will be.

While speaking softly, he kicked left at Alvarez, sideways, as does a cow, but with terrible force. Just at the instant his leg straightened his heel struck the side of the captain's knee. You could hear the joint pop open and the cartilage rip loose with a screech like a huge plastic egg carton being crushed, and you knew The Tiny Perfect Policeman was never going to walk normally again.

As Alvarez went down, Clarence went at him. Granted a mere two seconds more, he would undoubtedly have used another grip to kill his man.

The two soldiers were late. They were putting fresh magazines in their guns. The other man who struck suddenly and unexpectedly was the Syndic, who dove forward past me and carried Clarence to the ground in a flying tackle. I will never know how he moved so fast or from where he summoned up the strength to fight Clarence. If the rest of the meek are like him, I guess they are going to inherit the earth after all.

The pair of them rolled on the ground. The Syndic, pudgy little middle-aged man that he was, kept his grip on White Indian, who cursed him and tried to butt him with his head.

They tumbled over each other on the pale earth, rolling into Dark Horseman's blood while the two soldiers moved in with guns ready.

Alvarez, his face green in the agony of his torn leg, never lost his capacity for rational thought.

"Don't shoot the Syndic," he ordered.

He could afford to take out Dark Horseman. Shootings under the Law of Escape had been a commonplace of police work since the last century, when President Díaz first introduced the police forces to Mexico. But Alvarez could not afford to have the town's only official killed, much as he might have preferred that to happen.

The soldiers circled, waiting for their shot at Clarence, and the Syndic kept himself entwined with their target. He was a bold, brave, tenacious little man. And even I, scared out of my mind, didn't do all that shabbily. I was the one who got in among the bodies and the blood and sapped Clarence behind the ear with a brick, laying him out stone cold unconscious, which is a whole lot better than stone cold dead.

That was when Little Margaret wandered up the beach and found so many new things to pray about.

Alvarez gave me White Indian to pack home in an army truck. He made it clear that White Indian wasn't a prize for me to keep.

CHAPTER 19

FOR THE CONVENIENCE
OF THE REPUBLIC

Foreigners . . . have the right to the guarantees listed in Chapter 1, Heading 1, of the present Constitution; however the Executive of the Union has the exclusive power to order out of the national territory, immediately and without the necessity of previous legal proceedings, any foreigner whose presence he judges to be inconvenient.
—From Chapter 33, Political Constitution of the United States of Mexico

When village people came to the iron gate at my garden wall, they would stand outside and speak through the hand-hole, saying plaintively, "Wolf Man. Hello, you are there, Wolf Man? Well, good morning, Wolf Man?"

If I didn't answer, often as not they would sit on the concrete step and wait awhile before resuming. To the gringo ear it was like listening to water dripping into a tin dishpan.

Gringos were different. When they came to visit they hammered on the big gate with the heel of the hand and made it clang while neighbours on both sides watched in horror. It was true what people said. Gringos were quite barbarous.

Staff Sergeant Fitzgerald was a third type. He just reached his hand through the hole, slammed back the bolt and strode in. He opened the living-room door with the same authority and was in one of my living-room chairs almost before I realized he had arrived.

It was not the kind of morning on which I write about a land of song and flowers existing on the outer limits of probability. I almost told him to get the hell out and sit on the front step and sing, as other people did.

I wondered how he had arrived so soon after the event. It isn't easy to get transported into rural Mexico in the space of twenty-four hours. It turned out that when he left Mexico City he knew only that the army was sweeping for the drug cache and that a shrimper captain or two had been arrested. He learned of the previous day's bloody happenings only when he found Alvarez in the hospital, where doctors were trying, not too optimistically, to shape some sort of knee for him to stump around on for the rest of his life.

Brought here from Santander by Turnaround John, Fitz made it plain that he didn't plan to stay. "There's nothing to be gained by me peering up a dead horse's ass" was the way he put it.

I made him a raw fish cocktail and took him to the bedroom where Clarence lay whitely.

The White Indian's eyes flew open and, all bright-eyed and bushy-tailed, he said, "Hi, there. How are you doing? Say, how did the Syndic get involved in all that?"

"I'm just visiting," said Fitz, "trying to find out what you've been up to," but White Indian dropped off again before Fitz stopped speaking.

We went back to the living room, whereupon his voice followed us. "Hi, there. How are you doing? Say, why was the Syndic there?"

"He has been saying the same thing at least once every half-hour since yesterday afternoon," I said. "That and pooing and peeing for me to clean up. I am thinking of finding a bigger brick and hitting him harder."

I had called the kid doctor over when I first brought Clarence back from the beach, and he had solemnly reported that White Indian had a concussion and would surely get better, unless, by chance, he died. I didn't need a doctor to tell me that people will live unless they die. Anybody passing by on the street could have told me that. But I supposed I couldn't complain. The young man had charged me only the normal rate for a doctor's house call, the equivalent of $1.50 U.S.

The village was, of course, awash in stories, most of them wrong, and a constant procession of people came to the gate, some in idle curiosity but most, I found, out of a genuine affection for Mr. Clarence, The White Indian.

The Fragment, I discovered in the morning, had spent the entire night outside the front gate, wrapped in his thin serape.

Before he was obliged to leave for school, which started at eight, he brought his mother over with her remedies. They were what you might expect. She burned feathers under Clarence's nose, gave me some concoction of lime juice and verdigris from a corroded battery to pour down his throat or into his hair, and for good measure placed an open knife beneath his bed. Knives cut the pain of women in childbirth, so why not ensure that White Indian suffered no needless pain? I thanked her and said I thought the knife was every bit as effective with men as with women.

We had buried Dark Horseman that morning, hurriedly, in a grave for which no marker was ready. I had bought a plain coffin for him so that he would not go to the soil wrapped in a blanket as had the little brother who died in the Blue Norther.

"Poor bastard," I said. "He's got six feet of earth. The only thing his country ever gave him."

"He shouldn't have switched sides," said Fitz. "Is it any wonder Alvarez was so angry?"

"The tiny perfect murderer."

"Have a little understanding, Macdonald."

"Understanding! For God's sake, I was there! The Dark Horseman walked out with his hands over his head."

"Law of Escape," said Fitz. "If you don't approve of it, at least try reminding yourself how grateful you are that you can walk the streets of the cities in this country and feel safer than in New York or Los Angeles or Detroit."

"Balls," I said.

"Then try reminding yourself that this is not your country."

"Alvarez is a rotten bastard."

He sighed. "Let me tell you a story, Mac. Alvarez has a teen-age daughter whose milk teeth never came out, so she has the most frightful set of double buck teeth you have ever seen on a human being. He and his wife saved money for her to go to an orthodontist, but the wife took sick and all the money went for her hospitalization. The little daughter cried herself to sleep for a year and a half. All that time, one of Alvarez's superior officers was building a $2.5 million home in the Polanco district on a $65-a-week salary."

"Eat your fish," I said.

"I guess it's a thing civilians can't understand," he said.

I made coffee for both of us.

I went over the whole story again for him, telling everything I knew or surmised, almost like writing another report, my last chatty note.

It ended with my telling him about the knife under White Indian's bed and the candles burning for him in the church.

"Poor, superstitious bastards that they are," he said. "But as I tell my Mexican friends in Mexico City, look, it's not your fault you were born Mexican and I am not going to hold it against you."

"You're a pawky man, Fitzgerald."

He grinned. We were sympathetic, we two.

He left to see the Syndic because, he said, that was one hand he had to have the honour of shaking, the other hand being Clarence's. I tidied up Clarence's bed. He woke with a slightly different expression on his face and I said, "Say something, Clarence."

"Something!" he shouted "Something!" He laughed and went back to sleep again.

Fitz returned after half an hour, looking even more mournful than usual, and said he was going back to Mexico City. "Even out of uniform, I think maybe it's best that I'm not here for the next act. Our friend Clarence is being Thirty-threed. You can be the official witness."

"I heard somewhere about Thirty-threeing."

"Article 33 of the Mexican Constitution. He is being expelled from Mexico. For the good of the republic. They have the very strongest case against him. No evidence has been brought so there is none to refute. No jury has sat so there is no decision to appeal. People here can move with remarkable efficiency sometimes.

"Somebody will read a paper over him, I suppose, and he'll be taken to the airport and put aboard a plane and the Mexican government will pay for his one-way ticket outbound. You can go to the airport with him."

I went to the liquor cabinet, pulled out a bottle of tequila and poured us both a shot. He cut some limes and brought salt.

"What a lousy business it all is, Fitz. Two men dead, Dark Horseman and a young soldier, neither of whom deserved it. At least one career ruined. Two or twenty or maybe two hundred men corrupted. All because governments can't remember what Cato said in the Roman Senate two thousand years ago: 'The more the laws, the more the criminals.' "

"Philosophy is a bit over my head. I'm a policeman."

"And clearly police work is not what I was cut out for."

"I'm not telling you anything I didn't tell the commissioner. We had no business using amateurs like you, not even just for writing chatty notes. Civilians shouldn't be put out in a place like this. We are the ones who are paid to be shot at."

"Well, at least from a police view it was a success. You got all that Mexican Brown and you got Number One besides. I suppose a bit of death and sorrow doesn't count for much against that."

He looked at me, with that face like a scorpion's vulva, and I wondered if he was going to make another of his outrageous jokes.

"Why are you looking at me that way?"

He just kept looking.

"I'll be damned! It wasn't Wilbur."

"Wilbur wasn't high enough up the scale to kiss the hem of Number One's robe. He couldn't pick Number One out of a crowd of two with any reliability."

"I keep getting educated in this place."

"Mac, the Wilburs of the drug world are common as clouds in a summer sky. A man is retired, respected and suddenly out of money, which he never expected to be. He loses the farm on the stock market. Or his trust company collapses. He can't believe what's happened to a quiet, careful law-abiding citizen like him.

"Wilbur did what he never thought he'd do; he ran out of money. He had it all in a Mexican bank, and the collapse of the peso ruined him. Wilbur also had a powerful need, a wife with cancer.

"So typical. Somebody explains to the guy that all he needs to do is take one little step aside and everything will be as it was before. Think of it, Mac. Restored. The Wilburs don't want to make fortunes. They just ask to be put back on square one so they can play the honest game all over again.

"He ran one tiny little shipment across the border, as we now know. Just enough that they had him harpooned. For the big score, which could have bought him a suite of rooms and four doctors in Johns Hopkins, he was to be their gofer in this operation."

"Son of a bitch," I said.

"Do you have a wife dying of cancer?"

"I didn't mean it that way. I was talking about how this old world turns."

"It turns as it has always turned, grinding down the meek and the poor."

"All right, tell me. I've earned it. Who was Number One?"

182

He licked some salt, slapped back a tequila, and puckered his lined face on a lime again. After some thinking, he let the words fall out of his mouth.

"We will probably never know who Number One was. Never. Just maybe, just possibly, in some other operation years from now, another deal in another country, he'll turn up and tell us about it. Or, what's just as possible, he'll tell us when the stuff has been made legal, at which time he'll be standing for election somewhere, besides being a bank president and a patron of the arts."

"I thought you weren't a philosopher. Come on, Fitz. You people have some idea."

"If we have an idea, that's all it is. We have not one shred of evidence, not even enough to hold him overnight in Mexico, and in this country you don't need much more than a suspicion for that. Number One, if he was ever here, is shiny clean, and not a clue will stick to him."

"Fitzgerald, who is he?"

"Yes. You deserve an answer." He paused so long that I thought he might leave it at that, admitting that I deserved to know but refraining from telling me. He talked to his glass.

"The received wisdom is that it's the professor, Jon. And we've got you to thank for that. It was there in your first note, your long, chatty note, you called it."

"Be damned if I know what I said."

"You gave us all the names and descriptions for checking and we did it and so did Interpol. Everybody checked out. The Pretty Little One was smart but she's poor and always will be poor. The Syndic was what he seems. So was Mr. Ochoa and Henry the drunk. Wilbur was Wilbur, although we failed to find out that his money had run out.

"Even the professor checked out, in a way. He happens to be a master of the English language. He can write better applications for grants than any other human being."

"Go on."

"With a computer it isn't hard to add up the money he made from his many grants. It was comfortable, and it adds up to more because he is an internationalist: he holds passports for four countries, never spends more than three months in any one so he pays taxes to none of them.

"It was comfortable money, but it just wasn't enough to afford the most expensive whore in Beirut."

"Phoebe Nell."

"Or Beatrice Rendal-Knowles or Sarah, Daughter of the Bedouin Feran. Take your pick. She has ID papers for all. That was the one anomaly in your note. You mentioned that Pretty Little One and her daughter called her The Cunt. We thought maybe they were better judges of women than you, so we concentrated on getting all of her identities instead of stopping at the first one. It took a lot of time."

"She seems to have screwed every man in the village."

"She missed a couple," he said. "But this is Mexico. You know what a clutter things are always in. No job ever gets completed. She did her best to accommodate everybody. I guess she is one of those women who fuck some men for money, some for love and some for curiosity. Here it seems to have been mostly curiosity."

"Why didn't the professor object? Was he as obtuse as I was?"

He looked at the label of the tequila bottle as if the answer were written there for him to read aloud.

"You have a grand gift, Mac. A lot of policemen would envy you. You don't know answers but you sure as hell know the questions to ask."

He pinched his lower lip and looked up at the ceiling fan. "I said the received wisdom is that the professor, who hasn't left a solid clue for us to use, was the Number One of the operation. That was the finding of our research group, whom we pay because they are so much more clever than ordinary policemen."

"And you don't trust the experts."

"Couldn't pour piss out of a boot if it had a hole in the toe and the instructions written on the heel."

"All right, smartass, you tell me who he was."

"I'm not all that smart, but I'm smart enough to know that it was almost certainly Sarah, Daughter of the Bedouin. Forget the dumb blonde bit. She was here protecting a big investment. She wasn't the professor's pet. He was her decoy. Think back to your long, chatty notes. Who got Clarence drunk? It didn't work out because instead of blabbing to her he scared hell out of Wilbur instead. But it was Sarah who knocked White Indian off the wagon.

"Who turned up so often where White Indian and Dark Horseman were? Who was so interested in what Wilbur was doing in his yard?

Who questioned you so closely? Above all, who arranged to have pillow talk with just about every man involved in the operation, you excepted for some reason? You must have been a father figure.

"It explains how she could screw everybody in sight without Jon raising a whimper. It also explains why she is taking a flight from Mexico City to Havana today, while he is still dinking around here trying to get somebody to buy an old car from him. He probably doesn't know he's been dumped yet."

"I am bitched, buggered and bewildered."

"The women do it to all of us, Mac. The trouble started when we invented washing machines and clothes dryers and the other labour-saving devices. It gave them too much time for thinking."

We drank to that.

In what time for thinking he and I had left, I burned up a few seconds and said, "Fitz, the fact is, none of you know who Number One was or even if he was here."

"I told you that in the first place," said Fitz. "Why won't you listen to what is said to you? What is it about you civilians?"

After he left, Clarence started talking about the greatest hangover known to the human race. Even his hair hurt. He said he'd been awake before Fitzgerald left, but he hadn't felt like shaking hands with any policeman. I tried to tell him he'd been Thirty-three but he drifted back to sleep again, and I left the aspirins beside him on the bedside table and went up to the penthouse bedroom.

A burro honked. Six dogs barked and fought. The neighbours' fighting cocks began crowing. The creature that says "Who He" began saying "Who He." On somebody's radio, a man sang about silver moonlight, golden dreams and love that is forever and ever. All the familiar bedtime noises of the village were there to lull me into sleep.

But I didn't sleep. I was tired, but there was no sleep for me. Finally I remembered Winston Churchill's practice during the big war, said, "To hell with everybody" and promptly went to sleep. But the sleep I finally found was fitful and in the morning I awoke crying about cruel dreams I could not remember.

CHAPTER 20

"REMEMBER ME, ANGEL"

Truly, do we live on earth?
Not forever on earth, only a little while here.
We merely dream. All is a dream.
Is anything stable and lasting?

Where are we going? Where are we going?
In the beyond, will we find Death or Life?
Is there anything which lasts?
On earth,
Only the sweet song,
The beautiful flower.

—Ancient Nahuatl poem

That morning, after I had shooed Angel off to the Chicago Martyrs Primary School, White Indian was well enough to talk about how he planned to kill Captain Alvarez, and it was hard to get him to listen while I explained that he was being kicked out of Mexico and wasn't ever going to be allowed to come back. His concussion hangover was cruel. His eyes were the colours of the American flag.

I was grateful for Consuela, who breezed in and came directly to one point I failed to make.

"At least Dark Horseman is dead and out of it," she said. "That is something for which we must thank Captain Alvarez."

"What in hell are you talking about, for Christ's sake?" he said. He was in very bad shape. One did not use profanity in front of ladies in San Sebastian. Men had other faults. They had most of the faults known to the human race. But seldom that one.

"Because it was merciful," she said. "Can you imagine it? That beautiful big animal, put into a cage and left for twenty-five years?"

Like her mother, Consuela had a gift for bringing life's affairs into a clear focus. I took her idea and ran with it.

"Think of it, Clarence," I said, as if I had thought of it myself, which I had not. "Think, man. They say we are the cruellest society in all of history because of the way we raise our poultry. But at least we kill those poor creatures after a few weeks. What was that man going to do for a quarter of a century?"

"There was no reason for him to die thinking he'd been betrayed by his best friend," said Clarence.

Nobody could answer that, so I made coffee, and Consuela, who, like everybody else in the village, knew now of the deportation order, went again directly to her point.

"My mother cannot come to say good-bye to you. You understand how it is. She has nothing to do with politics, ever. She wants you to have this."

She reached inside her blouse and brought out a large brown envelope, which had been used once already in the Mexican mail system. Consuela gave a little smile. "She knows that Canada is very cold, and you may need to buy a warm jacket as soon as you get home."

He opened the flap and couldn't restrain a gasp. Neither could I, who could also see. It was stuffed with $50,000 notes. There must have been the equivalent of about five thousand American dollars. Clarence was going to go home with a grubstake.

He closed the flap and tossed the package carelessly on a deck chair.

"You can tell your mother I accepted in the Mexican way with a nod of my head," he said. "Have coffee."

When we drank he said, "Where did she find so much, Consuela?"

"She has her own ways."

"I will return it to her, of course. But of course, she already knows that. Anyway, you tell her that I will write to her very soon."

"Don't do that," she said.

"There is no harm in a letter. The authorities won't stop it."

"Please, do not write my mother."

"Why?"

"As I am sure you know, my mother cannot read or write, and it embarrasses her terribly to have to ask me or Arturo to read to her."

"I didn't realize."

"She cannot even write her own name. When we go to the bank I make her X sign for her while she lays a finger on the top of the pen. All my mother knows are figures. Figures and people are all my mother understands."

"Of course. I see."

As they walked to the gate he said, "Your mother is a great woman, Consuela."

"Some mothers are too great," she said. "Like yours. You are so much in love with her that you can never be a husband to a living woman. What a shame."

She turned in the walkway and faced him. "Of course, you could have married a Mexican girl, because we are taught from birth to submit to our mothers-in-law. You could have married me, Clarence. But you did not. You are . . . there is no exact Spanish word, but the English have a term for it. You are a horse's ass, Clarence."

She reached up her hand, pinched his cheek, kissed him full on the lips, and walked away and out the gate, back straight, hair and hips swinging. She never looked back. He choked on what he could not utter.

If she had looked back, just one time, the whole San Sebastian story might have had a different ending. But she didn't.

"Clarence," I shouted. "In the name of God, run after that girl! Never let her go." But I was silent, of course; the shouting was all inside my head. You cannot arrange another man's life for him. You can arrange his death. Alvarez had reminded us of that. But you cannot arrange his life.

Far away up the street, the sun still made bright lights in long black hair.

He stood like a man whittled from an old stump. When she was no longer to be seen, he came back into the patio, one step at a time.

"Did I ever tell you how my father died?" he said. "He committed suicide. It's a failing of our people. We have one of the highest suicide rates of any people on earth."

"There is no sickness worse than self-pity, Clarence."

He shook the demons off his shoulders. "Yes, you're right. Mother used to say that. Thanks, Mac."

He went into his bedroom for a while and came out with a piece of paper in his hand.

"Well, asshole, " I said, "what are you going to do about the Cream

Puff? They won't let you take that on the airplane, you know."

"It's time I had a Lamborghini," he said. "I'm going diving in the North Sea again. I'll find the money lying there on the bottom. So, here's papers transferring Cream Puff to you. Sell her and use the money to send Angel to a decent school. Maybe there's one somewhere in the country run by the Jesuits under some disguised name."

"You don't mean it."

"I do at this minute, and you take me up on it right now, before I get selfish and mean in the white man's way and change my mind." He put the papers in my hand and folded the hand over them. "Will you do it for me?"

"Done," I said. We shook on it.

Clarence said, "It won't be as easy as you think. He's puny, but he's got spirit. He'll want to keep the car and let boarding school go. Like the sainted Don Miguel Hidalgo. The cry from the heart against Spain isn't the only reason Hidalgo is loved here. Did you know he was a poor kid, and the others at the seminary raised money to send him to Mexico City University? Hidalgo got in a card game on the way to Mexico and lost every centavo. Style, man, style. Like this kid."

"He will go to boarding school. I will see to it. But tell me, how in hell am I supposed to sell a car down here that came in on a six-month tourist permit?"

"Your noses! There is nothing in this entire world that you can't find a buyer for in Mexico. Sell it to the kid doctor. His daddy, I hear, buys him weekend flights to Aspen for skiing. You'd have no trouble getting twenty-five to thirty grand American from them. That will put him in a good boarding school."

"You're a generous man, Clarence."

"There is no such thing as generosity. There are only debts."

I wondered who the debt was owed to. Probably a little boy named Clarence Trelegis, who lived on an Indian reserve many years ago in the special age called childhood.

He went out on the street, which he wasn't supposed to do, and found the boy coming back from the school. Fragment had skipped classes. They came in and walked the patio together, the dark-faced golden-haired man and the little dark boy, talking, but what they said I will never know, except that I am sure White Indian did not tell the kid that he was giving him millions and millions of Mexican dollars.

In mid-afternoon the officials came, like troubles, like bananas, in a bunch. The municipal president from Santander had come as if for an official function. It was a foolish and unnecessary gesture, but then he was a foolish and unnecessary man. There beside his bodyguard was Alvarez, whiter, thinner, smaller than before, on crutches, with one leg cased in white plaster that did not have friendly notes from fellow patients pencilled on it.

They came to the house. Everything had been arranged for the movement to be fast and formal. Alvarez's bodyguard and chauffeur, the Sergeant, had arranged that with me. All was designed to occur so swiftly and with such absence of emotion or stress on everybody's part that it could end almost as quickly as it began.

The village people had other ideas. Somebody I would not need a long stick to touch had put the word out. They were gathering by the time the Sergeant came to make the first arrangements, and he observed, as he left, that The White Indian appeared to have more votes in this village than the president of Mexico.

There were twenty or so people on the street and more hurrying to join them when we came out through the gate in late afternoon. The sea breeze had exhausted itself and the palms no longer rattled their dry bones. Alvarez was white, stiff and in more than one kind of pain.

The municipal president was an inoffensive sort, a hardware merchant in the city of Santander who had become a PRI politician. You were reminded of George Ade's acid comment: "Every now and then, an innocent man gets sent to the Legislature." He was a fellow who meant well, feebly.

He mumbled an expulsion order from a document to Clarence, who nodded, and to Captain Alvarez, who looked more than ever like a porcelain doll.

We were about to enter the captain's car when an angel flew overhead. That is, no music, no barking of dogs, no cocks crowing. Even the clouds of little green Catalinas ceased to chatter.

"One moment," said a great, large voice.

The Syndic came over to join us at the side of the street, walking at a slow pace of his choice. He looked as he had always looked—two buttons off his shirt, his bellybutton poking over his old cotton pants, his bare feet in the loose sandals of the peasant. Only the voice had changed. It was deep and compelling, and even the bloodless Alvarez could not forbear to stop and listen.

"There is a thing I wish to say," said the Syndic.

"With your permission, Syndic, this is an official federal matter," said the president of the Santander municipal council.

"With your permission, I am the syndic of San Sebastian de Hidalgo, and when things are done in this pueblo, I will speak, and no other person shall speak."

He had come up beside us. He hitched his pants closer to the navel with a fast clutch, and while we waited for him to speak, he waited too, with that gift given to only a few politicians, the gift of making people wait to hear your words. When he spoke, his voice was a full octave lower than usual.

This is one of the reasons, unfair though it may be, that women have so much difficulty in politics. When a woman is excited, she tends to squeak. A man will squeak if frightened, but in the grip of other emotions his voice will drop an octave and give comfort to all who hear him. Tucked into the deeply buried ancestral archives of the mind is the belief that the deep, calm voice keeps the saber-toothed tiger away from the cave for one more night.

"I will now speak to the people who are here on this street," he said, and again he waited, as did we all.

"We in this village of San Sebastian de Hidalgo have an order from the chilangos of Mexico City. It is an order that our friend Mr. Clarence be sent away from Mexico.

"This was a surprise to us in this village. We did not think the government people even knew where San Sebastian de Hidalgo was.

"We have only 4 million bureaucrats in Mexico. We are a poor country. Four million is all we can afford. We thought they were all too much occupied with counting knots in the bulrushes to care about us."

There was laughter in the street, and the president of Santander Council felt impelled to intervene.

"Syndic," he said, "I do not care to associate myself with you while you are drinking."

"And I do not care to associate myself with you when I am sober," said the Syndic.

I liked the Syndic and perhaps loved him, but I was sorry for the municipal president. He was a decent enough man who was being done terrible, irreparable harm.

There were no newspapers in the village, no radio station, no generally accepted public records. Records were in the minds of the people. In those minds they were indestructible.

Everything said here this afternoon was being recorded in memories. It would be repeated, not accurately but with much exaggeration, throughout the district. It would be told with gestures, with elaborations and with an extravagant and intentional malice. The president was not going to survive the system that in Canada we call the moccasin telegraph. He had spent his entire capital of dignity this day, and it had been overturned and scattered at his feet. In this community, a man could lose almost everything—his home, his job, his looks. But he could never surrender his dignity.

"I would like to say something about this man, this Mr. Clarence of the Three Lakes," said the Syndic. Where, I wondered, had he heard and why had he remembered that Clarence's great-great-granddad had come from the hill country of old Mexico?

"I know this man very well. He is a man with many faults. He drinks, and becomes foolish."

There was a hum of approval and understanding.

"He has strength. He has dignity. He has courage, and what is a man without courage? Is this not true?"

There was a murmur.

"He has other characteristics. He has troubles with women. Perhaps he is alone in this?"

Laughter.

"When he drinks too much he does stupid and silly things. But he never does the stupid and silly things for the wrong reason." The Syndic pointed at Clarence. "Have you ever heard of a better man than that?"

From the patch of dark, silent faces across the street there rose a breath, less than noise, more than a sigh, like the first rustle of a strong wind before the trees begin to shake.

I recognized most of the faces. Turnaround John was there. So was the lagoon fisherman, Twenty-one John, named because he had a second vestigial small toe on one foot. The old couple who had a soft drink stand in the plaza had come; he was very tall and she was short and fat so they had the collective nickname of Ten. There was my neighbour, Juan Diego, and Skinned Rabbit, the man who drove the water truck. Among them, to my surprise, was old Mrs. Jiménez,

Widow of Montero, who had once chased us off her property because she thought we were Mormon missionaries. It was she who now stepped forward and shook her cane in the air above her white head.

"Long live Don Cuauhtemoc!" she shouted.

I could have wept for joy for him. Here he was, throwing away everything he had ever worked for, and he was gaining everything that he ever wanted. He was a don.

It was a title with no equivalent elsewhere. The government could not bestow it. You could not buy or inherit the title. It was the gift of the common people to bestow or withhold, and they did it by their own private whim and, like the monarchs of old, never deigned to give reasons for their choices.

Juan Diego was next. "Hurrah, Don Cuauhtemoc."

There were other voices. "Hurrah, Don Cuauhtemoc!" "Rise up, Don Cuauhtemoc!"

I saw his old mother in the crowd but could read no meaning in her little black eyes and did not know if she was now gratified about the son she named Cuauhtemoc or if she had reached an age when all the vanities of men were seen to be the foolish things they are.

As for the Syndic, he did not appear to hear the honorific used, but that, of course, is part of being a man called a don.

"Mr. Clarence is an ordinary man, a humble man, like you and like me. He is an honourable man.

"What, then, is honour?

"Honour does not demand a palace in which to live. Honour is at home in very humble places and among humble people."

I thought that in Clarence he had a poor candidate for humility, but the people shouted, "Rise up, Don Cuauhtemoc!"

He turned to Clarence. His words were ending. You could sense that, as it should be sensed in any good speech.

"I say this to you, Mr. Clarence. As far as I am concerned, you are a Mexican. My house is your house and my country is your country."

The two men went into a double embrace, kissing each other first on the left and then on the right cheeks while their tears ran down their faces.

The people shouted, "Hurrah, Mr. Clarence!" and "Long live Don Cuauhtemoc!"

"It's time to go, Clarence," I said, touching his arm. He turned his wet face to me. I had never seen an adult Indian cry before. Their glands dry up, or something. But he was crying.

"Yes, Mac," he said. "Yes, it's time to go."

I got into the back seat of Alvarez's car. The driver helped Alvarez get into the front, which he did with much difficulty. Clarence was about to get in beside me when he spotted Fragment in the crowd, standing alone. His mother probably did not have anything suitable to wear, again.

For God's sake, Clarence, handle this. Clarence did, because here, in the navel of the moon, all things are larger and brighter than off stage—all colours, all cruelties, all angers, loves and prides; all larger than life.

Among men, it was all centred on what the Catholics call the deadly sin of pride, but it was not for me, a foreigner, to judge them wrong in that.

"Remember me, Angel," he called across the street. "You think I am like another father to you but that is not so. I am like a brother. I am like a younger brother."

He switched his style of speech and instead of addressing the child as "thou" he called him "you." Normally an adult will use the *you* form only to mock a child, but in the way Clarence spoke, nobody took it as mockery.

"You will be a great man in Mexico some day, Angel. But always, I ask you, remember me, your brother, your little brother, Clarence of the Three Lakes."

The boy was again as I had seen him the first day on the plaza, small, dark and proud. He inclined his head a centimetre, no more, and raised it again, his face impassive but his soul shining out of his eyes.

"Get in the goddamn car, Clarence," I said, using English, which foreigners say is the language of the goddamn.

We moved away as gracefully as a large car can on a small, bumpy street.

So ended the great Mexican opera. As one might expect—with heroism, with song, with love and strong spirits, but with no solution, no resolution.

Why couldn't the almighty governments of this world have left this little village alone? It was government's passion for creating crimes where none had existed before that had led to all the cruelties, the betrayals and the broken hearts.

Only the Syndic has emerged better off than before, and in our materialistic society he too would have been classed as a loser. The boy now had fortune of which he did not yet know, but whether that meant joy or sorrow for him was in the laps of gods in whom I do not believe.

Because we were moving slowly, the voice of a servant girl singing came clearly through the open window. It was Esmeralda López, who was sweeping the pathway to Mr. Ochoa's house.

Esmeralda had had rickets as a child and her legs were so bowed that she was almost a cripple, but she had a lovely face and voice.

> Voice of my guitar
> Waken me in the morning
> I wish to rejoice
> In my lovely land, Mexico.

Clarence sang along with her.

"Silence," said Alvarez. There was a vein throbbing at the side of his temple. His face had a band of red showing across the eyes, and his lips were pressed so tightly that they had whitened. The captain's fuse was short, and hissing.

Clarence continued, louder, as Esmeralda's voice faded behind the car.

> Mexico, beloved country
> If I should die when I am far from you

The driver joined in the singing.

> Let it be said that I am only sleeping
> And that I shall return to you.

The driver had an exceptional voice. He had that quality you find in performers such as Harry Belafonte, Ed McCurdy and Nana Mouskouri. Every note was true, every word precisely spoken . . . and all with sincerity, with love. He was a great baritone. All six feet of him had gone into supporting vocal chords, and all his soul had gone into music.

Alvarez, no longer The Tiny Perfect Policeman, shouted. It was

195

the first time I had ever heard him raise his voice.

"I said SILENCE!"

He could have saved his breath to cool his porridge. They both kept singing.

> Then bury me in the mountains
> In the shade of the flowering trees
> Cover me with the earth of my country
> Which is the true cradle of man.

White Indian sang for the hell of it. He had lost all he could lose. There was nothing more to be taken from him except perhaps his life, if he pushed Alvarez too hard.

For the policeman at the wheel it was different. He was losing his patron, the man who had the power to lift him out of poverty and give him a fingerhold on the middle class. The Sergeant was tearing up his lottery ticket, his chance to see his children become teachers, clerks or bureaucrats; to see his wife have an electric washer and dryer. He had everything to lose. He sang because he was a Mexican.